AGRIPRENEURSHIP FOR EMPLOYMENT AND EMPOWERMENT OF WOMEN IN RURAL AREAS

Dr G. Valentina

GenNext Publication

ISBN: 978-93-8022-260-8

Price: ₹ 940/-

First Published, 2015

Published by

GenNext Publications
5, Ansari Road, Daryaganj
New Delhi - 110002
Ph. 9212142040
E-mail: gennext@hotmail.com

Laser Typesetting : Rajender Vashist, Delhi
Printed at : G. Print Process, Delhi

Cataloging in Publication Data–DK

Courtesy: D.K. Agencies (P) Ltd. <docinfo@dkagencies.com>

Agripreneurship for employment and empowerment of women in rural areas / G. Valentina.
pages cm
Contributed articles.
Includes bibliographical references and index.
ISBN 9789380222608

1. Women in agriculture--Government policy--India.
2. Entrepreneurship--India. 3. Agricultural industries--India. 4. Rural women--Employment--India. 5. Sustainable agriculture--India.
I. Valentina, G., editor.

DDC 338.10820954 23

Contents

Theme-II: Technologies for Women Empowerment and Employment

Theme-III: NGO Interventions and Case Studies on Agripreneurship

Theme-IV: Government Initiatives and Policy Framework for Agripreneurship and Rural Development

ABSTRACTS

Theme-I: Agripreneurship for Women Employment and Empowerment

Theme-II: Technologies for Women Empowerment and Employment

Theme-III: NGO Interventions and Case Studies on Agripreneurship

Theme-IV: Government Initiatives and Policy Framework for Agripreneurship and Rural Development

Acknowledgements

Rapid expansion of Self Help Group activities promoted across the country has led to entrepreneurship development. Entrepreneurship development is a part of the programme enunciated by the Government of India in its most spelt out programme called *Swarnajayanthi Gram Swarojgar Yojana* (SGSY) which was genuinely inclined to promote self-sufficiency in the poor women of Self Help Groups from the rural areas. At the outset the women have been able to successfully mobilise the social and economic resources and gain a livelihood which helped them in overcoming poverty. Women were involved in the farm based and also the non-farm based entrepreneurial activities. The present book is a compilation of the entrepreneurship activities of the women entrepreneurs involved in the agriculture-based activities and their problems and prospects.

At the juncture where we decided to compile this book, we are aware of the difficulties of presenting a cohesive picture of women entrepreneurs in the Indian society. In the process, we also found the task even more challenging as literature was not available on the problems and prospects of the women entrepreneurs.

It would not have been possible for us to complete this work without the constant encouragement and patience of my father Mr Franklin Bullabbai, my mother Mrs Vijayam and my husband Mr Dominic D Oliveira. I gratefully acknowledge their support in helping me reach a conclusion.

Over a period, we have benefited from interactions with various agrientrepreneurs and the activities I record my sincere thanks to all.

I thank the National Institute of Rural Development in helping me understand the dynamics of the concept through a workshop. I also extend my heartfelt thanks to Ms Deepa who assisted me in compiling the papers and the Centre for Agrarian Studies in facilitating to work on the concept.

Dr G. Valentina

List of the Contributors

Ambrose, D.S., Chairman,Indian NGOs Network (INN), 219, 12th East Cross Road, MKB Nagar, Chennai – 6000039.

Aum Sarma, PhD(IIT), Associate Dean and University Head (FMP), Acharya N.G. Ranga Agricultural University . College of Agricultural Engineering, Sangareddy, Medak (dt), AP, Emailaumsarma@gmail.com

B. Dayakar Rao, Principal Scientist & Consortium PI (NAIP-Millets Value chain), Directorate of Sorghum Research (DSR), Rajendranagar, Hyderabad-500 030 (AP).

Bhama Venkataramani, Dilip Ambarkhanel, Ardhendu Shekhar Singh1director@ssbf.edu.in,dilipambarkhane @ssbf.edu.in, shekhar.ardhendu@ssbf.edu.in

C.S.Rama Lakshmi, IFS Commissioner, Department of Sericulture, Managing Director, SERIFIED, Government of Andhra Pradesh, Hyderabad-500 004.

G Valentina, Assistant Professor, Centre for Equity and Sociial Development, National Institute of Rural Development: myvaluei@gmail.com

Huchhe Gowda, Assistant Professor, Department of Studies in Economics, Rani Channamma University, Vidyasangama, PBNH-4, Belagavi-591156, Karnataka (State), India. e-Mail: hgowda_smtd@rediffmail.com

Jayaram Killi, Director, CMSA in Society for Elimination of Rural Poverty (SERP).

K. Dattatri, Chari, Zonal Project Directorate, Zone V, CRIDA Campus, Santoshnagar, Hyderabad.

M. Savita, Krishi Vigyan Kendra, Hadonahalli, Bangalore Rural District, Karnataka email: savitagkvk@gmail.com

M. Vinaya Kumari, P. Kanaka Durga, Faculty, MANAGE.

Narendra J. Zende, ARTI, Phaltan, Dist. Satara, Maharashtra

P. Naidu, U Ghate, H N Behera, R. Ingle. CCD, Director of CCD (The Covenant Centre for Development, www.ccdgroup.org); Contact-ccdnorth@gmail.com, pulinydu@gmail.com

R. Chinnadurai, Assistant Professor, Centre for Planning, Motoring and Evaluation, NIRD.

Sathyavani Gandham, Panchayat Secretary, West Godavari District.

Shivakumar, C., Chief Project Coordinator, Green Foundation.

V. Suvarna, District Programme, Co-ordinator, A.P. Mahila Samatha Society.

Vilas Jadhav, Subject Matter Specialist (Agri Extension), Programmed Coordinator, Krishi Vigyan Kendra, Kosab Hills, Thane, Maharashtra.

Y.L. Prema Kumari, Ex Chief Manager, Andhra Bank.

Introduction

Over the years India is bogged down with Agrarian crisis including agricultural problems of production, productivity, poor rate of interest, employment, underemployment and disguised unemployment and concerted efforts have been made in addressing these issues. The attributable reasons for the crisis seem to be glaring in terms of withdrawal of the public investments in agriculture, migration of men to more lucrative urban employment, liberalisation policy, droughts, crop failure, and unsatisfactory insurance schemes, notwithstanding some agony and decline of rural livelihoods, especially that of women. The other sectors too failed to absorb them into productive employment to restore their livelihoods. Studies on rural employment flagged their findings proclaiming that, on an average, a rural labourer gets work for not more than 15 days in a month. In order to address these myriad issues, the Government of India made many interventions, and to mention a few like self-employment through SGSY, Food for Work Programme and MGNREGS, which gained applause in the recent instances. Wage employment programme is providing jobs to more number of women and helped in reducing the financial burden marginally by providing wage employment of 52 days per annum. On the other hand, policies of liberalisation gave way to Feminisation of Agriculture which specifically entails women's increasing participation in agricultural labour force, whether as independent producers, as unremunerated family workers, or as agricultural wage workers; as self-employed. In other words, an increase in the percentage of women who are economically active in rural areas; an increase in the percentage of women in the agricultural labour force relative to men, either because more women are working or because fewer men are working in agriculture. Therefore, the rural female work participation rate rose to 27.2 per cent in the year 2004-05. With these developments taking place on ground, women are seen contributing as labourers in various agricultural activities like weeding, in preparation and application of green and farmyard manure, crop management, playing a pivotal role from planting to harvesting and post-harvest operations in agriculture and allied industrial sectors (depending on the region and crops), thereby employing as many as 89.5 per cent of the total female labour in agriculture sector [FAO]; in forest-based small-scale enterprises women constitute 51 per cent of the total employed in rural production.

The scenario is changing fast with modernisation, urbanisation and development of education where business and opportunities of employment for women have increased drastically. On the one hand, there is feminisation of agriculture and on the other, women labour participation rates have been declining from 2004-05 to 2010-11 leading to an emerging trend of defeminisation of agriculture which supports the fact that the women labour participation rate has further plunged to 18 per cent by the decadal year 2010-11. Reports from NSSO also support (the economists) that nine million jobs meant for women have been lost in the rural areas and this reduction in the female labour force participation rate explains the movement of the women from labour oriented jobs to more decent and well paid employment as can be seen through agri-preneurship entailing women's involvement in agri- entrepreneurship.

The term women agri-entrepreneurship means—Entrepreneurship is an act of business ownership and business creation that empowers women economically increase their economic strength as well as position in society. It is estimated that presently women entrepreneurs comprise about 10 per cent of the total entrepreneurs in India. Agripreneurship is frequently used in the context of education and small business formation, and a significant portion of agribusiness activity in the country is the result of small and medium enterprises. Such enterprises capture opportunities that arise all along the farm in the supply chain. An agripreneur undertakes a range of different activities involving economic development and of human capital that can be shaped by training. According to J.A. Schumpeter, "Woman who innovates, imitates, or adopts a business activity is called woman entrepreneur." We have examples of various states in India like Kerala wherein, in the year 1975–76 the numbers of Industrial units run by women entrepreneurs was 73. It has increased to 4,190 in 1993–94. The women entrepreneurs in Kerala are now at the top of all industries right from readymade garments to high tech computers (Kuruksehtra, June 1998). Silli is one of the best examples where 15,000 women are involved in Knitting, mushroom cultivation and pickle making etc. In recent years, the entrepreneurship especially involving the women SHGs has gained wide popularity. Most of the programmes are aimed in this direction only as the rate of becoming entrepreneurs in women is more compared to men. (Renzulli et a1. 2000). According to ILO Statistics the growth rate was highest in the Tamil Nadu state of India which was 18 per cent in 2001.

Entrepreneurship is a turf where men are the prime players but women have also established their role and place in this field too. Women who were once up on a time the bread winners for the family have now become the bread earners and have excelled. However, the women entrepreneurs face challenges due to mushrooming of the multinational companies, which is the greatest deterrent to rural women entrepreneurs. Secondly, patriarchy and illiteracy have been major barriers and hindrance in the development of entrepreneurship in women. In addition to these challenges (According to the economist) the uneducated rural women are considered to have a Low Ability to Bear Risk, lives a protected life, taught to depend on male members from birth, not allowed to take any type of risk and Economically they are not self-dependent. Lack of access to Infrastructure and Rampant Corruption also constitute the other problems for the rural women entrepreneurs and they have to depend on intermediaries to get the things done, especially marketing and sales in the business which gives rise to business fallacies where the intermediaries usurp major part of the surplus. Lastly Lack of cooperation from the financial institutions discourages the women entrepreneurs further. Therefore, the women entrepreneurs in India are handicapped in the matter of organising and running businesses on account of low levels of skills and for want of support system. But the trend is changing. Women across India are showing interest to be economically independent. Women are coming forth to the business arena with ideas to start small and medium enterprises. They are willing to be inspired by role models—the experiences of other women in the business arena.

Against the existing scenario and considering that two-thirds of the Indian population is employed (either directly or indirectly) in agriculture sector, agripreneurship in Indian agribusiness stands out as an imperative for generating employment in the country. Agripreneurship is a key factor with a potential to transform the rural livelihoods by providing sustained employment and is also a prime driver of Indian economy. Thus, sustainable agripreneurship ventures are seen to have a potential to promote job-led economic growth in rural areas by harnessing technologies for environmentally sustainable and socially equitable development which can provide a decent livelihood.

The role of women entrepreneurs has thus been especially relevant in the present situation encompassing large scale unemployment that the country faces and the small scale industry which provides platform for providing more than 80 per cent of the employment. The myth that women cannot engage in productive employment is dispelled today with Women's Self-Help Groups housing several female-run businesses establishments, producing everything from organic pickles to school bags made of scrap fabric. At the Organic Shop, women sell their products to local customers, establishing a niche market for organic goods. Against the myriad intervention of the women entrepreneurs this book provides a platform for understanding the problems and prospects, experiences and best practices of women entrepreneurs.

A major objective of this book was to identify the critical issues of women in Agri-entrepreneurship and discuss on various issues regarding problems and prospects of women Agri-entrepreneurship in rural India.

The papers presented in the book are based on basic research which is action research oriented. All facts and problems discussed in this seminar are the opinions of the respective authors.

The book is a compendium of experiences from 40 participants attending the seminar belonging to the Government sector as well as the Non-Governmental sector, representing various states of Andhra Pradesh, Maharashtra, Karnataka, Orissa, Chhattisgarh and Chennai etc.

The paper presentations were made bringing in experiences, challenges and prospects and best practices by senior Bureaucrats from the Government, Professors from CRIDA, Agriculture Universities, Management Institutions like Symbiosis, MANAGE, KVKs, Women Trade Union Organisations, SERP and prominent NGOs like ARTI, APMS (Andhra Pradesh Mahila Samakhya), Green NGO, VRUTTI, SEED and Banks.

The papers focused on the Agrienterprises undertaken by the women (Agripreneurship) and the experiences drawn on the canvas were from the SHGs, cooperatives, individual entrepreneurs, public-private partnerships etc.

The following four major themes have been considered in the book.

A. Agripreneurship for Women Employment and Empowerment

1. Women Empowerment for Sustainable Sericulture in Andhra Pradesh - Mrs C.S. Rama Lakshmi IFS.
2. Women Entrepreneurship Development Through Millets Processing Technologies - Dr B. Dayakar Rao, N. Kachui, K. Kalpana, K.N. Ganapathy and J.V. Patil.
3. Entrepreneurship development of tribal women through KVK activities - Prof Vilas Jadhav.

Women Agri-Producer Companies for Sustainable Rural Development in Northern and Eastern India - Dr P. Naidu, U. Ghate, H.N. Behera, R. Ingle Entrepreneurship Development Among Rural Women Through Krishi Vigyan Kendra - Dr K. Dattatri, Chari Dr Appaji, Dr G. Rajender Reddy and Dr N. Sudhakar.

4. A Study of Women Vegetable Street Vendors in Karnataka - Dr Huchhe Gowda.

B. Technologies for Women Empowerment and Employment

1. Agripreneurship in food processing – A Sustainable Livelihood Approach for Women Empowerment - Ms M. Savita, Mr K.N. Srinivasappa S. Mr Ganeshamoorthi, Ms B.G. Vasanthi and Ms B.V. Manjula.
2. Meeting the Challenge of Agripreunership with Participatory Guarantee System as an Entry for the Organic Market- Mr Shivakumar, C.
3. Collective Farming - APMS experience.

C. NGO Interventions and Case Studies on Agripreneurship

1. Production of Sugarcane Saplings: A Successful Arti Technology for Women Agripreneurship in Western Maharashtra - Mr Narendra J. Zende, ARTI, Phaltan, Dist. Satara, Maharashtra.
2. Market Linkage for Sustainable Empowerment of Women Entrepreneurs - Dr Bhama Venkataramani, Dr Dilip Ambarkhanel, Ardhendu Shekhar Singh.

D. Government Initiatives and Policy Framework for Agripreneurship and Rural Development

1. Empowering Women Farmers Through Agripreneurship Under Mahila Kisan Saskthikaran Pariyojana - Mr Jayaram Killi, Mr Raidu, D.V. IAS (Rtd).
2. Case Studies on Women Empowerment Through Micro Finance with Special Reference to Andhra Bank - Smt Y.L. Prema Kumari.
3. Entrepreneurship Development Through Agripreneurship In India - Dr Ambrose, D.S.
4. Impact of Self Help Approach on Women Empowerment - A Comparative Analysis on SC and non-SC Women From Selected States - Dr R. Chinnadurai.

5. Government Initiatives and Policy Framework for Agripreneurship and Rural Development - Dr K.A. Swamy.
6. Entrepreneurship in Women for Pro-Poor Growth and Gender Equality - Ms Sathyavani Gandham.
7. Agripreneurship Development and Employment Generation Under Agri-clinics and Agri-business Centers Scheme in Andhra Pradesh - Ms M. Vinaya Kumari, Ms P. Kanaka Durga.

THEME-I: AGRIPRENEURSHIP FOR WOMEN EMPLOYMENT AND EMPOWERMENT

1

Agripreneurship for Employment and Empowerment of Women in Rural Areas

Dr G. Valentina

1. Introduction

Over the years India has been bogged down by Agrarian Crisis involving problems of production, productivity, unemployment, under employment and disguised unemployment and has made concerted efforts in addressing these issues in the rural areas. The attributable reasons for the crisis seems to be glaring in terms of withdrawal of the public investments in agriculture sector, migration of men to more lucrative urban employment, liberalisation policy, non-cooperation of the natural resources in embedding sustainable agriculture systems, subsequent droughts, crop failure, and umpteen other indicators further adding to the agony and decline of rural livelihoods leading to loss of livelihoods, and poverty and especially of the women. Poverty being such a challenge in the rural areas and a matter of concern for Government of India, it was addressed through anti-poverty and other developmental programmes. Consequently, the Eleventh Plan became remarkable in expanding the scope and coverage of flagship programmes and making development programmes a part of the target. Accordingly the Government of India spent more than Rs 156,000 crore on MGNREGA programme, about Rs 39,000 crore on ICDS, Rs 69,000 crore on NRHM, and almost Rs 78,000 crore on SSA and NRLM still has a budget of Rs 3915 crore. Further to improve the present status of women in Agriculture and to enhance the opportunities for her empowerment, Government of India has announced "Mahila Kisan Sashaktikaran Pariyojana" (MKSP), as a sub component of the National Rural Livelihood Mission (NRLM) and decided to provide support to the tune of Rs 100 crore during 2010-11 budget. Though these programmes were successful to a certain extent they did not make a significant dent in meeting the emerging crises.

Diversification in the Agriculture policy and policy on Liberalisation of the Government paved the way for the creation of high paying jobs for men in the city, slapping higher rates of taxation on agriculture and abolition of fertiliser and seed subsidies expounded on the beliefs that liberalisation and free markets will encourage growth in agriculture through privatisation and the main intention here was to shift away from agriculture imports and encourage export-led growth. This strategy of the policy proponents entailed a reduction in the budget and the tariffs, which ramified and led to instability of farm income. The resulting impact was on the farmers who firstly began to grow conservative crops and relied on wage labour; secondly, before the onset of liberalisation, facilities like credit, input assistance in terms of fertilisers and seeds etc., and marketing were facilitated by the government were replaced by private mechanisms and along with these, the governmental institutions which were otherwise beneficial to farmers were slowly obliterated; thirdly, Small farmers who once upon a time depended on these institutions reduced their productivity due to non-availability of adequate infrastructural arrangements, all these aspects impacted the agriculture negatively affecting the livelihoods of rural population. These interventions paved the way for the movement of men from villages to cities leaving behind the women in the villages who were ordained additional responsibilities of performing the farming activities as also taking care of the family. As a result woman's participation in agriculture has been on the rise. In the garb of rising participation of women in agriculture and with about 50 per cent constituting the women population in the country, entrepreneurship in agriculture for women became a way out in providing alternate livelihoods.

2. Agrarian Crisis in India, and the Feminine Face

Increasing women's involvement in agriculture facilitate emergence of a new terminology specialising on Feminisation of Agriculture which refers to an increase of women's participation in the agriculture sector which is measurable new paradigm is vastly seen in the developing countries. The IAASTD describes this phenomenon as 'the feminisation of agriculture'. But it is linked with a multitude of factors such as distress outmigration of rural men in favor of 'non-agriculture sectors', leaving women to undertake the production activities which are labour-intensive usually growing cash crops; growing number of women-headed households; increased 'casualisation' of work; unprofitable crop production due to stagnating agricultural economy (Feature Article: Notes from the field: feminisation of agriculture in the eastern Gangetic plains August 14, 2012; Posted by south Asia masala in : India, Lahiri-Dutt, Kuntala, trackback). This phenomenon gained a special relevance during the year 1960 and became pronounced during liberalisation period, giving a feminine orientation to the institutions associated with agriculture which gained a gendered color and affected women in all spheres of activity relating to her involvement in agriculture. Therefore, the plough which was once upon a time a male-dominated farming implement became the domain of a female agriculture worker who utilised these technologies while working on their own farms Surprisingly this trend continued during liberalisation period also despite the abolition of the taxes (and subsidies) on agriculture.

But this trend led to a decline in agricultural incomes: firstly, due to discriminatory practices applied on wage payments for men and women and this distinction resulted in unequal distribution of rewards in the market, establishing higher payments and gainful opportunities of work to men all-round the year, while relegating the women to the status of labourers, seasonal workers or are left with temporary jobs to nurture on, which called for lower levels of skills and therefore accommodated in low wage rates. Discriminatory practices in the cultural system has also denied female small-scale farmers the same access as men do have to fertiliser, seeds, credit, membership in cooperatives and unions, and technical assistance which deters the potential for gains in productivity and has a huge impact on food security. Greater involvement of women is also seen in allied activities of agriculture in which 93 per cent of women are employed in dairy production in India today but it is surprising to note that 75 per cent of memberships in dairy cooperatives are taken by male registrations (Sujaya, 2006). Conventionally, women's livestock rearing activities are viewed as an extension of domestic work relegated to the works around the house. In agriculture production due to gender stereotypes, some products were recognised as belonging to women and some to men—the "big things", like coffee and tea plantations and control over big animals, belonged to men; while the "small things", involving lesser status jobs like vegetables production and rearing small animals, belonged to women (Nathan, Reddy and Kelkar, 2008). Secondly, Structural adjustment of 1990s and subsequent exorbitant raise in feminisation of agriculture led to poverty and food insecurity as only limited yields of low quality were achieved in order to compensate for lack of fertilisers and other inputs.

Thus, with Feminisation of agriculture getting rampant and gaining ground season after season we are left with questions on ownership and control of small holder women farmers over the land, access to water, credit, and agricultural inputs; the constraints in accessing markets and marketing opportunities. Provision of food and nutrition security; Impact of global and national market on Women ; policies, formulation of programmes and investments made by Union and State Governments for their development, all these aspects stand out as serious concerns in dealing with women in agriculture and answering these questions seems to be a difficult task.

3. Employment of Women in Agriculture

According to various studies across the country developments taking in women employment have altered the status of women in agriculture (main findings of the study conducted NRMC India—Small holder Women Farmers in India) and in large parts of Asia majority of agricultural labour force in small-scale and subsistence farming is comprised of women which is also evident in the statistics.

- More than 46 per cent of agricultural labourers are women.
- 85 per cent of rural women workers are in agriculture (2007 Report of the Sub-Group).
- Almost a third of the women are cultivators {(2001 Census) more than 56 per cent of cultivators are women (Uttaranchal with high migration of men to the plains)}.
- Women comprise close to 33 per cent 'cultivators' (a census category, implying farmers with land) and
- 47 per cent of agricultural labourers.
- 70 per cent are agricultural workers (the world over),
- 80 per cent are food producers, and
- 10 per cent involved in basic food stuff processing
- 60 to 90 per cent undertaking rural marketing;
- Women make up for more than two-third of the work force in agricultural production (FAO, 1985).
- Agriculture and allied industrial sectors employ 89.5 per cent of female labour. [FAO].
- 18 per cent of the farm families (NSSO Reports) are reported to be headed by women.

Though the proportion of labour force working in agriculture declined over the 1990s, the proportion of women working in agriculture increased, particularly in developing countries (FAO). Despite the visibility of women's involvement in agriculture work, women have remained invisible as they are not grounded in marketing the products.

On the contrary feminisation has also evidenced an outcome that women seem to be moving away from agriculture

(Feminisation of Agriculture as an Effect of Male Out-migration: Unexpected Outcomes from Jhapa District, Eastern Nepal; By Hom Nath Gartaula, Anke Niehof and Leontine Visser) and the decline in women's employment in rural areas has been there since long despite high economic "growth" (Neetha N of the Centre for Women's Development Studies). Comparing employment data of two consecutive surveys conducted by the National Sample Survey Organisation (NSSO) in 2009-10 and 2011-12 shows that in the continuing employment crunch in rural areas, the most vulnerable sections like women are getting eliminated, (Amitabh Kundu). "Three decades ago, in 1983, about 34 per cent of women in rural areas were working which has steadily declined and now stands at just short of 25 per cent. But the decline in the past two years is shocking - it is the most drastic decline ever seen," (Neetha N of the Centre for Women's Development Studies). Even while considering subsidiary work (short term, supplementary work), women's employment numbers still show a huge decline of 2.7 million in two years. This reflects the fact that women are no longer getting long term and better paying jobs, and are forced to take up short term and transient works. But the root cause of this jobs crisis in rural India is attributed to "A decline in public investment in agriculture and extension work for dissemination of knowledge coupled with increasing mechanisation," (V.K. Ramachandran, professor of economic analysis at the Indian Statistical Institute, Bangalore). Severe slowdown in expansion of irrigation and supply of electricity to rural areas also constitute reasons for causing jobs to dry up. But today with the feminisation of agriculture the scenario is undergoing a change; firstly, with increasing population there has been a fragmentation of the land and the small size of agriculture land gave in a dependency to the farmer community on subsistence agriculture. Since this system was becoming unviable it pushed the women to take up employment as local wage labourers where men migrated for wage labour to the cities. The small sizes of the land, low access to land, labour, and non-availability of other production inputs, have secured a very low potential for women to gain in the market.

But such involvement (because of the non-availability of men in the house) of the women have also established positive avenues for accessing social networks in the vicinity and firmed up their decision-making skills on - choice of crops, application of fertiliser, time of irrigation, hiring of labour, and investment in capital goods and inputs, credit and technology etc. Yet one is still to guess the amount of control that a woman would exercise over the remittances and it stands out as an enigma to capture the cash income flows within poor households and whether or not the incomes from absentee males empower the women. However, evidences magnify that, women's rights remain severely restricted as cultural barriers prevent women from exercising their right to own property, or their right to access water, livestock and machinery. Access to education, information and political participation is also restricted, whilst opening a personal bank account obtaining a loan is often not possible (IBID). According to FAO if women enjoyed the same access to productive resources as men, farm yields could be raised by 20–30 per cent, increasing the overall agricultural output in developing countries by 2.5 to four per cent. Besides increasing women's income, this gain in production could lessen hunger in the world by 12–17 per cent.

4. New Deal for Women

There is a need for a new deal for women in agriculture (M.S. Swaminathan, *The Hindu*, April 19, 2005- NCF) facilitating necessary inputs and credit support which can bring in ample scope for increasing resource inputs and contribute to increasing production. For example, in an IFAD project in Bangladesh on Aquaculture Development women were trained exclusively in (fish) aquaculture and provided credit for initiating commercial fish culture in ponds which were owned by their men. With the technical knowledge and credit system in place the women were able to transform the pond aquaculture from a semi-subsistence mode of utilisation to a regular commercial mode, and an increase in productivity of more than 50 per cent (Nathan and Jahan, 2004). Similarly, women in the state of Andhra Pradesh who utilised the micro-credit to take lands on lease that were fit for cultivation, developed them into regular cultivation lands establishing higher productivity than earlier. In 2003-2004, the Krishi Vigyan Kendra (Agriculture Science Centre) in Andhra Pradesh, which monitored 40 women-run dairy units noted that "the average milk yield increased from 380 to 610 liters per dairy, with a net increase in profit of Rs 3,20,000 to Rs 5,80,000 per unit per annum" (DARE/ICAR, 2003-2004:178). In another intervention by the Deccan Development Society (DDS), it encouraged the women groups to use their savings and credit to take the land on lease who (groups) developed 1,000 acres of common land in and around their villages by raising neighborhood forests in 28 villages. Currently they own the tree *pattas* (title deeds) in their own names. Leasing in land as a group makes the women stronger in the lease market. They are also able to lease larger areas of land (Agarwal, 2003).This women-centred management system both provided larger household benefits, through more fuel and fodder production and increased income from sales of grass seeds, etc.; it also increased forest cover and tree diversity (Nathan and Shrestha, 2004). And an overall review of forest regeneration movements (Kelkar, Nathan and Walter, 2003) showed that when women were mobilised there was a greater impact on forest cover and environmental regeneration which otherwise suffered conversely. Thus, the new deal ordaining the status, management and ownership and transformation of household resources helps in increasing the productivity especially when they are under-utilised.

Contrarily when these resources are not opened access to women they are constrained by their inability to access credit on time since the land remains in the names of men, and their signatures are mandatory before gaining access to credit. Subsequent delays rope in consequent losses due to failure to procure and use inputs on time which is evidently reported in studies conducted in Pakistan and Nepal which have left women as de facto farm managers.

5. Agri-Entrepreneurship

In the new deal agri-entrepreneurship is the need of an hour for achieving sustainable "Livelihoods" and it is the root of human development and economic growth is "livelihoods" rather than "jobs." Today agri-entrepreneurship is adding the economic profits and cost-benefit ratios to Agricultural produce. Defining Agri-entrepreneurship, it is viewed as any business in the agricultural industry, which includes production of agriculture, food, natural fiber, the environment and natural resources it also includes the production of food item (Food grain—Fruits—Vegetables- Flowers), processing, and supply of agricultural goods which range from Corn to Cornflake, Fruits to Fruit juice and Cotton to Cloth. Apart from these products, bi-products of farming like fuels derived from farm waste and farming equipment, machinery, chemicals etc., also form a part of Agri-business activity. These are usually 'small and medium enterprises' and they form the backbone of the national economy. However, an assessment of the application of farm technologies in these activities is not more than 20-30 per cent. The use of information and communication technology (I&CT) for reducing the gaps and increasing productivity is the need of the hour (Wani, 2005). In the 21st century, Information Communication Technology (ICT) is utilised in the Agri. Business applications like—Kisan kiosk, Krishi related web site, Agri business portals and many more. For a successful career in Agri. Business the farmers should focus on producing the products based on the market demands and keeping pace with the Science and Technology innovations i.e., ICI, Green House, Sprinklers/Drip irrigation, Tissue culture etc., which play a crucial role in Agripreneurship.

Agro–entrepreneurship is seen as one panacea in overcoming unemployment problem in the rural areas and generating employment opportunities. It is also seen as a platform in solving problems viz. (a) reduce burden on agriculture, (b) generate employment opportunities for rural youth, (c) control migration from rural to urban areas, (d) increase national income, (e) support industrial development in rural areas, (f) reduce pressure on urban cities, etc.

6. Agripreneurship, Employment and Empowerment of Women in Agriculture

Gains of feminisation have resulted in entrepreneurial ventures for women. Thus, Entrepreneurship which is considered a turf where men are the major players, women entrepreneurs have proved their mettle. Women who were earlier the bread makers have now become the bread earners and they are doing a great job. According to J.A. Schumpeter, "Woman who innovates, imitates, or adopts a business activity is called woman entrepreneur." Today women from poor families (Eastern Gangetic plains) are accepting jobs at lower wages; jobs that were formerly done only by men, such as land preparation, cultivation of crops, spraying pesticides, harvesting, post-harvest processing and marketing of the products. In a situation in Chhattisgarh, as the monsoon season leaps in (Jaideep Hardikar) women are increasingly seen taking the role of farm managers. Evidently these expressions of changing work roles are the changes in the traditional gender division of farm work. Despite allocating substantial amount of time for domestic work, rural women have empowered themselves in the absence of men where they are managing small budgets and taking household decisions. Additionally these opportunities have facilitated women's movement to the local market to sell their products (Kalamkar S.S.A., Shende N.V.B). Obviously women's adoption of the agricultural works has been more wage-based involving agricultural processing and investment of more time in cash-crop production (*ibid*).

The Scenario has further undergone a change with modernisation, urbanisation and development of education and business. The opportunities of employment for women have increased drastically. As per the estimates women entrepreneurs comprise about 10 per cent of the total number of entrepreneurs in the country. Examples available are from various states in India like Kerala wherein, in the year 1975-76, the number of Industrial units run by women entrepreneurs was 73. It has increased to 4, 190 industrial Units in 1993-94. The women entrepreneurs in Kerala are now at the top of all industries right from readymade garments to high tech computers (Kurukshetra, June 1998). In the state of Jharkhand, Silli (legislative assembly area) is one of the best example where 15,000 women entrepreneurs belonging to "Gunj Pariwar" (NGO) are involved in knitting, mushroom agriculture and pickle making Industry etc. In recent years entrepreneurship involving women SHGs gained wide popularity. Most of the developmental programmes are aimed in this direction only as the rate of becoming entrepreneurs in women is more compared to men. (Renzulli *et a1.*, 2000). According to ILO Statistics the growth rate was highest in the state of Tamil Nadu which was 18 per cent in 2001.

Agro-processing is another sunrise sector in which women have an important role to play in the Indian economy. According to estimates, in developed countries the total work force engaged in agro-processing sector (directly or indirectly) is around 14 per cent. However, in India, only about three per cent of the work forces find employment in this sector revealing the vast untapped potential for employment in the sector. However, the Food and Agriculture Organisation (FAO) considers that feminisation has serious implications for the producers' economic agency and productivity and farm income. Agro-based industries are usually the medium and small enterprises where middle level services are provided by groups or co-operatives from the rural areas including the repair and maintenance services provided by the artisans at individual level. Agriculture and industry have traditionally been viewed as two separate sectors. Traditional definition of agroprocessing industry refers to the subset of manufacturing that processes raw materials and intermediate products derived from agricultural sector. Agro-processing industry involves a transformation of the products originating from agriculture, forestry and fisheries (FAO). Agro-processing could also be defined as a set of techno-economic activities carried out for conservation and handling of agricultural produce and to make it usable as food, feed, fiber, fuel or industrial raw material. Hence, the scope of agro-processing industry encompasses all operations from harvesting till the materials reach the end users encompassing, activities like packaging, quantity, quality, pricing, branding, marketing and sales. Inadequate attention to agro-processing sector in the past put both the producer and the consumer at a disadvantage and it also hurt the economy of the Country. In view of its large potential for growth and implied socio–economic impacts, potential for employment and income generation.

Following Agro-processing initiatives offer a good hope for future:

(1) Food processing and packaging

(2) Preservation of seasonal vegetables

(3) Preservation of seasonal fruits

(4) Seed processing and preservation

(5) Use of solar community dehydration centres for seeds

(6) Selective farming for vegetables and flowers seedlings

(7) Processing feed and fodder for the animals

(8) Technology applications

While promoting entrepreneurship in agriculture different types of enterprises can be considered cutting across various levels like:

1. *Farm Level:* At the individual family level, each family can be treated as an enterprise optimising production by utilising the technologies, resources and demand of the market.

2. *Service Providers:* Different types of services get into demand for optimising agriculture outputs and these include input procurement, hiring of implements and equipment's like tractors, seed drills, sprayers, harvesters, threshers, dryers and technical services such as installation of irrigation facilities, weed control, plant protection, harvesting, threshing, transportation, storage, etc. Similar opportunities exist in the livestock husbandry sector for providing breeding, vaccination, disease diagnostic and treatment services, apart from distribution of cattle feed, mineral mixture, forage seeds, etc.

3. *Input Service Providers:* Many prosperous entrepreneurs are involved in providing critical inputs such as bio-fertilisers, bio pesticides, vermicomposting, soil amendments, plants of different species of fruits, vegetables, ornamentals, root media for raising plants in pots, agricultural tools, irrigation accessories, production of cattle feed concentrate, mineral mixture and complete feed. There are also entrepreneurial ventures on sericulture, fisheries in rural areas.

4. *Post production Processing and Marketing of Farm Produce:* Post-production operations require high levels of technology inputs which can be handled by People's Organisations like self-help groups, sugar cooperatives, dairy cooperatives and fruit growers' cooperatives in many

States. These ventures involve processing of the agriculture produce and they need good professional support for managing the activities and compete with other players in the markets, particularly the retail traders and middlemen.

For example BAIF has been promoting livestock husbandry, particularly dairy husbandry as an important activity for sustainable livelihood in rural areas. Promotion of dairy husbandry was preferred since all the small and large land holders in rural areas own cows and these animals stand in generating gainful self-employment in times of severe under-employment. BAIF's strategised on utilising the low productive cows for producing high yielding cows through crossbreeding. These animals start producing milk at the age of three years and yield about 2500 kg of milk per lactation and such cows fetch Rs 15, 000-20,000 and generate a net income of Rs 5000-7000 per annum. In addition to economic returns the cattle supply the farmyard manure and boost agricultural production. Simultaneously the supply of bullock power is strengthened. This programme has benefitted 15 lakh families in 25000 villages. Initially when this programme was floated more than 65 per cent of the families were with their income below the poverty but now at least seven-eight lakh families are able to maintain two-three crossbred cows and have come out of poverty. Thus, Dairy husbandry has become an important supplementary activity in the sugar belts of Western Maharashtra. However, in places like Gujarat and Rajasthan, where there is an uncertainty in the agricultural productivity due to erratic rains, dairy husbandry has turned out to be the major source of livelihood. Establishing mobile livestock breeding and extension services by employing trained para-vets has been the objective of the programme. The para-vets provided door-to-door services by creating awareness and motivation in addressing problems related to livestock management apart from proving breeding services, using frozen semen of superior sires. Today young farmers in Western Maharashtra maintain nearly 15-20 cows and the cowshed are connected to the biogas plant.

In addition, many of them have also started supplying cattle feed, mineral mixture, seeds for forage production and other inputs required by the dairy farmers. These para-vets earn Rs 4000-5000 per month, within two-three years of establishing their service. In about eight-10 years, they are able to enhance their capabilities and reputation and earn Rs 8000-15000 per month. Milk collection and decentralised processing at the block level or in small towns and installation of milk processing units of 15000-20000 liters capacity has a good scope for this activity. Promotion of agri-horti-forestry on degraded lands is another intervention of BAIF which is primarily organised to rehabilitate tribal and small farmers popularly known as Wadi in which fruit crops such as mango, cashew, custard apple, tamarind, etc., are being grown. Here the tribal women learnt grafting and nursery management techniques and started rising grafted plants in their backyards. A minimum support price of Rs 15 is offered by BAIF, they are also allowed to sell in the open market. Today the tribals in Vansda block produce more than 10 lakh grafted mangoes per year. Associated with this project has been the production of vermicomposting, servicing and maintenance of hand pumps, drip irrigation units, repair of pump sets, production of housing materials, food processing and trading.

7. Problems of Entrepreneurship Development

Though entrepreneurship in agriculture provides a large canvas for generation of opportunities for employment there are many problems inherent in the system which either make of mar the entrepreneurial activity because of which the rate of success of entrepreneurship is very low in India. Firstly absence of adequate knowledge, resources, technology and connectivity with the market, it becomes difficult for the illiterate small holders to handle agriculture activities and promote enterprise development. Creation of adequate awareness among the farmers and the users, about the benefits of these services is essential which can be in the form of technical and business information, information on marketing agencies, suppliers of critical inputs and equipment and research stations who are involved in the development of modern technologies. Secondly, knowledge on legal provisions/ restrictions and obstacles, which have an impact on the promotion of fair trade, practices. However, the women entrepreneurs face challenges which are embedded in the system itself like the Growth of Mall culture which is the greatest deterrent to rural women entrepreneurs. Secondly, India being a patriarchal male dominant society financing the ventures run by women is considered risky. Thirdly illiteracy is found to be another major barrier and is an hindrance in developing awareness on the technologies related to entrepreneurship. Which disables them from involving themselves in research and gain the necessary training (UNIDO, 1995, p. 1). In addition to these challenges (According to the economist) the uneducated Rural women are considered to have a Low Ability to Bear Risk, lives a protected life, taught to depend on male members from birth, not allowed to take any type of risk and Economically they are not self-dependent. Lack of access to Infrastructure and Rampant.

Corruption also constitutes the other problems for the rural women entrepreneurs. They have to depend on intermediaries to get the things done, especially marketing and sales in the business which gives rise to business fallacies like where the intermediaries usurp major part of the surplus. Lastly Lack of cooperation of the financial institutions discourages the women entrepreneurs further. Therefore, the Women entrepreneurs in India are handicapped in the matter of organising and running businesses on account of low levels of skills and for want of support system. But the trend is changing. Women across India are showing interest to be economically independent. Women are coming forth to the business arena with ideas to start small and medium enterprises. They are willing to be inspired by role models-the experience of other women in the business arena.

8. Government Programmes for the Promotion of Agro-Entrepreneurship in India

Recognising the feminisation of women and her increased participation in the Agriculture work process the Government of India has also promoted training and development cum employment generation programmes for the women to start their entrepreneurial ventures, which was evidently reflected in the seventh five-year plan, in a special chapter on "Integration of women in development" in which emphasis was given to treat women as a specific target groups in 'all major development programmes of the country; devise and diversify vocational training facilities for women to suit their changing needs and skills; increase their efficiency and productivity through exposure to appropriate technologies, equipment's and practices; provide marketing assistance for the products of women entrepreneurs and involve women in decision-making process.

Subsequently during the Eight Five-Year Plan the Government of India devised special programmes to increases employment and income-generating activities for women in rural areas by launching the following programmes:

(i) Prime Minister Rojgar Yojana and ED programme was introduced to develop entrepreneurial qualities among rural women.

(ii) 'Women in agriculture' scheme was introduced to train women farmers owning small and marginal holdings in agriculture and allied activities. And to generate more employment opportunities for women KVIC took special measures in remote areas.

(iv) Women co-operatives schemes were formed to help women in agro-based industries like dairy farming, poultry, animal husbandry, horticulture etc., with full financial support from the Government.

(v) Other schemes like integrated Rural Development Programs (IRDP), Training of Rural youth for Self-employment (TRYSEM) etc., were started to alleviated poverty and 30-40 per cent reservation was also provided under these schemes to women.

During the Ninth Five-Year Plan it was realised that Economic development and growth cannot be achieved fully without the development of women entrepreneurs. Therefore, Government of India introduced the following programmes and schemes for promoting women entrepreneurship:

(a) Trade Related Entrepreneurship Assistance and Development (TREAD) scheme lunched by Ministry of Small Industries to develop women entrepreneurs in rural, semi-urban and urban areas by developing entrepreneurial qualities.

(b) Women Component Plant, a special strategy involving budgetary allowances adopted by Government to provide assistance to women entrepreneurs.

(c) Swarna Jayanti Gram Swarozgar Yojana and Swaran Jayanti Sekhari Rozgar Yojana were introduced by government to provide reservations for women and encouraging them to start their ventures.

(d) New schemes named Women Development Corporations were introduced by government to help women entrepreneurs in arranging credit and marketing facilities.

(e) State Industrial and Development Bank of India (SIDBI) also introduced schemes to assist the women entrepreneurs like;

(i) Mahila Udyam Nidhi

(ii) Micro Cordite Scheme for Women

(iii) Mahila Vikas Nidhi

(iv) Women Entrepreneurial Development Programmes

(v) Marketing Development Fund for Women

Formation of Consortium of Women entrepreneurs of India was encouraged, comprising of different bodies such as NGOs, voluntary organisations, Self-help groups, institutions and individual enterprises from rural and urban areas which provide a platform to assist women entrepreneurs in developing new, creative and innovative techniques of production, finance and marketing.

Adequate arrangements were made for the Training programmes which were designed specially for self-employment of women like:

(i) Support for Training and Employment Programme of Women (STEP).

(ii) Development of Women and Children in Rural Areas (DWCRA).

(iii) Small Industry Service Institutes (SISIs)

(iv) State Financial Corporations

(v) National Small Industries Corporations

(vi) District Industrial Centres (DICs)

A special fund was also created by SIDBI for entrepreneurial development of women in rural areas under Mahila Vikas Nidhi grants where loans are provided to women starting their entrepreneurial venture in the fields of spinning, weaving, knitting, embroidery products, block printing, handlooms handicrafts, bamboo products etc. Similarly, Rashtriya Mahila Kosh was set up in 1993 to grant micro credit to poor women at reasonable rates of interest with very low transaction costs and simple procedures.

9. Strategy for Promotion of Successful Enterprises

Considering the present problems faced by the entrepreneurs engaged in agri-business, it is necessary to create a congenial atmosphere in the field. Some of the important pre-conditions for successful agri-business are presented below:

1. There should be a unanimous option among government officials and farmers about the need and benefits of promoting self-employed youth or private entrepreneurs to facilitate the farmers to enhance agricultural production and profitability.
2. The Government should discontinue the practice of providing free services in those sectors where the work has been assigned to private entrepreneurs.
3. The technical skills and ability of the entrepreneurs should be evaluated to ensure high standards. There should be a monitoring agency to check the quality of the services and the charges collected from the farmers to prevent exploitation.
4. To popularise the services of the entrepreneurs, the Agricultural Extension Agencies and Farmers Organisations should give wider publicity about the services available to the farmers. Such publicity can enhance the credibility of the services provided by the entrepreneurs.
5. The Government should encourage the entrepreneurs by introducing various concessions and incentives.

6. Networks of entrepreneurs may be established to share their experiences. These networks can also establish a close link with Research Institutions and Universities to become acquainted with the latest research findings and seeking solutions for their field problems.

Such direct marketing can be promoted throughout the country. This can be done by allocating some common places in the towns for weekly markets, where farmers can bring their produce, as is done in Andhra Pradesh through Ryat (farmers') bazaars. To facilitate easy transportation of farm produce, buses plying to villages should have additional storage space. The commodities sold in farmers' market should be exempted from octroi and other taxes. Additionally promotion of weekly markets, seasonal fairs for agricultural commodities can also be organised during certain fixed periods every year when farmers can bring their produce in bulk.

10. Conclusion

Increasing women's participation in agriculture can be interpreted as more women working in agriculture than were found previously; Secondly, men are working less, making way to greater participation of women. Thirdly, it may also mean neither has changed but recent data have only begun to capture women who have already been working in agriculture. Indeed, a major problem of Indian farmers is that, as agriculture is considered as a family tradition, a majority of the farmers continue to practice what their forefathers or their neighbors practiced. There is a need for change. Agriculture must be considered as an enterprise, which should have a sound management back-up giving emphasis to women entrepreneurship. Promotion of agro-based enterprises in rural areas through women ensures food security as people in the local areas possess the required skills. Such businesses have a ready demand in rural areas with ample market opportunities. With a strong agro-based programme, non-farm activities can also be initiated when the women entrepreneurs are more experienced and capable of taking risk and can manage the programme better. Promotion of direct marketing by establishing close interaction between producers and consumers will further enhance the benefits for women entrepreneurs while encouraging a large number of unemployed rural youth to turn into micro-entrepreneurs and traders. Technological empowerment of women in agriculture (a current programme in India) has to be backed up with unmediated asset ownership of women; a process to enhance agricultural management skills and knowledge; a wide spread gender sensitisation in rural areas through information and communication technologies, which help to develop a social understanding of women as producers, farmers and economic contributors. In other words, women's unmediated control and ownership of land, new technologies, and irrigation and management skills give them and their households a livelihood with dignity. These if done hand in hand, are stronger measures in overcoming poverty. Usually entrepreneurship in agriculture is high jacked by outsiders in the absence of local entrepreneurship leading to exploitation and deprivation of employment for the farmers. Considering the growing unemployment in rural areas and slow growth of agricultural sector, it is necessary to tap the opportunities for promoting entrepreneurship in agriculture, which in turn can address the present problems related to agricultural production and profitability and employment. It is suggested that agro-based entrepreneurship mission and the agro-based entrepreneurship education should go hand in hand. Mass employment generation is possible with agri-based industrialisation. With better industrial and entrepreneurial education discipline, entrepreneurs will naturally take advantage of the vast human resource availability. With these issues in the background the seminar is conducted with the following themes in consideration.

- Theme-1 Agripreneurship for Women Employment and Empowerment
- Theme-II Technologies for Women Empowerment and Employment
- Theme-III NGO Interventions and Case Studies on Agripreneurship
- Theme-1V Government Initiatives and Policy Framework for Agripreneursip and Rural Development

References

1. Step Taken By Government to Develop Women Entrepreneurs in India, Sameer.
2. Feminisation of Agriculture as an Effect of Male Out-migration: Unexpected Outcomes from Jhapa District, Eastern Nepal; By Hom Nath Gartaula, Anke Niehof and Leontine Visser; Published by The Social Sciences Collection.
3. Women in Agriculture; Feature Article: Notes from the field: feminisation of agriculture in the eastern Gangetic plains August 14, 2012;Posted by southasiamasala in : India, Lahiri-Dutt, Kuntala, trackback;Kuntala Lahiri-Dutt.
4. Women and Agriculture; Caroline Sweetman; Migration, agriculture and women.
5. Feminisation of Agricultural Labour in India;Kalamkar S.S.[a], Shende N.V. Gokhale Institute of Economics and Politics, Pune-411 004, Maharashtra;[b] Department of Agricultural Economics and Statistics, Dr PDKV, Akola, Maharashtra; Online published on 24 November, 2011.
6. The Feminisation of Agriculture in Asia: Implications for Women's Agency and Productivity; Govind Kelkar; UNIFEM South-Asia Regional Office; New Delhi, India, 2009-04-07.
7. The Cost of Revolution; Research Paper; nrmc India Smallholder Women Farmers in India: A Research Study.
8. The agroprocessing industry and economic development.
9. Quality control and standards, agro-processing, industry infrastructure in india.
10. Commercial farming; Trading; Carrying and Forwarding agents‡ Agricultural marketing Information Technology Enabled Services (ITES) for agriculture & allied activities.
11. Non-performing assets and Financial Recovery; janmonibarman's blog; Friday, 28 June 2013; agripreneurship.
12. Entrepreneurs Experiences in Agriculture; *N.G. Hegde;* Presented at the VII Agricultural Science Congress at the College of Agriculture, Pune, February 2005. 16-18.

13. Feminisation of Agricultural Labour in India; Kalamkar S.S.[a], Shende N. V.[b]; A Gokhale Institute of Economics and Politics, Pune 411 004, Maharashtra Department of Agricultural Economics and Statistics, Dr PDKV, Akola, Maharashtra; Online published on 24 November, 2011.

2

Women Empowerment for Sustainable Sericulture in Andhra Pradesh

C. S. Rama Lakshmi

Abstract

Employment of women has been recognised as an effective strategy for their socio-economic empowerment for sustainable sericulture. In crop related activities, a clear cut division of labour was observed along gender lines with some common activities for both men and women. Involvement of farm women in agricultural activities, types of tools/equipment/machine used by them, their working pattern and drudgery reduction is widely studied to benefit the women folk. A woman on an average is engaged for 135-145 days in a year in rearing related activities including cocoon harvesting as against 90-105 days in case of man. Women play a leading role in growing world's silk production which means their participation is central in any programme to improve farming strategies in realising healthy cocoon crops. Women empowerment further results in generating networks and partnerships to support such of those activities wherein the role of women is well pronounced. An attempt was made to measure the extent of women involvement in sericulture development through documenting the success stories and a few awards were given to different categories of women sericulturists of different regions of Andhra

Pradesh. As a token of recognition and appreciation to the Women Stakeholders in the Sericulture Industry, an Award "Pattu SERI" is given to the best performers on the eve of the International Women's Day by Department of Sericulture, Government of Andhra Pradesh. Those details are discussed in detail in the paper.

Introduction

Women though delicate and soft in nature have a stronger and bolder heart and it is historically proved that, since ancient civilisation, women in India played decisive role in household. Though having modest personality confining them to the house, women are recognised as the backbone of the domestic front and society, besides silently supporting men in decision-making and planning. There is a wrong notion that women do not contribute in economic activities as they are normally confined to their household work. The contribution of women, particularly the rural women have attained much more than their male counterparts in some societies. Almost all the work, right from maintaining the family, cultural and social affairs are looked after by the women. The rural women in particular play an important role to take up employment primarily to supplement their family income which is particularly true in the field of sericulture, agro-forestry and farming. But economic contribution of the women often goes unrecognised and is usually considered, an extended part of her normal household duties, they require more attention and importance so that their work in silence gets recognised.

Sericulture an agro-based cottage industry is a combination of biological and technological aspects involving three major activities viz., mulberry leaf production, Cocoon production and Raw Silk production. It is a unique combination of on-farm and off-farm activities. Landless and skilled work forces generally attend non-farm activities. Besides, by-product utilisation ensures additional income generation. Hence, sericulture industry provides ample scope for both on-farm and non-form activities.

Income Sharing in Sericulture Sector

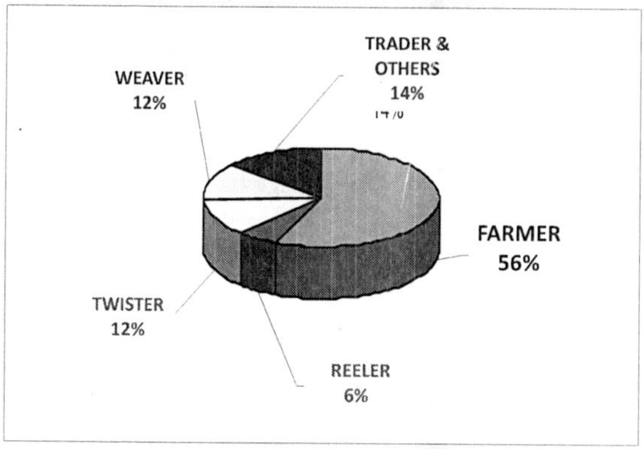

Role of Women in Sericulture

Women workers have limitations to involve themselves in such type of work, which involve literacy, skill up gradation and staying away from home. These aspects necessitate providing job for less educated population of women at local places in decentralised way preferably within their household and hence, Sericulture could be the best alternative to provide gainful employment opportunity especially to women.

Despite the prevailing notion of 'inside—outside dichotomy', the farm sector of late is witnessing a growing phenomenon of feminisation of agriculture with greater integration of women in economic activities.

As it is said "Silk for the women, by the women". Sericulture and Women do connect with each other in several ways for eg., 53 per cent of women participation in sericulture, 57 per cent of the gross value of silk flows to cocoon producers where women participation is high, 70 per cent of women participation in rearing, reeling and weaving sectors, 70 per cent of world silk consumption by Indian women, 80 per cent of silk is consumed by Indian woman. In Rural and Semi Urban areas of Andhra Pradesh, a large number of women folk are working with full force in the various activities related from soil to silk. Some of the noteworthy awardees and their contributions are as follows:

Case Studies of Women Seripreneurs

Best Mulberry Farmers

Smt. Manubolu Venkataratnam of Pedavegi is cultivating mulberry since 2009-10 in 6.5 acres of mulberry and rearing is undertaken in two rearing sheds five crops of CB and six crops of Bivoltine hybrid. With an average yield of 68 Kgs/100 dfls she has earned Rs 9.25 lakhs which has motivated the farmers of her area to establish sericulture as their occupation. Similarly, Smt. Panchada Gayatri of N.N.Patnam has been cultivating mulberry since 2009-10 in 2.0 acres with five crops of CB and two crops of Bivoltine hybrid. With an average yield of 60 Kgs/100 dfls, an amount of Rs 1.69 lakhs is realised per year.

Further, Smt. K. Sakunthalamma of Thimmapuram village of Anantapur district has been cultivating Mulberry since 2003 in an area of 2.5 acres and rearing is undertaken with bivoltine hybrids (10 crops per year). An annual income of Rs 4.00 lakhs is realised as her income along with cocoon production. She has raised mulberry saplings worth Rs 2.00 lakhs as an additional income generating activity. Smt. Nagaratnamma of G.V.Palem, Madakasira of Anantapur District has been undertaking bivoltine rearing since 2001 in 2.5 acres of mulberry with an average yield of 76 Kgs per 100 dfls and has realised an annual income of Rs 2.50 lakhs.

Best Tasar Farmers

Kum. Keta Nagamani of Nuguru village of Khammam district of AP has been undertaking Tasar culture since 2010-11 with the production of 36,000 seed in three crops and 50,000 cocoons were harvested and realised a net income of Rs 1.05 lakhs. In addition, she looks after the young age Tasar silkworm rearing centre sanctioned by the Government of AP. Further, she has established Lakshmi Devi Tasar Silkworm rearing unit in Venkatapuram during 2011-13. Despite several hurdles, Kum. Nagamani could increase her income by four to five times from Tasar Silkworm seed production. At a young age she could accomplish her set goals.

Best Seri Poly Clinics

Smt. Kasukurti Jyothi of Bapulapadu village of Krishna district has been practicing Sericulture since 2007-08 in an area of 3.50 acres of mulberry and earns an annual income of Rs 5.09 lakhs. Due to lack of availability of inputs in her area, she has established a Polyclinic with the support of the Department with the name "Rythu Mitra Seri Poly Clinic". She is a farmer-cum Women entrepreneur worth emulating with a business turnover of Rs 3.3 lakhs.

Best Seed Producers (Chawkie Rearing Centre)

Smt. Akiveeti Jyothi of Cumbum village of Prakasam District is the wife of the Sri Balasubramanyam, Asst. Sericulture Officer of Government of AP. She is responsible for spreading sericulture activity in more than 300 household in Prakasam Dist. With a monthly income of Rs 40,000 she is the source of motivation for many families of Giddalur division. Along with the production of very good quality chawkie worms, she works as voluntary extension agent, encouraging many farmers to take up Bivoltine crops in the entire area. Mrs Jyoti has been a source of inspiration to all other Sericulturists of Prakasam district.

Best Silk Reeler

Smt. S. Reshma Begum of Kummaravandlapalli of Anantapur District established a reeling unit having 10 Basin Multi End Reeling Unit and 400 spindle twisting unit in 2011 with annual silk production of 22-25 MT. In addition, she has established a twisting unit for which the Sericulture Department extended the helping hand and provided the space during establishment. She is involved in changing the fortune of the fellow women in the neighborhood by imparting training in reeling and twisting.

The Sericulture was found to be more remunerative than other cash crops such as cotton in Atmakur District of Nalgonda district. Sri Gurumurthy is very vocal in stating that his wife is the central figure behind the success of their sericulture enterprise.

Mrs Jyothi of Cumbum village of Prakasam District, an innovative women entrepreneur deserves a salute for her commitment and leadership quality that gave her unique identity as she believed in concept of learning by doing and asserts the following reasons for her success in sericulture.

- Assured chawkie quality at her CRC.
- Technical guidance through Audio-visual aids that developed confidence among the farmers.
- Regular personnel visits to farmers fields.
- Supplying chawkie on credit basis. Farmers generally pay the chawki cost after selling the cocoons of that particular crop.
- With an assured cocoon yield of 65-70 Kgs from CB and 60-65 kgs of Bivoltine hybrid.

Due to the efforts of Mrs Jyothi, mulberry acreage in her village increased from 10 to 300 acres within six years. Artificial diet was introduced on an experimental basis in Jyothi CRC for the first time which has resulted in revolutionising sericulture activities in that area.

The success of Mrs G. Nagaveni has ignited the passion for taking up sericulture among many women. She is a member of SHGs with 3.5 acres of mulberry plantation, harvesting of 230 Kgs of cocoons per month in 11-12 crops and earns an income of Rs 3.6 lakhs per year. Through this income obtained from sericulture, within a span of five years she purchased immovable assets like residential house, mini chawkie rearing hall, rearing shed and mini mounting hall and an additional land of 2.0 acres was purchased. Influenced by these benefits they have developed interest in sericulture and have determined not to give up sericulture at any cost.

Smt. Jayamma of Atmakur village of Nalgonda district has replaced four acres of cotton field with V1 mulberry in August 2011. She has felt that sericulture as more profitable since the labour requirement is slightly higher in case of cotton crop. After taking up sericulture, in the very 2nd crop has earned an amount of Rs 56,300 which has improved their financial status. She stood as successful progressive sericulturist and a source of inspiration to many farmers in Atmakur (S) mandal.

Smt. Rajani of Patimatla (v) of Nalgonda district practiced sericulture since 2010 in an extent of two acres of mulberry, she could maintain an average yield of 62 Kg./100 dfls and has earned an income of Rs 1,84,900 per year. Enthused by this income she is very confident and wishes to continue sericulture activity after thoroughly analysing the returns. The bimonthly income from the sericulture enterprise has created confidence in herself and her family.

Smt. Savitramma of Parigi village of Anantapur district has established the fact that women can be a successful entrepreneur. With 2.5 acres mulberry and 1.5 acres of cash crops she manages all the activities with lot of confidence. By realising an amount of Rs 3.2 lakhs through bivoltine rearing in eight crops, she continues to inspire the fellow women and immensely satisfied with the earnings from sericulture and has turned out to be a source of inspiration in her locality.

Some of the success stories of Women farmers in Sericulture Sector indicate that high returns and Staff support motivated them to take up sericulture, the bimonthly income with high profitability has attracted their attention and has been inspirational factor for many other women in their locality.

Agriculture is the single largest livelihood system in Asia contributing to about 30 per cent of the GDP and it is needless to say that Sericulture is a part of it. Sericulture in India as seen is a sustainable farm based economic enterprise empowering the rural poor because of its relatively low requirement of fixed capital and higher returns on investment. Further, the changes in employment and income opportunities in rural areas may be brought about by selecting a highly labour intensive and high income yielding cropping pattern and sericulture continued to be one such sector which plays a vital role in generating gainful employment opportunities, more so to womenfolk.

In addition, the Department of Sericulture, Government of Andhra Pradesh is making an all out effort in attracting women folk in large number to take up sericulture so that Andhra Pradesh will take a step forward in occupying first place in silk production in the country.

References

C.S Rama Lakshmi, IFS., (2012) "Potentiality of Seri culture for poverty alleviation in dry land areas of Andhra Pradesh" Indian Silk Magazine, February 2012, Volume-2, pp. 20-24.

C.S Rama Lakshmi, IFS, (2012) "Joint Family can make wonders in Sericulture" Indian Silk Magazine, June 2012, Volume-3, pp. 10-12.

C.S Rama Lakshmi, IFS, (2012) "Mrs Nagaveni, a Sericulturist Worth Emulating" published in Indian Silk Magazine, November 2012 Vol. 3 (51 old) No. 6, pp. 14-16.

C.S Rama Lakshmi, IFS, (2012) "Innovative Practices: Wealth out of Seri Waste" published in Indian Silk Magazine, April 2013/Vol-III (51 old) No.12. (pp. 10,11).

www.seri.ap.gov.in

www.csb.gov.in

Report of the working group on Textiles and Jute Industry for the Eleventh Five Year Plan (2007-12) published by Government of India, Ministry of Textiles.

Annual Report of Sericulture Department, Government of Andhra Pradesh for the year 2011-12.

Success Stories of Women farmers in Sericulture Sector published by Department of Sericulture, Government of Andhra Pradesh in 2012-13.

G.Sandhya Rani (2006)—"Women in Sericulture" ISBN 81-8356-098-9.

3

Women Entrepreneurship Development Through Millets Processing Technologies

B. Dayakar Rao, N. Kachui, K. Kalpana, K.N. Ganapathy and J.V. Patil

Abstract

Processing intervention in millets has created a wide scope of women entrepreneurship in the country. To imbibe the skills and knowledge of newly developed processing technologies and value addition process remains a challenging factor due to various social and financial imperatives. It requires lot of policy measures so that women can be actively involved in value addition throughout the value chain for sustainable growth in processing vis-à-vis commercialisation across traditional and non-traditional consuming regions. This paper identifies the various constraints both tangible and intangible that hinder women entrepreneurship development in millets, and suggest measures towards profitable and sustainable approach so as to empower them for better income and better contribution to the society.

Keywords: *Millets, Sorghum, Women, Entrepreneurship, Processing*

Introduction

Women Entrepreneurship is an act of business ownership

and business creation that empowers women economically; increases their economic strength as well as position in society (Deshpande and Sethi, 2009). The entrepreneurship development of women in millets can be best described as women's participation in the value addition from farm production to processing and marketing. Women in rural areas make up over half of the low paid agricultural labour (Riebschleger and Fila, 2009) and so is their role in value addition of the farm produce. Traditionally in rural areas, woman stays as housewife whose responsibilities are confined to household activities. However, with the change in lifestyle and increasing cost of livelihood such as education, health, and welfare, the role and responsibility of women has dramatically changed in both urban and rural areas. The most common and vital enterprising activity for women in rural and urban areas is food processing.

Millets are in the family of cereals grown globally with differential importance across continents and within regions of the world. They form a diverse group of small grains cultivated in diverse and adverse environments, mostly in the dry, semi-arid to sub-humid drought-prone agro ecosystems. They are small grain cereals which including sorghum, pearl millet, and other small millets and these are known for their hardiness and adaptation to low input and harsh environments. Total utilisation of millets across the world, is mainly human food, animal feed, seed and processing and other uses. Diversified uses of these crops for food, feed and industrial purposes are expected to promote demand for millets in the future, and thereby improve quality of life in rural India, besides benefiting urban consumers.

Millets possess unique nutritional and functional properties that can lead themselves to the development of healthy and nutritious foods at low costs. Sorghum and pearl millet are gluten-free, have unique phenolic compounds, which are being identified as antioxidants. Unique health foods that have high levels of insoluble dietary fiber, phytates and phytochemicals could be made from sorghums with high levels of catechins, flavonoids and harder-to-digest proteins. The starches in sorghum are released more slowly than those in other cereals and so it is considered beneficial to diabetic patients. In India, it is estimated that eight per cent of population are affected by diabetes, and the consumption of millets helps diabetic and obese population (fiber rich content; slow digestibility) and promotes natural intake of Zn or Fe as well as prevents mineral malnutrition. Millets, especially finger millet is a rich source of calcium which promotes development of bones in children. However, there is a limited awareness on health benefits accrued by millets consumption.

The utilisation of millets pattern was traditional and the skill required, made the consumption of millets restricted to a limited section of population. Millets consumption declined due to rapid industrialisation, urbanisation and increased income levels. Its levels across the major millet growing countries, especially in the urban areas, are waning. Another reason for decreased consumption is because of the labourious and time-consuming process involved in preparation. These resulting in the shift towards more convenient/ processed products of fine cereals like rice and wheat from the sorghum. So far millet processed foods are not significantly exploited to commercialise their importance as health or prophylactic food, despite offering well-balanced composition of carbohydrates, proteins and minerals together with high dietary fiber.

Value addition in food processing sector has high degree of inter-dependence with forward and backward linkages and can play an important role in accelerating economic development. The preparation and production of millet value added foods using processing interventions would initiate the production units and small scale in rural and urban areas to raise the income level of housewives and also the economic status of the growers.

Integrated millets value chain approach plays a key role in harnessing sustainable model to create demand of millets in the country. National Agriculture Innovative Program (NAIP) is chosen as a vehicle to facilitate accelerated and sustainable transformation of Indian agriculture in support of poverty alleviation and income generation. It is done by collabourative development and application of agricultural innovation by the public research organisations and other stakeholders. Thus, entire set of actors are involved in "Production to Consumption

System (PCS) value chain" mode and helps in rural income augmentation and employment generation through post-harvest processing and value addition. Directorate of Sorghum Research (DSR), under the NAIP project has initiated the on-farm production, processing intervention, nutritional certification, promotion and marketing of sorghum in the Indian market. The attempt enabled to bring all the stakeholders in production to consumption system value chain on a common platform and link poor dry land farmers with market as well as consumer.

1. Empowerment of Women at Farm Level

Value addition at farm level is one of the most effective approaches to women empowerment, especially in the case of millets/sorghum. Since the marketable surplus is generally low, at the same time there is no proper channel available for procurement of the grain, processing at urban level is not reliable if not impossible especially for the small scale processors unless it is for large or medium scale processors. Therefore, it will be profitable if processing is taken up at the farm level wherein the desired quality and quantity of raw material is readily available for the production. Most of the post-harvest processing operations are performed at urban sites resulting in increased cost of transportation and storage requirement besides loss of some important byproducts and post-harvest losses (Bakane *et al.*, 2013). Processing at farm level has the following advantages with regard to capital and marketing the final products. The entrepreneurship development therefore needs to give priority at the rural sector, while in urban sector women can take the key role in promoting and marketing them as convenient and health foods for all age groups. The processing of sorghum/millets is simple, in a sense any interested person can learn and start their own food processing; with less than rupees one lakh capital investment; and can be marketed in both the rural and urban market. With the advancement in technology, and the increasing demand of convenient foods in both the urban and rural market, the women can take lots of advantage if provided with proper orientation on setting up of small scale processing especially in the farm areas.

5. Millet Processing Skills and Knowledge

In order to take up millet/sorghum processing and marketing profitable, the entrepreneur will gain both the skill and knowledge on the machineries, processing technologies and promotion and marketing technique. This can be attained by offsite and onsite training.

a. Off-site Training

Off-site training which includes all the post-harvest management training comprising of supply chain management, nutritional significance of the end products, processing, promotion and marketing. The main objective of offsite training is to disseminate the basic knowledge that is required to take up millets processing and to motivate the trainee. Such trainings are conducted by inviting the subject matter specialists from either private or public institutions as the topic covered under such training is vast. After completion of off-site training, on-site training follows.

b. On-site Training

On-site training involves demonstration of primary and secondary processing at the processing labouratory. This will be given by the experts by showcasing the processing technologies developed for easy adoption of technologies by the entrepreneurs and to decrease the risk involved in start-up by offering access to capital and one-on-one technical and managerial assistance (Paula, 2001). It also provides platform to entrepreneurs to take advantage of the proven and commercialised technologies developed by the coordinating institute.

6. Advantages of Millets Processing

a. **Convenience:** Another advantage is that the raw materials (grain) are readily available. Since the marketable surplus of sorghum is generally low, the vendors come and buy the surplus grain directly at the farm at the minimum possible price. In other words, the farmer does not have any bargaining power which brings low revenue to the farmers. Alternatively, if the women can take up processing at farm level, the value of the produce will be much higher, and will impact employment and earning during the off season.

b. **Low capital:** Processing of millets can be taken up even with low investment (below 1 lakh rupees), such as flour and rawa. Women can start sorghum processing by forming into groups such as SHGs, Women Group etc., in the rural areas.

c. **Increasing Demand for Convenient Foods:** The increasing demand of convenient food products has been on the rise in both urban and rural alike. Millets are the traditional staple diet for millions of people, which has huge market potential in the traditional areas if available to them in the form of ready-to-cook and ready-to-eat food.

d. **Low Marketing Cost:** The millets value added products have high acceptability by the traditional staple diet followers if available in ready-to-eat and ready-to-cook foods, reduce the promotion expenditure unless it is for special packaging to attract the buyers.

e. **Market expansion:** Market expansion is considered in the broader sense implying the increasing awareness of health and nutrition foods and yearning for convenient foods among the populace. Millet processing therefore can bring enormous employment and business opportunities to the women by exploring and fully utilising this nutrient rich crop into developing market product, by either replicating or developing various ready-to-eat and ready-to-cook food products as per the local choice and demand.

7 Constraints in Women Empowerment

a. **Education:** According to 2001 proceedings going to press in 2014 would sound better with 2011 census figure, the literacy rate of female is 53.7 per cent with 72.9 in urban area and 46.2 per cent in rural area (Census 2001). The figure implies difficulty to impart or spread the awareness on the different processing technologies that have been developed under various research programmes, especially to the rural women who are the major stakeholders in the supply chain.

b. Society Perception: Generally in India, women are not given much importance when compared to men, whether it is in family business or leadership in the society. About 90 per cent women talent goes waste due to the negligence and non-supporting nature of family members (Savita Kumari, 2012), lacking both moral and financial support. This has become a bottleneck to actually motivate them to learn different technique on value addition in millet and to involve them in the processing business.

c. Lack of Information on Processing Technologies: Processing of sorghum/ millets was considered to be very difficult due to inconvenience in preparation and low shelf life. With the advance in technology and various processing interventions, these inconveniences have been removed. However, the spread of knowledge on such processing technologies is in the initial stage. Most farmers still practice subsistence farming as far as cultivate sorghum and millets is concerned, only meant for their own food and cattle need feed. There is still long way to go for spreading the awareness on millet processing unless the entrepreneurs are directly encountered with the developer (in case of sorghum processing, DSR is the developer).

d. Lack of Policy Intervention: Unlike fine cereals, millets have the disadvantage of nil subsidies to the cultivators that resulted in low or no marketable surplus (sorghum grain)- the raw material for processing. Millets being a dry-land crop, the cultivators are mostly marginal farmers who could hardly invest or take the risk to start processing.

e. Lack of Financial Issues: Lack of inheritance rights, less access to capital, low exposure to business, investments, saving issues and other decision-making issues are constraints in expansion of women entrepreneurship.

f. Market Situation: Consumers' perception is one key area

where the newly developed products need to focus on its marketing strategy. The pilot commercialisation of sorghum products at Hyderabad on a pilot scale has proved the feasibility and profitability of sorghum/millets processed foods. However, the actual market situation will vary from region to region, and so far the MIS (Market Information System) of sorghum and millet products are not established. The entrepreneurs require innovative promotion strategies during or prior to marketing in the target market.

8. Challenges in Entrepreneurship Development of Women in Millets Processing

a. Integrated Approach: Entrepreneurship development in millets requires sustainable linkage of producers (farmers) and processors (entrepreneurs) in compliance with the market condition. Such linkage can ensure consistent supply of desired quality and quantity of raw materials to the processors, and better price to the farmers.

b. Gender Neutral or Women-Specific: Entrepreneurship development in millets processing can be taken up irrespective of gender. However, when women empowerment is concern, the question arise as to how far the women-specific approach has greater impact in terms of number of participation, learning, and starting processing business after the training.

c. Policy Sensitisation: Most of the millets are new to the entrepreneurs and people in general. The nutritional, health benefits and potential to employment generation through millets in the country, needs to be sensitised to the policy makers to popularise millets across the country to build confidence among those interested in taking up millets processing.

Conclusion

Value addition at farm level, training on processing techniques, information on financial issues market, and government policies will facilitate women empowerment in millet processing.

References

1. Bakane, P.H., Borkar, P.A., Khedkar, M.B. and Dange, M.M. 2013. Rural entrepreneurship development through agro processing. Agriculture Update, 8 (1 and 2): pp. 314-316.
2. Census 2001: http://censusindia.gov.in/Census_Data_2001/India_at_glance/literates1.aspx
3. Deshpande, S and Sethi, S. 2009. Women Entrepreneurship in India. Shodh, Samiksha aur Mulyankan (International Research Journal)—ISSN-0974-2832 Vol. II, Issue-9-10 (Oct.-Nov.-2009)
4. Joanne, R and Fila, B. 2009. Voices of women in rural India: Empowerment, entrepreneurship, and education. Journal of Contemporary Rural Social Work, 1 (1).
5. Paula, K. 2001. Promoting Women's Entrepreneurship Development based on Good Practice Programmes: Some Experiences from the North to the South. International Labour Organisation. ISBN 92-2-112341-3
6. Savita, K. 2012. Women Entrepreneurship in India. International Indexed and Referred Research Journal, June, 2012. ISSN- 0974-2832, RNI-RAJBIL 2009/29954; Vol. IV ISSUE-41

4

Entrepreneurship Development of Tribal Women Through Krishi Vigyan Kendra Activities

Vilas Jadhav

Abstract

Since ancient times women have been playing a crucial role in family as well as in farming. But their contribution has not been identified fully and acknowledged. In the present scenario of globalisation, liberalisation and privatisation in agricultural sector also, the sustainable development and empowerment of farm women is considered as a key factor for development of any country. According to the 2011 census of India, women constitute half of the total population. Participation of women in economic activities is now emerging as a universal phenomenon. Advancement of information and communication technologies created many opportunities for the development of talents of women in entrepreneurship activities. Krishi Vigyan Kendra, funded by a renowned institute, Indian Council of Agricultural Research provides vocational training programmes to the farm women in self-employment. A study was conducted during 2013–14 in Dahanu, Jawhar and Palghar tehsils of Thane district of Maharashtra state. From each tehsil, two adopted villages were selected based on highest number of farm women who participated in vocational training programmes which was organised by Gokhale Education Society's KVK Thane (MS) and involved in self-help group activities. From each village 20 farm women (i.e., total 60 farm women) were selected by following simple random sampling procedure and information was collected and analysed. The results of the study revealed that, more than (56.60 per cent) of farm women were illiterate with middle aged with semi medium level of income. Half of the respondents belonged to medium mass media utilisation category. Low to medium achievement motivation was observed in more than 50 per cent of the farm women may be because of illiteracy and ignorance. Further majority (71.60 per cent) of the farm women regularly attended training and 62.50 per cent of them occasionally participated in extension activities. Whereas it is noticed that majority of the farm women were self-motivated as to join SHG since it is a good means to save money. The preparation of sapota products, poultry keeping, goat rearing, vegetable cultivation, papad making and vermi- culture on small scale basis were the major activities adopted by more than half of the farm women pursuant to motivation efforts through training and demonstration. It was highlighted from the results that, financial condition of majority (73.33 per cent) of farm women was improved, followed by social status (68.33 per cent) and increased level of confidence (61.66 per cent) among farm women towards entrepreneurship are the major benefits derived after joining as the members of SHG as expressed by themselves. The women entrepreneurs well managed their time for their daily household and entrepreneurial activities. Participation of women in SHG activities motivated them to take up an enterprise for the self-employment generation. Hence policy makers and administrators have to give priority to formation of women SHG and provide financial assistance for establishing their own agro based enterprises.

Key words: Entrepreneurship, Empowerment, Sustainable development, Self-help Group, KVK, ICAR, Demonstration, Training.

Introduction

"You can tell the condition of a nation by looking at the status of its women" ***- Jawaharlal Nehru.***

The emergence of women entrepreneurs and their contribution to the national economy is quite visible in India. The number of women entrepreneurs has grown over a period of time, especially in the 1990s. Women entrepreneurs need to be lauded for their increased utilisation of modern technology, increased investments, finding a niche in the export market, creating a sizable employment for others and setting the trend for other women entrepreneurs in the organised sector. While women entrepreneurs have demonstrated their potential, the fact remains that they are capable of contributing much more than what they already are. Women's entrepreneurship needs to be studied separately for two main reasons. The first reason is that women's entrepreneurship has been recognised during the last decade as an important untapped source of economic growth. Women entrepreneurs create new jobs for themselves and others and also by being different. They also provide the society with different solutions to management, organisation and business problems as well as to the exploitation of entrepreneurial opportunities. The second reason is that the topic of women in entrepreneurship has been largely neglected both in society in general and in the social sciences. Not only have women lower participation rates in entrepreneurship than men but they also generally choose to start and manage firms in different industries than men tend to do.

Rural women play a vital role in farm and home system. She contributes substantially in the physical aspect of farming, livestock management, post harvest and allied activities. Her direct and indirect contribution at the farm and home level along with livestock management operation has not only helped to save their assets but also led to increase in the family income. She performs various farm, livestock, post harvest and allied activities and possesses skills and indigenous knowledge in these areas. The women were empowering themselves technically to cope with the changing times and productively using their free time and existing skills for setting and sustaining enterprises. They were engaged in starting individual or collective income generation programmes with the help of self-help group.

This will not only generate income for them but also improve the decision-making capabilities that led to overall empowerment.

Advantages of Entrepreneurship among Rural Women

Empowering women particularly rural women is a challenge. Micro enterprises in rural area can help to meet these challenges. Micro-enterprises not only enhance national productivity, generate employment but also help to develop economic independence, personal and social capabilities among rural women. Following are some of the personal and social capabilities, which were developed as result of taking up enterprise among rural women.

- Economic empowerment
- Improved standard of living
- Self confidence
- Enhanced awareness
- Sense of achievement
- Increased social interaction
- Engaged in political activities
- Increased participation level in gram sabha meeting
- Improvement in leadership qualities
- Involvement in solving problems related to women and community
- Decision making capacity in family and community

Agricultural production of the Thane district mainly depends upon tribal women. They are engaged in tedious jobs like rice transplanting and harvesting of rice as well as grass cutting which is the main economic source. It means tribal woman has significant role in home as well as farming activities.

Tribals are still using the traditional practices that cause low income and less productivity as compared to other communities. This is one of the main reasons for their poverty. In order to upgrade their socio-economic status, the only option today is to improve their agricultural productivity through the adoption of improved technologies. In the attempt to boost the overall agricultural productivity tribal women play a key role in changing the traditional practices. Therefore, the role of women should be given emphasis so that the desirable changes can be brought about in lifestyle of tribal masses.

Keeping these things in mind, the KVK, Thane (MS) started its intervention. KVK has given an opportunity with due attention to their specific farming responsibilities and arranged various vocational training programme for promoting women participation and contribution in agricultural production. After providing training programmes many farm women started agricultural based enterprises individually as well as SHGs for their self-employment.

Entrepreneurship development and income generating activities of KVK are a feasible solution for empowering women. They generate income and also provide flexible working hours according to the needs of home makers. Economic independence is the need of the hour. Participation in income generating activities helps in the overall empowerment of women. Empowering women through training, demonstration, education, ideas, consciousness, mobilisation and participatory approach can enable them to take their own decisions, make them self reliant and self-confident.

Thus, to investigate the entrepreneurship development of tribal women through KVK activities, the present study was undertaken with the following specific objectives:

(i) To study the socio-economic profile of tribal women

(ii) To analyse the economic gains derived by the women after starting enterprise.

(iii) To study the entrepreneurial behavior of tribal women

Methodology

The study was conducted in Dahanu, Jawhar and Palghar tehsils of Thane district of Maharashtra state. The three tehsils are selected purposively because many villages from these tehsils were adopted by KVK due to feasible and smooth functioning of various mandatory activities. Two villages from each tehsil i.e., six villages were randomly selected. One group of each village i.e., six groups which were trained by KVK on Sapota product preparation, vermiculture preparation, vegetable cultivation, *papad* making, goat rearing and poultry keeping enterprises. Six villages from three tehsils 60 women entrepreneurs engaged in concerned enterprises since last five years was drawn for the study. Thus, total respondents were 60 women selected for the study. The interview schedule was pretested. Personal interview technique was used for data collection. The data collected from the respondents were processed and tabulated. Frequency and percentages were used for statistical methods. The correlation coefficient was employed to interpret the data.

Result and Discussion

i. Socio-economic Profile of Tribal Women

The information on socio-economic profile of tribal women entrepreneurs obtained in the study area is presented in the following Table 1:

Table 1: Socio-economic Profile of Tribal Women

Sr. No.	*Particulars*	*Respondents*	
		Frequency	*Percentage*
1	Age		
	Young (18–35 years)	09	15.00
	Middle (36–50 years)	46	76.66
	Old (Above 51)	05	08.34
	Total	**60**	
2	Self- Education Status		
	Illiterate	34	56.60
	Primary	18	30.00
	High School	08	13.40
	College	0	0.00
	Total	**60**	**100.00**
3	Marital Status		
	Married	56	93.34
	Unmarried	0	0.00
	Widow	04	6.66
	Total	**60**	**100.00**
4	Family type		
	Joint	09	15.00
	Nuclear	51	85.00
	Total	**60**	**100.00**
5	Land Holding		
	Landless	11	18.34
	Marginal	42	70.00
	Small	07	11.66
	Medium	0	0.00
	Large	0	0.00
	Total	**60**	**100.00**

Sr. No.	*Particulars*	*Respondents*	
		Frequency	*Percentage*
6	Occupational pattern		
	Farming	31	51.66
	Agricultural labour	26	43.34
	Wage	03	05.00
	Service	0	0
	Own business	0	0
	Total	**60**	**100.00**
7	Annual income (Rs) **Before Training**		
	Rs. 20,000/- to Rs. 50,000/-	42	70.00
	Rs. 50,000/- to Rs. 75,000/-	12	20.00
	Rs. 75,000/- to Rs. 1,00,000/	04	06.66
	Above Rs. 1,00,000/-	02	03.34
	Total	**60**	**100.00**

Majority of the tribal women i.e., 76.66 per cent were in middle age group. It was also found that, 15.00 per cent of the beneficiaries are in young age group and only 8.34 per cent belonged old age group in the study sample.

Regarding education status, it can be inferred that on an average 56.60 per cent of the sample women entrepreneurs were illiterates and only 30.00 per cent and 13.40 per cent of them had schooling up to primary and High school level respectively.

It could be seen that about 93.44 per cent of the were married while 6.66 per cent were widows in the study sample. With regard to composition of nucleus family it could be observed from above Table that 85 per cent of the sample beneficiaries have a nuclear family system while 15 per cent were joint family in the study area.

The status of land holding position of the sample respondents revealed that 70.00 per cent belonged to marginal land holding category followed by 18.00 per cent in landless and 11.66 per cent of them small land holding category.

Majority (51.66 per cent) of the respondents had farming as their main occupation followed by both agricultural labour (43.34 per cent) and wage earning (05.00 per cent) in sample. Regarding annual income, table shows that before enterprise started the 70.00 per cent of the respondents having income of Rs 20,000 to 50,000 followed by 20.00 per cent were in

Rs 50,000 to 750,000 . 6.66 per cent and 3.34 per cent respondents were having income of Rs 75,000 to 1,00,000 and above 1,00,000 respectively.

ii. Analyse the Economic Gains Derived by the Women after Starting Enterprise.

Gokahale Education Society's Krishi Vigyan Kendra, Dist. Thane (MS) provided one month duration vocational training programme to persons as per their interest and need. The particular women started their enterprises involving SHGs. The economic gains derived by the women entrepreneurs are as given in following Table:

Table 2: Economic Impact of Various Enterprises

Sr. No.	*Name of Group*	*No. of Women Entrep-reneurs*	*Name of Enterprise*	*Year of Star-ted*	*Average Annual Income per group Rs. (Before Training)*	*Average Production of enter-prise (Kg)*	*Average Gross Income received (Rs) (After Training)*	*Individ-ually Profit gained per Year (Rs)*
1	Amrut Madhuri	09	Preparation of Sapota products	2005	37,800/-	2146 Kg	4,29,200/-	47,688/-
2	Bhagavati Mahila Bachat Gat	10	Vermiculture production	2006	26,500/-	58942 Kg	3,53,652/-	35,365/-
3	Aadishakti Mahila Bachat gat	10	Vegetable production	2006	31,750/-	27400 Kg	3,83,600/-	38,360/-
4	Vimal Bachat gat	11	Nagali Products	2007	25,750/-	748 Kg	3,36,600/-	33,660/-
5	Vaishnavi Bachat gat	10	Gaot Keeping	2007	27,400/-	120 Nos	3,85,000/-	38,500/-
6	Sushila Bachat Gat	10	Poultry Keeping	2007	24,960/-	4850 Nos.	3,88,000/-	38,800/-
	Total	**60**			**29,026/-**		**3,79,342/-**	**38,779/-**

It is reveals that, 09 women entrepreneurs of Amrit Madhuri group engaged in Preparation of sapota products enterprise who received gross income of Rs 4,29,200. It means the individual member got Rs 47,688 per year. In case of Vermiculture production enterprise, the Bhagavati Mahila group received gross income Rs 3,53,652 i.e., the individual member yearly got Rs 36,365. In case of vegetable production from Aadishakti mahila group received Rs 3,83,600 gross income and indicates individual member earns Rs 38,360 per year. Regarding nagli products namely papad, satwa, biscuits etc the Vimal group received Rs 3,36,600 and their individual earns Rs 33,600 per year. While poultry keeping business, the Sushila group received Rs 3,88,000 and got net profit Rs 38,800 per person per year.

On an average, women entrepreneurs earned Rs 38,779 per year which were 34 per cent more income than they got before training received i.e., Rs 29,026 per year. All these entrepreneurial work was done in the remaining time of household work.

(iii) Entrepreneurial Behavior of the Women Entrepreneurs

The overall Entrepreneurial behaviour score of the respondents was worked out by summing up the scores obtained on five dimensions namely decision-making, risk orientation, management orientation, economic motivation and self-confidence. The data in respect of overall Entrepreneurial behaviour presented in Table 3:

Table 3: Distribution of Respondents According to their Overall Entrepreneurial Behaviour

Sr. No.	*Category*	*No. of percentage*
1	Low	19.00
2	Medium	62.00
3	High	19.00

It reveals that majority (62.00 per cent) of the respondents had medium Entrepreneurial behaviour The others were found equally distributed in low and high categories. The average score of the respondents was 101.71 which also indicates medium Entrepreneurial behaviour.

It can be discerned for these results, that, by and large, the women entrepreneurs almost had fairly good Entrepreneurial behaviour. This might be due to their better scoring on almost all the parameters selected to measure the Entrepreneurial behaviour. When looked in the context of their enterprises, these finding lead to conclude that the women entrepreneurs might have been efficiently managing the operations related to their enterprises.

Conclusion

It could be concluded from the findings that, this study has brought to limelight the personal and socioeconomic characteristics of women entrepreneurs. On the basis of this, it would be possible for the extension worker and other agencies to identify the prospective entrepreneurs. This would help in making the job of extension worker easier and would also save their time. Secondly, special efforts need to be made to convince these traditional entrepreneurs about newly recommended technologies by organising the practical oriented training classes in the villages, where the particular agricultural enterprise is run extensively. Thirdly, younger entrepreneurs having higher self-confidence, decision-making after training received by KVK, so some of these characteristics should be manipulated suitably, wherever possible to improve the Entrepreneurial behaviour.

References

1. Anonymous (1998): A study of Entrepreneurial behaviour of youth. A report of the Agricultural Extension, Agricultural Economics and Agricultural Statistics subcommittee, Dr Balasaheb Sawant Konkan Krishi Vidyapeeth, Dapoli.
2. Patil A. S. (1999): A study of Entrepreneurial behaviour of the vegetables in Raigad district. M. Sc. (Agri) Thesis (Unpublished), Dr Balasaheb Sawant Konkan Krishi Vidyapeeth, Dapoli.
3. Suresh K. (2008): Impact of micro Finance on empowerment of rural women—a case study of dairy enterprise in the tank management project area of North Karnataka. M. Sc. (Agri) Thesis (Unpublished), Department of Agricultural Economics College of Agriculture, Dharwad University of Agricultural Sciences, Dharwad.

4. Ram Naresh Thakur (2009). "Rural Women Empowerment in India" in Empowerment of Rural Women in India Kanishka Publishers, New Delhi.
5. Shobana Nelasco and Junofy Antorozarina (2009) "Rural women empowerment through Self Help Groups" in Empowerment of Rural Women in India Kanishka Publishers, New Delhi.

5

Entrepreneurship Development among Rural Women Through Krishi Vigyan Kendra

K. Dattatri, Chari Appaji, G. Rajender Reddy and N. Sudhakar

Abstract

Women play a vital role in agriculture as they are involved in majority of farm operations viz. Sowing, transplanting, weeding, harvesting, storage and marketing of farm produce. Women constitute 43 per cent of agricultural workforce in developing countries. Most women are unpaid family workers and work on the family farm irrespective of crop and women engaged in the production and trading of cash crops are a minority. Further the average farm size in India is about one hectare. Due to average small sized farms men in the family migrate to urban areas for seeking employment to feed the family members for increased wages leaving agriculture to women. Fifty two to seventy five per cent of women engaged in agriculture are illiterate and lack improved skills. In addition to farm operation women need to take care of home and children care responsibility. Often young girls assist their mothers in house hold activities. Generally women don't have financial freedom as the ownership title of lands is in the name of men. Due to above situation the women economic condition is poor. Likewise women suffer from gender based inequalities in areas of access to inputs.

Therefore, the Krishi Vigyan Kendras operating in Andhra Pradesh and Maharashtra (78 No.) states, conducted skill oriented training programmes on income generation and entrepreneurship development for rural women during the years 2008–09 to 2012–13. A total of 3321 training courses were organised by KVKs involving about 0.96 lakh farm women during 5 years. Training Programs Conducted for rural women during 2008–09 – 2012–13 in Zone – V (A.P. and Maharashtra).

The training programmes include value addition of field crops, cereals, millets, pulses, oilseeds, and fruit crops, viz., Aonla, Pomegranate, Citrus, Banana, medicinal crops, promotion of dairying through fodder cultivation, azolla cultivation and feeding, production of vermin compost etc. In case of non-farm activities, training programmes on hand embroidery, zardosi, bathik printing fabric painting, quilt bag, and jute bag making, crochio wire bag making, handicrafts from Mesta fibre etc. After imparting training fallow up and spot guidance was given in establishing the units. Exposure visits were arranged to established units. Facilitated in getting finance from ATMA, NABARD and other financial institutions.

As a result of the above efforts, women trainees have established different units in various districts of Andhra Pradesh. and Maharashtra.

Due to the training programmes rural and farm women have started the enterprises and earning an average income of Rs 1000 to 4000 per month and supporting their families. Income generated from these enterprises sustained their lives, families and living standards have improved.

Introduction

The basic concept underlying the definition of entrepreneurship is innovativeness, an urge to take risks in the face of uncertainties and an intuition i.e., a capacity of seeing things in a way which afterwards prove to be true. Entrepreneurship means a quality destined to increase production spontaneously.

Entrepreneurship depends on certain personality traits viz.; perception of market factors, independence and a high need for influencing others, involvement, decision-making, access to and control over resources, calculated risk taking, need for achievement, placing family and friends next to business etc., increases probability of an entrepreneur emerging out successful.

The present status is that women have important role in income generating activities of agriculture, but have little control over income. They are largely engaged in small scale activities and have better access to local market, often at price discount. The challenge is to aggregate the small scale production and improve the access to markets. This needs capacity development for access of women to technology, financial services and markets.

One of the main objective of Krishi Vigyan Kendras (Farm Science Centers) established by Indian Council of Agricultural Research (ICAR) is to empower the rural women by imparting latest technical knowledge on agriculture and allied fields to improve their farms, vocations and enterprises.

Thematic Areas for Training of Rural Women in Krishi Vigyan Kendras

- Design and development of low cost diet
- Gender mainstreaming through SHGs
- Household food security by kitchen gardening and nutrition gardening
- Income generation activities for empowerment of rural women
- Rural crafts
- Value addition
- Women and child care
- Design and development of high nutrition efficient diet
- Minimising nutrient loss in processing, storage
- Dairy management
- Sheep and goat management

- Poultry management
- Feed and fodder management

Krishi Vigyan Kendras (78) operating in Andhra Pradesh and Maharashtra states, conducted skill oriented training programmes on income generation and entrepreneurship development for rural women during the years 2008–09 to 2012–13. A total of 3321 training courses were organised by KVKs involving about 0.96 lakh farm women during five years (Table 1):

Table 1: Women Entrepreneurship Development Courses Organised

Year	*Andhra Pradesh*		*Maharashtra*		*Total*	
	NC	NP	NC	NP	NC	NP
2008-09	212	5552	256	5641	468	11193
2009-10	280	8389	357	10486	637	18875
2010-11	255	6799	349	10340	604	17139
2011-12	460	15643	380	10792	840	26435
2012-13	375	12576	397	10685	772	23261
Total	**1582**	**48959**	**1739**	**47944**	**3321**	**96903**

In the farm sector trainings are given on value addition of field crops, cereals, millets, pulses, oilseeds, and fruit crops, viz., Aonla, Pomegranate, Citrus, Banana, medicinal crops, promotion of dairying through fodder cultivation, azolla cultivation and feeding, production of vermin compost etc., while in the non farm sector trainings are provided on hand embroidery, zardosi, bathik printing fabric painting, quilt bag, and jute bag making, crochio wire bag making, handicrafts from Mesta fibre etc., After the completeion of the training the participants are given follow up and spot guidance in establishing the units. Exposure visits are also arranged to establish the units and facilitation is made on accessing the financial institutions like ATMA, NABARD.

With such a follow up effort, (women) trainees have successfully established different units in various districts of Andhra Pradesh and Maharashtra. The details are discussed below table-2 and 3.

The data presented in Table 2 shows that five women from Ahmednagar and Solapur District have taken up papad making as enterprise and are earning an average income of Rs 1.20 to 3.00 lakh per annum. The product is sold in the local market, exhibitions and *melas* organised at various places. *Papads* are prepared with green gram and black gram flour, flavoured with corriender, spinach, black pepper, cumin, garlic etc.,

In Jalgaon district, where banana crop is cultivated in large areas, enterprise on value addition of banana through preparation and marketing of banana chips was started by two enterprising women Ms Malathi Dake and Ms Shoba Vani. The banana chips with different flavours like *pudina* (mint leaves), tomato etc have been their specialty. The produce is sold through an outlet opened by them in Jalgaon towns and through outlets in other towns not only in the district but also other districts where their product is gaining popularity. On an average they are earning three to 3.5 lakh through marketing and sale of banana chips.

Enterprise of value added Aonla products such as candy, *murrabba*, Jam, *Supari* etc., have been started by the women who have undergone training in these aspects in the KVKs of Beed, Aurangabad, Jalna, Ahmednagar and thane districts. Aonla, which is a rich source of vitamin C is cultivated in a considerable area in these districts and is available throughout the year. The net income obtained by the women through these enterprises is to the tune of Rs 1.8–3.5 lakh.

Ms Chaya Bhagat, an enterprising graduate in Ahmednagar district cultivates medicinal and aromatic plants and is processing them in the form of jelly, juices as also extracting oils. Medicinal plants such as Aloe Vera, Jamun, cucumber etc., are being cultivated and processed. These products are being marketed in Mumbai/Pune through the network of dealers and retailers. She earns a net income of over 2.0 lakh per annum. Ms Chaya has built her enterprise with the assistance of her husband who has encouraged her in all aspects. She also trains other women folks of the village and nearby areas in preparation of products. Ms Chaya also acts as master trainer for KVK Ahmednagar.

Table 2: Agri-based Enterprises Undertaken by Women Trainees

Name of Trainee / SHG	*District*	*Enterprise established*	*Annual income (Rs)*
Vishala Bele	Solapur	Pomogranate Juice centre	2.8 lakh
Vandana A Thombre	Solapur	Dall mill	2.7 lakh
Ranjana P Umbarkar	Ahmednagar	Papad Making	1.20 lakh
Gauraubai b Patil	Ahmednagar	Papad Making	1.25 lakh
Kasturbai S Patil	Solapur	Papad Making	1.38 lakh
Savitha Ashinde	Solapur	Papad Making	2.4 lakh
Mangal S.Yadav	Ahmednagar	Papad Making	3.3 lakh
Malathi U Dake	Jalgaon	Banana chips	3.36 lakh
Shoba Wani	Jalgaon	Banna chips/wafers	2.95 lakh
Nazia Shaik	Beed	Aonla candy, Murabba, Jam, supari	1.25 lakh
Mrs.S.Vijay Bhalekar	Aurangabad	Aonla candy, Murabba, Jam, supari	1.8 lakh
Ms.Sitabai R mohite	Jalna	Aonla candy, Murabba, Jam, supari	2.2 Lakh
SHG	Nandurba	Soyamilk, paneer etc.	2.4 lakh
SHG	Kurnool	Sorghum flour, rava,	1.50 lakh
Ms.Chaya K.Bhagat	Ahmednagar	Alovera, jamun, cucumber	2.0 lakh
Anitha R Kalpande	Buldhana	Safed Musli powder	3.36 lakh
Bhaya Lakshmi	West Godavari	Pickle making	1.25 lakh
Ms.Mangala Solanki	Ahmednagar	Aonla, soya products, pickles branded	3.5 lakh
Annapurna	Nandurbar	Neem Powder	.90 lakh
B.Shesharatnam	Prakasam	Bath powder	.36 lakh
Jyothi Amol Patil	Thane	Mango processing	1.10 lakh
Sharada G Patil	Thane	Aonla products	3.19 lakh
K.Ratnamala	Chittoor	Dairying	0.96 lakh
Swathi Ashok Katela	Thane	Goatary	0.54 lakh
C.Siva Parvathi	Chittoor	Sericulture	3.75 lakh
Manjula K umbhalkar	Amravathi	Mushroom	0.49 lakh
Durga Naykhore	Amravathi	Mushroom	0.49 lakh
Jyothi P. Koble	Akola	Veg. cultivation under shade net	4.0 lakh

Name of Trainee/SHG	*District*	*Enterprise established*	*Annual income (Rs)*
Sujata	Wardha	Veg. cultivation under shade net	2.5 lakh
Aruna Sanjay	Pune	Veg. cultivation & Marketing	3.6 lakh
SHG (tribal)	Osmanabad	Organic Veg. cultivation & Marketing	4-8.90 lakh
Umatai	Washim	Floriculture nursery	2.25 lakh
Kalyani Anil	Akola	Veg. cultivation & Marketing	2.2 lakh
Ms C. Bajamma	Karimnagar	Vermiculture & Compost	0.90 lakh
Ms Suvarna Kale	Ahmednagar	Vermiculture & Compost	4.8 lakh

Value addition to soybean through preparations of soya milk, *paneer*, tofu, *chivada* etc., are undertaken by the women trainees of KVKs in Nandurbar, and Ahmednagar districts. The women derive a net income of Rs 2.4-3.5 annually through marketing of these products made from soybean.

Preparation and marketing of value added products like sorghum Semolina (Rava), flour has been undertaken by women folk in Kurnool district which fetches them an income of about 1.5 lakhs per annum. These products are marketed in retail shops as well as super markets in Kurnool district.

Ms Anita Kalpande, a diploma holder in dairying, besides promoting dairy activities managing milch cattle, has 20 goats also in her farm. She also cultivates fodder crops apart from cultivation of *safed* musli, Anola etc. Through processing and marketing of *safed* muesli and Anola products directly without involving middle man, she is adding an additional income of Rs 3.36 lakh per annum.

In Chittoor district of Andhra Pradesh, women have started producing improved fodder crops and azolla in the farms to enhance dairy and reduce cost of production.

Sericulture, through producing and marketing of silk, has been taken up by Ms C. Shivparvati in Chittoor district. She earns an amount of 3.75 lakhs through this enterprise. Sericulture is also taken up as an enterprise in the district of Nalgonda in Andhra Pradesh by women. In Maharashtra, vegetable cultivation and floriculture in shade nets houses are undertaken. Exotic vegetables and cut flowers are being produced and marketed in Mumbai and Pune. Door to door delivery based on demand is also undertaken by the women of exotic vegetables and cut flowers.

For promotion of organic manures, production of vermin compost and marketing on commercial basis is being undertaken by women in Karimnagar and Ahmednagar districts adding an income to a tune of Rs 0.9 to 4.8 lakh per annum.

Table 3: Non-agri-based Enterprises Started by Women Trainees

Name of Trainee / SHG	*District*	*Enterprise established*	*Annual income (Rs)*
L. Chandrakala and others	Kurnool	Maggam embroidery	25000-30000
S. Mani,	Kurnool	Fabric Painting	30000
SHG	Karimnagar	Zardosi embroidery	35000
Master Trainer	Kurnool	Fashion Designing	25000
A.Padmavathi	Kurnool	Dyeing & printing	18000
Rekha vitne Pate	Beed		0.55 lakh
Sindhu Shyam nirmal	Jalgaon	Tailoring	0.36 lakh
Bhagya Lakshmi	Anantapur	Tailoring	0.28 lakh
Krajeshwari	Chottoor	Tailoring	0.62 lakh
Smt.Gayatri	Srikakulam	Mesta Handicrafts	1.58 lakh
SHG	Karimnagar	Jute bag making	12000
SHG	Kurnool	Quilt bag making	8000
SHG	Kurnool	Crichio wire bag making	6000
Indumati Pumbare	Solapur	Smokeless Chulla	0.55 lakh

Trainees who have acquired skills in the areas of tailoring, embroidery, batik printing and other areas, have started small scale enterprise to fulfil the family needs. These activities are taken up by the women in their leisure time, they earn Rs 18000-55000 per annum, for supporting their families.

Mrs Gayatri in Srikakulam district after successfully undergoing training in preparing of Mesta handicrafts has started her own enterprise and earns an income of Rs 1.58 lakh annually.

In Karimnagar and Kurnool districts women who have undergone training at the respective KVKs in the districts, have formed self-help groups and are preparing and marketing Jute, quilt, and wire bags. Amount of about Rs 6000 to Rs 8000 per woman in the SHG is distributed per annum as their share. These activities are taken up by the women using their spare time.

Conclusion

The enterprise taken up by rural women has not only generated income for their families but also created additional employment opportunities. Due to this the additional income thus generated by women is being used for provision of education to children, perusing higher studies. Women have invested money thus earned in purchase of household assets and jewellery. More number of special entrepreneurship development programmes need to be conducted by promotional agencies and development organisations with equal thrust on technology up gradation and entrepreneurial qualities.

6

A Study of Women Vegetable Street Vendors in Karnataka

Huchhe Gowda

Abstract

Women are significant contributors to the growing economy. But still the women's contribution in the total workforce remains unrecognised. Almost 400 million people—more than 85 per cent of the working population in India—work in the unorganised sector. Of these, at least 120 million are women. Unorganised sector work is characterised by low wages that are often insufficient to meet minimum living standards including nutrition, long working hours, and hazardous working conditions, lack of basic services such as first aid, drinking water and sanitation at the worksite and so on. Women working in the informal sector are not included in the official statistics and their work is undocumented and considered as disguised wage work, unskilled, low paying and does not provide benefits to the worker. India was one of the first countries in the world to give women the right to vote. The Indian constitution is one of the most progressive in the world and guarantees equal rights for men and women. Despite the advances women have made in many societies, women's concerns are still given second priority almost everywhere. They continue to face discrimination and marginalisation both subtle and blatant and do not share equally in the fruits of development.

Street vending is one of the largest categories of informal work employing women. The low costs of entry and flexible hours make street vending an attractive option for poor women; for many, it is the only option they have. Street vendors perform an important role in providing services to the urban population, especially the poor. The contributions of women street vendors are unfortunately hardly ever recognised. Hence the study was conducted, as this would throw light on the type of problems the women hawkers' face. Street food vendors play a prominent role in street food vending, vegetable vending, fruit vending and flower vending. Keeping this in mind, the present study was focused on street vendors by selecting women at random

Key Word: *Women, Population, Workforce, Nutrition and Informal Sector*

Introduction

Women are significant contributors to the growing economy. But still the women's contribution in the total workforce remains unrecognised. Almost 400 million people—more than 85 per cent of the working population in India—work in the unorganised sector. Of these, at least 120 million are women. Unorganised sector work is characterised by low wages that are often insufficient to meet minimum living standards including nutrition, long working hours, hazardous working conditions, lack of basic services such as first aid, drinking water and sanitation at the worksite and so on (Moghe, Kiran, 2007). Women working in the informal sector are not included in the official statistics and their work is undocumented and considered as disguised wage work, unskilled, low paying and does not provide benefits to the worker. India was one of the first countries in the world to award women the right to vote. The Indian constitution is one of the most progressive in the world and guarantees equal rights for men and women. Despite the advances women have made in many societies, women's concerns are still given second priority almost everywhere. They continue to face discrimination and marginalisation both subtle and blatant and do not share equally in the fruits of development.

The term 'unorganised' is often used interchangeably with the term 'informal', or employment in the informal sector. Strictly speaking, 'informal' is used to denote all forms of enterprises owned by individuals or households engaged in the sale and manufacture of goods and services operated in a proprietary or partnership basis and with less than ten total workers'. Further, in a sense workers who are not covered by the existing Social Security benefits and the workers in the formal sector without any employment/social security benefits provided by the employer (NCEUS Report, 2007).

The activities in the informal sector can be categorised into two sections: the self-employed and casual (non-permanent) labour. A major section of the self-employed; work as street vendors. The rise in the number of street vendors is largely due to the lack of employment in other sectors but it is also directly linked to the expansion of the informal sector in these countries (Bhowmik, K Sharit, 2005).

Approximately 2.5 per cent of India's total population exclusive source of existence is through street vending. A self-employed Vendor can be considered as a micro-entrepreneur who earns his living by selling products and services on the streets. Being in informal sector this is one of the most unorganised and unregulated professions in India with minimum policy intervention. Although a national policy was formulated in the year 2004 which was revised in year 2009 but the provisions in it are yet to materialise.

A street vendor is broadly defined as a person who offers goods or services for sale to the public without having a permanent built up structure but with a temporary static structure or mobile stall (or head load). Street vendors may be stationary by occupying space on the pavements or other public/private areas, or may be mobile in the sense that they move from place to place carrying their wares on push carts or in cycles or baskets on their heads, or may sell their wares in moving bus or other means of transport.

Street vendors form a very important segment of the unorganised sector in the country. It is estimated that in several cities street vendors count for about two per cent of the population. Women constitute a large segment of these street vendors in almost every city. Street vending is not only a source of self-employment to the poor in cities and towns but also a means to provide 'affordable' as well as 'convenient' services to a majority of the urban population (National policy of Urban Street Vendors, 2009).

The first and urgent need is regulation of their working conditions, the second is provision for conditions in which they are unable to continue to work, such as old age and disability, and the third is measures to help them overcome situations of insecurity, such as major illnesses and the liability of losing employment or being laid off at the will of the employer, for which they have no legal remedy.

Bhowmik, K Sharit (2005) opined that though the Asian countries have witnessed an increase in street vendors, their governments are by and large indifferent to the specific needs of this sector. Street vendors perform an important role in providing services to the urban population, especially the poor. Their contributions are unfortunately hardly ever recognised by the governments. Instead, the governments are more often than not hostile to them. This is a result of a broader issue concerning the informal sector as a whole. In most Asian countries the informal sector is very large and it constitutes the mainstay of the economy. Instead of protecting this sector and ensuring that its workers get their minimum dues, the governments are indifferent to their existence. Street vendors are an important part of the informal sector not only because of their numbers but because of the crucial roles they play in preserving this sector. The goods sold by street vendors are usually consumed by those in the informal sector, as they are cheap. Moreover, a significant amount of goods produced by small industrial units in the informal sector is marketed through them. In fact we have a situation where one section of the urban poor (street vendors) helps the other sections of the urban poor by providing them low priced goods and by marketing their products. Unfortunately, instead of recognising their contributions to the economy, governments view street vendors as encroachers or criminals.

Compared to men, female street vendors are more likely to operate in insecure or illegal spaces, trade in less lucrative goods, generate a lower volume of trade, and work as commission agents or employees of other vendors. As a result, they tend to earn less than male vendors (International Labour Organisation, 2002).

The number of street vendors in Indian cities has increased sharply during the past few years. It is now estimated that around 2.5 per cent of the urban population is engaged in this occupation. Studies on street vendors/hawkers are few and are focused mainly on some cities. In 2000, the National Alliance of Street Vendors in India (NASVI) organised a study on hawkers in seven cities which included Mumbai, Kolkata, Bangalore, Bhubaneswar, Patna, Ahmedabad and Imphal. This could be taken as one of the more comprehensive studies on street vending.

Need for the Study

Street vendors form a very important segment of the unorganised sector in the country. It is estimated that in several cities street vendors count for about two per cent of the population. Women constitute a large segment of these street vendors in almost every city. The role played by the hawkers in the economy as also in the society needs to be given due credit but they are considered as unlawful entities and are subjected to continuous harassment by Police and civic authorities. In most cities of India Street Vending is regarded as an illegal activity. There are municipal and police laws that impose restrictions on the trade. In most cases these laws do not directly prohibit hawking as a profession. They impose restrictions on the use of urban space for street vending. It is also necessary to study the nature of the trade in its totality. Hence the study was conducted, as this would throw light on the type of problems the women hawkers' face. Women vendors who are street food vendors play a prominent role in street food vending, vegetable vending, fruit vending and flower vending. Keeping this in mind, the present study was focused on street vendors by selecting women at random. Against this background, the present study has been undertaken with the following objectives.

Objectives

1. To study the socio-economic conditions of the women street vendors in Belgaum city of Belgaum district of Karnataka state.
2. To study the nature of street vending in terms of commodities sold; investment and earnings.
3. To study the problems faced by women street venders in the study area.

Methodology

The present study is based on primary and secondary data collected. This study has been conducted in Belgaum City of Belgaum district of Karnataka State. The primary data has been collected through structured interview schedule. A total of 50 women street vendors in ten busy streets of Belgaum city were selected for the study through random sampling method. The secondary data were collected from books, journals, research reports, and other published materials related to the street vendors. The collected data were consolidated and tabulated. The data were analysed by using the simple percentage and average wherever appropriate.

Results and Discussion

The results for the present study are discussed under the following headings:

Socio-economic Background of the Women Street Vendors

The Table 1 shows that majority (36 per cent) of the women street vendors were in the age group of 31-40 years. Women in the age group of 21-30 years and 41-50 years were equal number (20 per cent). The data analysis revealed that eight per cent of elderly women in the age group of 61-70 years were also working as hawkers. Insecurity and lack of family support compelled those elderly women to enter in the unorganised sector. The majority (40 per cent) of them were educated up to primary school level. Almost 36 per cent of them were illiterates. About 16 per cent of them had undergone elementary education and eight per cent of them were educated up to tenth standard. Street vendors are often those who are unable to get regular jobs in the remunerative formal sector on account of their low level of education and skills. Lack of proper education, training and experience make the women underprivileged and unskilled.

Table 6.1: Socio-economic Background of the Women Street Vendors

Particulars	Categories	No. of Respondents
Age	21-30 years	10 (20)
	31-40 years	18 (36)
	41-50 years	10 (20)
	51-60 years	8 (16)
	61-70 years	4 (8)
	Total	**50 (100)**
Educational Status	Primary	20 (40)
	Elementary	8 (16)
	Secondary	4 (8)
	Illiterate	18 (36)
	Total	**50 (100)**
Caste	Scheduled Caste	28 (56)
	Scheduled Tribes	8 (16)
	Other Backward Caste	14 (28)
	Total	**50 (100)**
Family Type	Small family	32 (64)
	Joint family	18 (36)
	Total	**50 (100)**
Family Size	1-4	18 (36)
	5-8	32 (64)
	Total	**50 (100)**
Family Income	Upto Rs. 2000	10 (20)
	Rs. 2001-Rs. 3000	28 (56)
	Rs. 3000-Rs. 4000	12 (24)
	Total	**50 (100)**
Locality	Urban	22 (44)
	Rural	28 (56)
	Total	**50 (100)**

(*Source:* Primary Survey).

(**Note:** Numbers in the parentheses indicate percentage).

Street vendors often are migrants and most of them are from underprivileged social segments of society. The study also unveiled the same. That is most of them (56 per cent) belonged to the scheduled caste, 16 per cent were schedule tribe and the rest (28 per cent) were from other backward communities.

More than half (64 per cent) were living in nuclear family system and the remaining (36 per cent) were in joint families. In most of the families (64 per cent) there were five-eight members and only 36 per cent of the families of the hawkers had five-eight members. As many women vendors had three or more children there were more than five members although they came under the category of nuclear family. More than half (56 per cent) of them had Rs 2001-Rs 3000 as their total family income and 24 per cent of them had Rs 3000-Rs 4000 as their total family income. Fifty six percentages of them lived in rural places and the rest belonged to the urban part of Belgaum.

Table 6.2: Nature of Street Vending

Commodities Sold	*No. of Street Vendors*	*No. of varieties sold*
Flowers	14 (28)	2-4
Fruits	12 (24)	3-4
Vegetables	10 (20)	2-5
Green leafy vegetables	8 (16)	2-4
Tiffin	4 (8)	2
Miscellaneous	2 (4)	2
Total	**50 (100)**	-

Source: Primary Survey.
(**Note:** Numbers in the parentheses indicate percentage).

Table 6.2 shows that most of the women street vendors were engaged in flower vending (28 per cent) and vegetable vending (36 per cent). Nearly 24 per cent of them were fruit vendors. Eight per cent of them sold ready to eat snacks. Women vendors from villages bought green leafy vegetables from their locality which are freely available in nature and also they brought eggs (country eggs) which are not usually sold in regular markets. Thus, these women vendors provide valuable service to the urban masses. The study revealed an interesting fact that almost all the hawkers who sold flowers were women. They used a table to display the flowers and a chair to sit upon. They were simultaneously tying flowers together farming a garland while selling. Most of the women hawkers sold fresh vegetables and fruits. They used to sit on road-side using polythene sheets to display the items which were to sold. They did not even have had temporary arrangements like umbrella to protect themselves from sun but sat on open place for the whole day. Only eight per cent of them prepared and sold snacks in their pushcarts. They were able to cater to the needs of the urban poor. They used banana leaves over the silver plates for serving food which was eco-friendly.

Table 6.3: Place of Procurement

Place of procurement	*No. of Street Vendors*
Market	34 (68)
Agricultural farms	10 (20)
Others	6 (12)
Total	**50 (100)**

Source: Primary Survey.
(**Note:** Numbers in the parentheses indicate percentage).

Table 6.3 reveals the place of procurement is concerned. It shows that most of the women street vendors (68 per cent) reported that they used to buy the commodities from the nearby farmers' market and main market of Belgaum city. Twenty per cent of them bought the items from nearby agricultural farms. Only 12 per cent of them like prawn sellers brought from men who were involved in inland fishing.

Table 6.4: Source of Investment

Source of investment	*No. of Street Vendors*
Borrowed money	30 (60)
SHGs	14 (28)
Own money	6 (12)
Total	**50 (100)**

Source: Primary Survey.
(**Note:** Numbers in the parentheses indicate percentage).

Table 6.4 shows that vendors took loans to sustain their livelihood. More than half (60 per cent) borrowed money from moneylenders and paid daily interest. About 28 per cent of vendors borrowed money from SHGs and only 12 per cent of them invested own money. They said that they used to rotate the money earned to pay the interest and repaying loans. One important observation is that the food vendors face the problem of investment. They depend mainly on loans from friends, family or moneylenders to run their business.

Table 6.5: Amount of Investment

Amount invested	*No. of Street Vendors*
Rs. 100 - Rs. 500	22 (44)
Rs. 501 - Rs. 1000	16 (32)
Rs. 1001 - Rs. 1500	12 (24)
Total	**50 (100)**

Source: Primary Survey.
(**Note**: Numbers in the parentheses indicate percentage).

About 44 per cent of them invested about Rs 100 - Rs 500 per day and 32 per cent of the women invested Rs 501 - Rs 1000 per day (Table 6.5). The monetary problem is compounded by the fact that the vendors have scarce resources for their trade and they need to obtain credit by borrowing. Most of the street vendors report having borrowed from money lenders who charge exorbitant interest rates.

Table 6.6: Earnings per Day

Amount earned / day	*No. of Street Vendors*
< Rs 200	24 (48)
Rs 201 - Rs 400	16 (32)
Rs 401 - Rs 600	10 (20)
Total	**50 (100)**

Source: Primary Survey.
(**Note:** Numbers in the parentheses indicate percentage).

Table 6.6 shows that most of the women street vendors (48 per cent) earned up to Rs 200 per day and 32 per cent of them earned between Rs 200 and Rs 400 per day. Only 20 per cent of them earned Rs 400 to Rs 600.

Table 6.7: Motivation Factor

Motivation Factor	*No. of Street Vendors*
To fight against poverty	34 (68)
To increase family income	10 (20)
Single earning member	6 (12)
Total	**50 (100)**

Source: Primary Survey.
(**Note:** Numbers in the parentheses indicate percentage).

The study revealed that the majority of the women (68 per cent) were forced to take street vending as a means of livelihood (Table 6.7). Lack of gainful employment coupled with poverty in both urban and rural areas pushed people in search of a better existence in the cities. About 20 per cent of the women stated that the income of their spouses were not enough to meet the day-to-day expenses of life. They could take only two meals per day. Nearly 12 per cent of them said that they were the single earning member of the family.

Table 6.8: Utilisation of their Earnings

Parameters	*No. of Street Vendors**
Household expenditure	20 (80)
Children's Education	12 (48))
Repay debts	18 (72)
Health care	4 (16)

Source: Primary Survey.
(**Note:** Numbers in the parentheses indicate percentage).
*Multiple response

Table 6.8 shows that the majority of them (72 per cent) stated that they used to repay debts with the money they earned and 80 per cent of them said that they used the money for household expenditure. About 48 per cent of them spent their earnings for children's education.

The interviewed street vendors suffer from different health problems. About one-third suffer from chronic diseases, another one-third suffer especially during rainy season. About 10 per cent have work related problems like skin diseases, respiratory diseases, headache, throat problems because of air pollution, or they suffer from burn-out syndromes because of overexertion and permanent psychological tensions relating to their business and livelihoods.

Table 6.9: Problems Encountered

Parameters	*No. of Street Vendors**
Lack of Infrastructure	20 (80)
Harassment by the Police	16 (64)
Lack of money to invest	18 (72)
Health Problems	9 (36)

Source: Primary Survey.
[**Note:** Numbers in the parentheses indicate percentage]
*Multiple response

(a) **Lack of Infrastructure:** Firstly, almost all (80 per cent) of the women street vendors used to sit on busy road-side without any temporary shed or covering to protect them from sun/rain. Secondly, they do not have access to toilet facilities during their working hours. Pregnant vendors and aged vendors suffer most of this unsatisfactory situation. They had to move to the public toilet which was far away from their place of selling. Many women used to control urination or drank little water to combat this situation. It is the responsibility of the State Government to provide them public toilets nearby, drinking water facilities and waste disposal and management system.

(b) **Harassment by the Police:** Nearly 62 per cent of them complained that they were threatened and harassed by police and municipal authorities. National Policy on Urban Street Vendors, 2009 also feel that public authorities often regard street vendors as a nuisance and as encroachers of sidewalks and pavements and do not appreciate the valuable services that street vendors render to the common man.

(c) **Lack of money to invest:** Most of the street vendors report having borrowed from money lenders who charge exorbitant interest rates. To promote access of street vendors to such services as credit, the services of Self Help Groups (SHGs), Co-operatives, Federations, Micro Finance Institutions (MFIs), Training Institutes etc., should be encouraged.

(d) **Health problems:** About 36 per cent of the women hawkers complained that they suffered from dust allergy, head ache and back ache. The mental and physical health of the street vendors has been affected. The SNDT-ILO study shows that 85 per cent of the street vendors covered suffered from ailments associated with stress. These include hyperacidity, migraine, digestive problems, lack of sleep etc.

(e) **Social Security:** Street vendors as a group belong to the unorganised sector of the economy. As such, they don't have access to Government-assisted social security. However, in some States, social security schemes such as Old Age Pension and other benefits are being provided through the Welfare Boards and similar bodies. But, their coverage of street vendors is very small. There are a few Non-Government Organisations (NGOs), who organise social security schemes for the street vendors (National Policy for Urban Street Vendors, 2009).

The Government gives Funeral grant, Educational incentives to the wards of registered beneficiaries and Maternity Benefits. During the year 2002-03, under the "Jana Shree Bhima Yojana" insurance scheme 1472 workers were enrolled (Labour Welfare Department, 2011). The present study revealed that the women street vendors were totally unaware of the Belgaum Unorganised Labourers' Welfare Society and the social security benefits. They did not know where and whom to approach to register and get help. Therefore, they should be educated about the policies of Government by the concerned authorities. Street vendors, being micro entrepreneurs should be provided with vocational education and training and entrepreneurial development skills to upgrade their technical and business potentials so as to increase their income levels as well as to look for more remunerative alternatives.

Policy Implications and Suggestions

Street vending is one of the largest categories of informal work employing women. The low costs of entry and flexible hours make street vending an attractive option for poor women; for many, it is the only option they have. Street vendors perform an important role in providing services to the urban population, especially the poor. The contributions of women street vendors are unfortunately hardly ever recognised. Their low income, double burden of having to work on the streets and look after the home and low level of unionisation make them the invisible section of street vendors. All urban plans demarcate public spaces for specific purposes such as parks and gardens, educational institutions, hospitals etc. Hawking also needs to be included in this so that proper infrastructure facilities can be provided. Women vendors associations should be created to initiate crèches and play schools. On the job training seminar for street vendors on issues of capacity building, State Women's Commission and Labour Welfare Department can organise marketing skills, business development and hygienic issues.

As with other informal workers, the ability of street vendors to improve their lives and working conditions rests on their ability to organise. Street vendors' organisations across the world have had some success in defending the rights of members, securing access to services, and influencing public policy. Like the National Association of Street Vendors of India, several regional associations should be initiated which can protect and promote women street vendors. Despite these positive developments, though, the vast majority of street vendors remain isolated, unprotected, and unorganised. There is an enormous need to build and strengthen all forms of street vendors' organisations, and to link them through national, regional and international networks. Women-friendly measures such as resting rooms, rest rooms are toilets in USA, separate toilets for women, transport facilities for women, violence-free working conditions, safe and hygienic working conditions not only ensures women to work fearlessly but also encourage women to participate in the work force. Measures such as provisions for solid waste disposal, public toilets to maintain cleanliness, aesthetic design of mobile stalls/push carts, provision for electricity, drinking water, covers to protect their wares as well as themselves from heat, rain, dust etc., storage facilities including cold storage and so on are the responsibility of the Government or Gender Component Cell to create a space to work with dignity.

References

1. Bhowmik, K Sharit, 'Hawkers in the Urban Informal Sector: A Study of Street Vending in Seven Cities of India'. National Alliance of Street Vendors of India. www.nasvi.org,www.streetnet.org.
2. Bhowmik, K Sharit (2005), Street Vendors in Asia: A Review, Economic and Political Weekly, May 28-June 4, 2005, 2005, pp. 2256-64.
3. Cohen, Monique, with Mihir Bhatt and Pat Horn (2000), "Women Street Vendors: The Road to Recognition" SEEDS, No. 20. p. 4.
4. Report of National Policy of Urban Street Vendors, Ministry of Urban Employment and Poverty Alleviation, Government of India. 2009. www.muepa/nic.in E.
5. Report of International Labour Organisation (2002), Women and Men in the Informal Economy: A Statistical Picture. Geneva: ILO. p. 52.
6. Moghe, Kiran (2007), InfoChange News and Features, < http://infochangeindia. org/index2. php?option= com_content &do_ pdf=1&id=6491.
7. Report on Conditions of Work and Promotion of Livelihoods in the Unorganised Sector, of the National Commission for Enterprises in the Unorganised Sector, Government of India (NCEUS), 2006.
8. Sakthivel, S and Pinaki Joddar (2006), Unorganised Sector Workforce in India -Trends, Patterns and Social Security Coverage. WIEGO.

9. Sharma, R.N. (1998), 'Census of Hawkers on BMC Lands', Tata Institute of Social Sciences, Mumbai.
10. Women in Informal Employment: Globalising and Organising Informal Workers in Focus: Street Vendors. WIEGO, USA.

7

Entrepreneurship Development Through Agripreneurship in India

D.S. Ambrose

Abstract

Women in India consistently lag behind the men in terms of access to education, health care, jobs etc. Apart from the economic and social inequality, women in India are victims of heinous crimes such as, dowry deaths, rape, molestation and immoral trafficking. As per the latest statistics:

- The female child sex ratio (0-6 years) is 914 per 1000 males.
- Rural female literacy rate only 58 per cent while rural male 78 per cent.
- Women employment in urban areas is only 13.9 per cent while. in rural areas is 29.9 per cent. With the rise in poverty, many women are forced to work in very low end and low paid jobs.
- Employment of women in organised sector is less than eight per cent.

Women especially in the child bearing age are often deficient in nutrition due to poverty. As a result the number of maternal deaths in India is one of the highest in the world and 87 per cent of all pregnant women in India are anemic.

India: Women's empowerment

Theme: Social and economic factors can contribute to women's empowerment.

Four of the main processes that could lead to women's empowerment, as defined by the evaluation, were:

- changes in women's mobility and social interaction;
- changes in women's labour patterns;
- changes in women's access to and control over resources; and
- changes in women's control over decision-making.

Changes in women's mobility and interaction. The evaluation found that women had become more mobile and begun to have new interactions with a range of officials. There was even a growing willingness on the part of group members to approach the Panchayats and Collectors with petitions or grievances. In all, the evaluation found that:

- 50 per cent of women group members had visited new places and travelled longer distances; 94 per cent had experienced new interactions with staff of institutions such as banks, district and block development organisations, NGOs and the project itself.

The study observed that this type of change was most likely to occur among women group members when:

- the women involved were heads of households or were older;
- the women involved had participated in training;
- their group members had accessed a bank loan;
- their group had undertaken community action initiatives; or
- their group had been organised into a federation and encouraged to participate in special events (such as Women's Day, Rural Women's Day).

Introduction

Agripreneurs and Agripreneurship Development

There is no single definition of the term "Agripreneur". However, an agripreneur may be thought to be someone who undertakes a variety of activities in agricultural to be agripreneur. For example, an agripreneur may start an agri-business, change a business's direction, acquire a business or be involved in innovatory activity in agricultural value addition. Thus, an agripreneur may undertake a range of different activities which have a common link - the perception of an opportunity and the willingness to do something to take advantage of it. Explicit in this is that the agripreneur is a risk-taker and has the opportunity to initiate and to implement decisions which deal with the uncertain agricultural business environment within which the firm operates. The business environment consists of many complex interrelated elements including: customers, competition, economic factors, social and demographic trends, government policy (both macroeconomic and microeconomic) and technology. In this paper I have identified five frameworks within which to analyse entrepreneurial activity. First, the Intuitive which stresses the personal psychological makeup of the individual to avail the opportunity; second, the Classical which highlights the importance of recognising opportunities; third, the Leadership which concentrates on a person's ability to motivate and direct people for success; fourth, the Management which looks at the importance of organising businesses by such means as developing strategies and improved decision-making; fifth, the Entrepreneurship looks at innovation within organisations. Within these frameworks of thought, the entrepreneur is responsible for identifying and meeting market needs. Entrepreneurs are often discussed in terms of starting a business. Research identifies a number of strategies necessary for successful entrepreneurial start-ups which include identifying unmet demand, developing new products which meet changing market conditions, producing, marketing and financial plans, weighing up risks and rewards and having the necessary resources to launch the business. Agripreneurship requires more than just the identification of new opportunities. Additional qualities such as imagination, commitment, decisiveness and self-confidence are also important elements of the entrepreneurial process. Thus, the agripreneur introduces change into the market place but must also be aware of the outside pressures for change which are being experienced as the result of other entrepreneurial activity.

The following table is adapted from Edward DeBono's lateral thinking principles (1990) and is applied to highlight the difference between the "Agricultural" of current approaches to Agripreneurship education and the "art" of agripreneurship education which is needed. The poor farmers have failed in agriculture but agripreneurs are becoming very successful by doing business in Agri Export Zones (AEZ) of India.

1. Agricultural is selective, whereas the Art of Agripreneurship is generative.
2. Agricultural moves only if there is a direction in which to move, whereas the art of Agripreneurship moves in order to generate direction.
3. Agricultural is mechanical, whereas the Art of Agripreneurship is provocative.
4. Agricultural is sequential, whereas the Art of Agripreneurship can make jumps.
5. Agricultural requires each step to be correct, whereas with the Art of Agripreneurship this does not need to be so.
6. Agricultural uses the negative to block off certain pathways, whereas with the Art of Agripreneurship there is no negative.
7. Agricultural excludes irrelevant information, whereas the Art of Entrepreneurship welcomes chance intrusions.
8. Agricultural has fixed categories, classifications and labels, whereas the Art of Agripreneurship there is no such constraints.

Agri-Entrepreneurship

Amidst the changing paradigms and demanding global structure, India, in order to remain a front-runner needs to primarily focus on the agriculture sector, the backbone of the economy. This specialisation is developing agripreneurs with distinct traits and skills to exploit opportunities galore in the field of agriculture. Among the various strategies to promote planned growth in this sector, focus on promoting viable enterprises is certainly helping to exploit its operational efficiency to the hilt.

Agri-business Development-Private Sector Role

Agriculture being vital for Indian economy, Government has very long played an important role. The time has come for private sector to come forward. Today, even Government is encouraging private sector participation by inviting trade bodies to suggest necessary reforms in Indian agriculture.

The Task Force highlighted the potential for global opportunities and India's competitive advantages in the context of WTO and Globalisation. Somehow, this initiative while preparing a document to completely transform Indian agriculture got new light through new policies and regulations prevalent in the country. In this document, many success stories have been presented, and final solution come with clear cut action plans for the future. It also started private sector role that could also complement and supplement the government efforts.

1. Many individuals, small business houses and large corporates were looking for new investment opportunities. In many sectors of the economy, not much scope was available. With the reducing interest rates, business plans with long gestation periods have acquired new relevance for the private sector. Agriculture Export Zones has become a new business opportunity for their entry at any investment level.
2. Agriculture being top priority, its business environment in terms of regulations, is also conducive. It attracts minimum taxes and gets maximum support. Reforms in agriculture have become top agenda for the government in the country.
3. Many private sector players engaged in agriculture related business activities have synergy in either backward or forward business linkages related to AEZ's.

4. Increasing demand for quality and convenience food by the world consumers has created new level of business opportunities.
5. Many interest groups and development agencies etc., have also identified Agriculture Export Zones as a new agenda that will create conducive Agri environment for healthy development in future.

Why India Promoting Agripreneurship: A Quick Perspective

In India, 52 per cent of total land is cultivable as against 11 per cent in the world. All 15 major climates of the world, snow bound Himalayas to hot humid southern peninsula; Thar Desert to heavy rain areas all exist in India. There are 20 agro-climatic regions and nearly 46 out of 60 soil types in the country. Sunshine hours and day length are ideally suited for round the year cultivation of crops. India is the centre for biodiversity in plants, animals, insects, micro-organism and accounts for 17 per cent animal, 12 per cent plants and 10 per cent fish genetic resources of the globe. In the livestock sector, India has 16 per cent of cattle, 57 per cent of buffalo, 17 per cent of goats and 5 per cent of sheep population of the world. Agriculture contributes 24.2 per cent to GDP, 15.2 per cent of total exports and provides employment to 58.4 per cent of country's work force.

- Agriculture remains a key sector of the Indian economy accounting for 25 per cent share in the gross domestic product (GDP) and about 13 per cent of the total export earnings.
- India is the second largest producer of rice and wheat in the world; first in pulses and fourth in coarse grains. India is also one of the largest producers of cotton, sugar, sugarcane, peanuts, jute, tea and an assortment of spices.
- In terms of the real value added, the Indian agriculture sector ranks third, after China and the United States.
- The share of agriculture in the total value added to the economy, at around 25 per cent, is still quite high. This implies that agriculture is likely to remain a priority, both for policy-makers as well as businesses, in the

foreseeable future and any move to ramp up the sector calls for a multi-pronged strategy.

- In recent years, there has been a considerable emphasis on crop diversification towards horticulture (fruits, vegetables, ornamental crops, medicinal and aromatic plants and spices), plantation crops (coconut, cashew nuts and cocoa) and allied activities.
- Creation of critical infrastructure for cold storage, refrigerated transportation, rapid transit, grading, processing, packaging and quality control measures open major opportunities for investment.
- Second highest fruit and vegetable producer in the world (134.5 million tonnes) with cold storage facilities available only for 10 per cent of the produce.
- Second highest producer of milk with a cold storage capacity of 70,000 tonne.
- Fifth largest producer of eggs. Investments in cold chain required to store 20 per cent of surplus of meat and poultry products during 10th plan requires Rs 500 Crore (US$100M).
- Sixth largest producer of fish with harvesting volumes of 5.2 million tonnes.

In a fast changing International Trade Environment, with a view to providing remunerative return to the Agripreneurs community in a sustained manner, efforts will be made to provide improved access to the produce / products of the agriculture and allied sectors in the International markets by setting up Agri Export Zones. The AEZ is expected to give a focus and direction for exports of key agricultural produce with potential from the country. It involves a detailed action plan for the development of a specified geographic areas for effecting systematically greater exports of a specific produce.

Agri Export Zone

With the primary objective of boosting agricultural exports from India, in March 2001, Government of India announced a policy of setting up of Agri Export Zones (AEZs) across the country. The Central Government sanctioned 60 AEZs comprising about 40 agricultural commodities till March 2005. These AEZs are spread across 20 states in the country.

Objectives

The objective of setting up AEZs is to converge the efforts made, hitherto, by various central and state government departments for increasing exports of agricultural commodities from India. The AEZ takes a comprehensive view of a particular produce/product located in a geographically contiguous area for the purpose of developing and sourcing raw materials, their processing/packaging, and leading to final exports.

The major components of this comprehensive concept are:

- Cluster approach of identifying the potential products and geographical region in which these products are grown.
- Adopting an end-to-end approach of integrating the entire process, right from the stage of production till it reaches the consumption stage.
- Integration of the activities of various agencies connected with the department of the product.

Agri Export Zones (AEZs)

AEZ are identified by the State Government, who would evolve a comprehensive package of services provided by all State Government agencies, State agriculture universities and all institutions and agencies of the Union Government for intensive delivery in these zones to develop agripreneurship. Private sector with proven credentials would be encouraged through entrepreneurship development to sponsor new agri export zone or take over already notified agri export zone or part of such zones for boosting agri exports from the zones. Services which would be managed and co-coordinated by State Government/Private sector and would include provision of pre/post-harvest treatment and operations, plant protection, processing, packaging, storage and related research and development etc. Nodal agency will supplement, within its schemes and provisions, efforts of State Governments for facilitating such exports.

The concept of the Agri Export Zone attempts to take a comprehensive look at a particular produce/products located in a contiguous area for the purpose of developing and sourcing the raw materials, their processing and packaging, finally exporting them. It is a part of agripreneurship development. Thus, the entire effort is centred on a cluster approach of identifying the potential products, the geographical region in which these are grown and adopting an end to end approach of integrating the entire process right from the stage of production till it reaches the market. The government helps agripreneurs in sourcing for raw materials, the setting up of processing facilities, providing finance at low interest rates and even matching with international buyers. The export zones mooted by the Agricultural and Processed Food Products Export Development Authority (APEDA) to increase international trade in agri-commodities are an attempt to take a holistic approach to encouraging trade in specific commodities located in contiguous areas.

The concept of AEZ can be summarised as "to produce what could be sold rather sell what is produced". It visualises identification of interventions in a project mode. By making all central, state governments and local agencies to work under one umbrella and comprehensively address all the issues relating to each stage of the entire value chain from farm to the ultimate consumer we can penetrate in to new markets in international scenario. Under AEZ India has successfully gone ahead to a large extend of private entrepreneurs. Traceability of the produce from the farmer to the end consumer is also very important in global trading.

Agri Export zones are concerned with A to Z of Agri-exports. The emphasis is on partnership on various agencies/ systems and convergence of interventions of various agencies like APEDA, Ministry of Food Processing Industries (MFPI), National Horticulture Board (NHB) etc. The focus will be on increasing exports of identified commodities, which is very important factor for entrepreneurship development.

The concept of AEZ's which aims to give fillip to agriculture exports through entrepreneurship development, comprises the following:

- Identifying a potential zone based on agro-climatic requirements for a particular crop.
- Integrating various assistance programmes of Central and State Government agencies and providing fiscal incentives to exporters.
- Implementing the same through involvement of private and public partnership and

Integrating all the activities till the produce reaches the market.

Measures Envisaged to Promoting Exports from such Zones by Agripreneurs

1. Financial Assistance to motivate entrepreneur: Both central as well as state government and their agencies are providing a variety of financial assistance to various agri export related activities. These extend from providing financial assistance for training and extension, R&D, quality upgradation, infrastructure, marketing etc. All these facilities have to be dovetailed and extended to promote agri exports from the proposed zones in a coordinated manner to promote agripreneurship.

2. Fiscal Incentives for the entrepreneurial support: The benefits under Export Promotion of Capital Goods Scheme, which were hitherto available to direct exporters, have now been extended to service exporters in the Agri Export Zones. Thus, even service provided to ultimate exporters will be eligible for import of capital goods at a concessional duty for setting up common facilities. They shall fulfill their export obligation through receipt of foreign exchange from ultimate exporters who will make payments from their account.

Exporters of value added agri products will be eligible for sourcing duty free fuel for generation of power, provided cost component of power in the ultimate product is 10 per cent or more and the input out norms are fixed by the advance licensing committee of the Director General Foreign Trade. In view of the power intensive nature of most of the value addition, almost all the exporters of the value added agriculture produce will become eligible for such facility.

Agencies involved in Sixty Agri Export Zones set up (AEZ) in India for Agripreneurship Development:

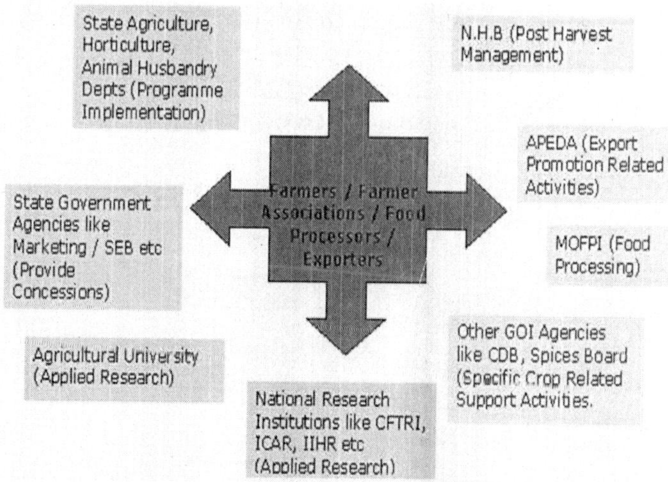

Need or Rational of Export Market

Investment required is estimated to be Rs 350 Crore (US$ 70M). In spite of the vast natural resources and abundant agricultural produce India ranks below 10th in the export of food products. Conservative estimates put processing levels in the fruits and vegetables sector at two per cent, meat and poultry at two per cent, milk by way of modern dairies at 14 per cent, fish at four per cent, bulk meat de-boning is to the tune of 21 per cent. Currently, the food processing sector, though in the nascent stage, constitutes 14 per cent of manufacturing GDP amounting to products value of Rs 2,80,000 Crores. It employs 130 lakh persons (13 million) and is supposed to increase at an annual rate of seven per cent.

Although Agri export zone will boost export but later on they will help to cater domestic market in a cluster form. Food chain clusters (See Figure) are formed with the participation of all stake holders such as farmers, seed growers, merchants, transporters, wholesalers, retailers, financial institutions, and insurance companies. Information sharing is essential for generating the efficiencies. The Internet and mobile communications are used to enable information and financial transfer between the stake holders. Also, recent advances in RFID technology will have tremendous impact in the management of the food chain particularly for source identification and tracking and also in providing supply chain visibility.

Food Supply Chain Cluster

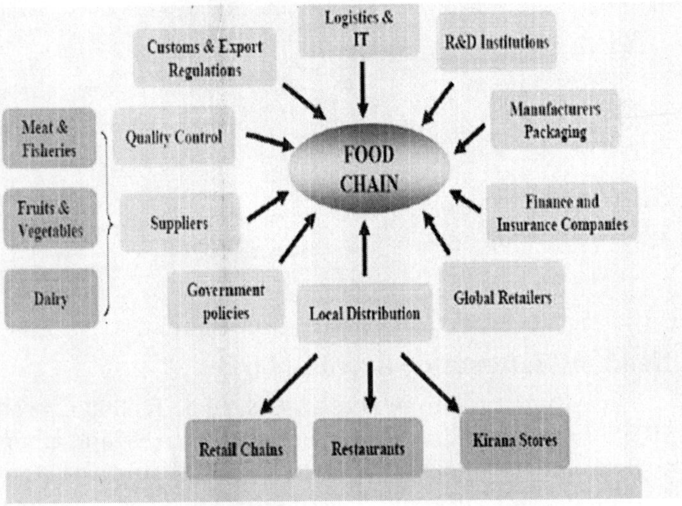

Present Status of India

State Governments identified product specific Agri-export zone for export of specific products from a geographically contiguous area and evolve a comprehensive package of services for delivery in these zones. Such services would include provision of pre/post-harvest treatment and operations, plant protection, processing, packaging, storage and related research and development, etc. The service providers as well as the setting up of common infrastructural facilities like sorting, grading, polishing, packaging, cold storage, transport equipment/ refrigerated vans, vapour and heat treatment plants, X-ray screening facility, etc., (Such activities also promoting entrepreneurship in these sectors) shall be entitled for EPCG Scheme. Agri exporters shall be entitled for recognition as Export House/Trading House/Star Trading House/Super Star Trading House on achieving a third of the threshold limit prescribed for exporters of goods.

Agribusiness v/s Agripreneurship Unlocking the Potential of India's Agribusiness through Agripreneurship

For India to achieve 8-10 per cent growth, agriculture must improve its growth rate to over five per cent. If more than seven per cent is not reached, no serious reduction of poverty can be achieved. India has major advantages including diverse agro climatic regions. On the supply side, India has a large pool of research manpower, large marketable surpluses and abundant raw materials for agribusiness. On the demand side, there is a huge growing market with consumption growth predicted to increase to 7.8 per cent. The problems of the agricultural sector include low levels of productivity, infrastructure and investment. There are weak linkages between research and extension, low seed replacement rates and an imbalanced use of fertilisers. Limited access to credit, insufficient risk cover, and quarantine and sanitary and phyto-sanitary standard infrastructure are other inadequacies of the system. The government is trying to improve the environment for investment. It intends to spend Rs 15,000 crore in the perishable sector on the backward and forward production linkages in horticulture. Priority sector lending and credit are expected to double in three years. The government is bringing 10 million hectares of additional land under irrigation. India is on track to becoming the world's leading food producer through a number of cross-sectoral initiatives and investment opportunities. Percy Barnevik, Honorary Chairman, Sandvik, Sweden, stated that the biggest potential in India is to mobilise 350 million people who live on less than one dollar a day Mobilising them into entrepreneurship will make a tremendous difference to India's economy. An NGO in Tamil Nadu has helped 80,000 women organise themselves into self-help groups. Thirty-five per cent of these 5,000 projects are agri-projects and 10 per cent are agri-related industrial activities. This programme, when replicated, may reach 1.3 million women and help four per cent of the state's population. Such projects provide social and economic empowerment to women and will also delay the migration to slum areas. Reema Nanavaty,

Director, Rural Development, self-Employed Women's Association (SEWA), India, said that farmers' contributions need to be recognised and should convert into agripreneurship. Agriculture is seen in a traditional manner and is not treated as an industry. Therefore, it is not attracting enough investment. There is a need for collective and joint cooperation among farmers to enter into farming and marketing contracts. Through the Agri-export Zone network, such initiatives reach 700,000 households. It is necessary to have agriculture stabilisation inputs and funds, a mechanism that provides solutions to marginal farmers in order to absorb such shocks as erratic rainfall. Farmers need to be given direct market access through collectives and cooperatives.

Results produced by Agripreneurs in sixty Agri-Export Zones all over India. These zones are set up on the basis of produce.

Results of Last Five Years Afford

1. Actual Export done by Agripreneurs in the year of 2005-2006 Rs 2107.00 Cr. (210.00 Million US Dollar) from Agri Export Zones.
2. Actual investment made by only Agripreneurs in the same period Rs 197.30 Cr. (19.3 Million US Dollar) in Agri Export Zones.

The 60 AEZs sanctioned by the Government envisaged an investment of Rs 1717.95 crores and export of Rs 11821.47 crores over a period of five years. Against these projections, these AEZs could mobilise an investment of Rs 449.90 crores and exports of Rs 2768.00 crores over the last three and a half years ending 31 March 2005.

The encouraging results of goal-oriented "Green Revolution", "White Revolution", "Yellow Revolution" etc., enthuse the agricultural fraternity of the country to set a new goal for "Agri-Export Revolution" which is not only the need of the hour but also a compulsion to strengthen and revitalise the economy of the country. While India holds an important position in the export market for a set of traditional agricultural commodities, new areas and new commodities are likely to emerge such as live animals and animal products, fruits, vegetables, floriculture, medicinal plants and processed agricultural products.

Solutions for Agri-entrepreneurs

Over the years, problems of unemployment, underemployment and disguised unemployment have plagued the country, especially the rural populace. Considering that two-thirds of the Indian population is employed (either directly or indirectly) in the agriculture sector, providing viable and sustainable business opportunities in Indian agribusiness is imperative for generating employment in the country. Sustainable agribusiness ventures can promote job-led economic growth in rural areas through harnessing science and technology for environmentally sustainable and socially equitable development. Entrepreneurship in sustainable agriculture is a key factor which has the potential to transform the face of rural India, the prime driver of our economy.

Holistic Approach

A holistic approach for cultivating entrepreneurship amongst rural communities at large is essential. This can be done through sustainable livelihoods that can be generated in the agriculture sector by providing business solutions that envelop natural resource management and innovative eco-technological principles. The 'Sustainable Livelihoods' approach, values wide range of activities people do to make a living, as well as assets and capabilities, they possess. In other words, the root of human development and economic growth is "livelihoods" rather than "jobs." While entrepreneurship has widely been viewed by policy makers and educators alike as the creative act of an independent businessperson, we are now learning that the roots of entrepreneurship extend deep into a community's civic structure

References

1. Breen, J.P. (2004) 'Enterprise, entrepreneurship and small business: where are the Boundaries?', *Int. J. Entrepreneurship* and *Small Business*, Vol. I, Nos. 1/2, pp. 21–34.

2. http://www.mofpi.nic.in/venturesetup/foreign
3. FAIDA Revisited Realising the potential, CII- Mckensey report, January 2004.
4. Business Strategies for Managing Complex Supply Chains in Large Emerging Economies: The Story of AMUL, Pankaj Chandra and Devanath Tirupati, Indian Institute of Management, Ahmedabad-380015, India, April 2003.
5. www.apeda.com/
6. www. Ciionline.org
7. *Indian Economic Survey*, 2006.
8. *Business India*, 24 issues from 2004 to 2006.

THEME-II:
TECHNOLOGIES FOR WOMEN EMPOWERMENT AND EMPLOYMENT

8

Agripreneurship in Food Processing—A Sustainable Livelihood Approach for Women Empowerment

S.M. Savita, K.N. Srinivasappa, S. Ganeshamoorthi, B.G. Vasanthi and B.V. Manjula

Abstract

Women perform 66 per cent of worlds work, produce 50 per cent of the food, yet earn only 10 per cent of the income and own one per cent of the property. The objectives of women Self Help Group (SHG) is to earn, save and utilise in such a way, so as to solve their day to day problems and to make themselves self-sufficient. By encouraging women SHG to engage in micro-enterprise that could be self-managed encourages management skills, risk taking, taking own decisions and earn their own income having a direct opportunity to experience various issues leading improving self-confidence and self-reliance. Thus, Krishi Vigyan Kendra, Bangalore Rural, initiated a Front Line Demonstration (FLD) on "Preparation of Jackfruit products: Branding and Market linkage" among the members of Divya Jyothi Mahila Self Help Group of Melekote cross village, Doddaballapur taluk, Bangalore Rural District. India stands second in production of Jackfruit in the world producing 14.36 lakh tonnes from 1,02,000 ha. In India, Karnataka ranks first in jackfruit production producing 2.6 lakh tonnes from 11,333 ha. It is an underutilised and over produced crop which lacks processing. Raw fruit marketing fetches low income, thereby processing of Jackfruit is promoted for enhancing the income. The members had undergone the hands on training on preparation of Jackfruit products through a vocational training programme, namely- Chips, Papad from raw unripe bulbs, whereas Halwa, Jam, RTS beverage from ripe bulbs and Mixture from rind. The SHGs were sensitised on nutrient composition of Jackfruit; Cost economics, importance of Hygiene and Sanitation in production unit, Marketing channels, Food Safety and Standards Authority of India (FSSAI) licensing and registration. They were exposed to marketing avenues of Jack products through organising an Exposure Visit to Mango and Jack Mela -2013 held at Lalbaguh, Bangalore. A unit was established by the members and supported by KVK by providing critical inputs such as weighing balance, sealing machine, foil sealer, labeling and packing materials. The experiences of this FLD model was shared among other farmers in the locality through organising a Field day and it created awareness about enhancement of income through processing of Jack. KVK guided the SHG in getting Market linkages such as exhibitions, fairs, local bakeries, National conference of KVKs and International Krishimela organised by UAS held at GKVK, Bangalore, and Mahila Mahotsava organised by IIHR, Bangalore on the eve of celebration of Women in Agriculture day at Lalbaguh. The group had a turnover of Rs 65,000 in six months by selling the products under the brand name "SIRI PRODUCTS" registered under FSSAI. Thus, the SHG realised a considerable income through the FLD model developed by KVK in processing of Jackfruit to value added products.

Introduction

Entrepreneurship development in rural people is increasingly being recognised as a means to overall development of the rural community as well as that of the country. The problem posing our rural masses is not so much in terms of creation of productivity and wealth as that of developing the capacities and ensuring utilisation of human potential in creating wealth. It is neither recommended nor possible to distribute all needed inputs to rural folk, to take advantage of growing commercialisation in the field of agriculture instead, motivational and capacity building inputs that promote entrepreneurship in the area of agriculture would go a great deal in mitigating their problems of unemployment and poverty. It is believed that ninety per cent scope of developing entrepreneurship in agriculture exists, as against the present only ten per cent is in place in rural areas (Jhamtani *et al.*, 2003).

Worldwide it is observed that small and medium enterprises create most of the jobs. In Indian context if full employment is to be created, we need to exploit the potential of small scale industries including those directly linked with agriculture such as value addition of crops, fruits and vegetables, diversification and value addition in agriculture as a whole.

There are as of now available numbers of technologies in agriculture and allied areas that provide opportunities to farmers to take a shift from subsistence farming to commercial and economically viable agriculture. To avail of these opportunities farmers need to be motivated and made aware of these along with development workers who also must comprehend the process of entrepreneurship development to help farmers avail the opportunities for diversification and commercialisation in agriculture and create viable enterprises.

Front Line Demonstration (FLD) is a unique extension activity. It empowers farmers/farmwomen to solve their problems learnt through FLD. It involves participation, interaction and joint decision-making. Farmers learn by carrying out activates themselves and through constant observation. A FLD followed by Hands on training programme one can see, learn, do and practice.

Women perform 66 per cent of worlds work, produce 50 per cent of the food, yet earn only 10 per cent of the income and own one per cent of the property (Geeta *et al.,* 2013). Hence, in 2004 the concept of Self Help Group came into existence in Karnataka for the overall upliftment of rural women in the existing society.

The objectives of women Self Help Group (SHG) are to earn, save and utilise in such a way, so as to solve their day to day problems and to make themselves self-sufficient. By encouraging women SHG to engage in micro-enterprise that could be self-managed encourages management skills, risk taking, taking up their own decisions and earn their own income having a direct opportunity to experience various issues leading to improvement in self-reliance and self-confidence.

India stands second in production of jackfruit in the world producing 14.36 lakh tonnes from 1,02,000 ha. In India, Karnataka ranks first in jackfruit production producing 2.6 lakh tonnes from 11,333 ha (Shree Padre, 2010). It is an underutilised and over produced crop which lacks processing. Raw fruit marketing fetches low income, thereby processing of jackfruit is promoted for enhancing the income.

Thus, Krishi Vigyan Kendra, Bangalore Rural, initiated a Front Line Demonstration (FLD) on "Preparation of Jackfruit products: Branding and Market linkage" among the members of Divya Jyothi Mahila Self Help Group of Melekote cross village, Doddaballapur taluk, Bangalore Rural District.

Methodology

A group named-Divya Jyothi Mahila Self Help Group of Melekote cross village, Doddaballapur taluk, Bangalore Rural District was selected to study the impact of developing entrepreneurial skills through Front Line Demonstration (FLD) on "Preparation of Jackfruit products: Branding and Market linkage".

A vocational training was organised for the SHG members comprising of demonstration and hands on training on preparation of various jackfruit products namely, Chips, Papad from raw unripe bulbs, whereas Halwa, Jam, RTS beverage from ripe bulbs and Mixture from rind.

The SHGs were sensitised on nutrient composition of jackfruit; Cost economics, importance of Hygiene and Sanitation in production unit, Marketing channels, Food Safety and Standards Authority of India (FSSAI) licensing and registration.

The cost economics of the demonstrated products were also determined.

They were exposed to marketing avenues of jack products for better understanding of the market demand through organising an educational Exposure Visit to Mango and Jack Mela -2013 held at Lalbaguh, Bangalore, as a part of vocational training programme.

The minimum critical inputs to establish a small production unit such as weighing balance, sealing machine, foil sealer, labeling and packing materials were made available under FLD funded by ICAR, New Delhi.

The SHG established a production unit in a separate building with essential facilities such as electricity and water supply. This production unit is registered under Food Safety and Standards Authority of India (FSSAI) for production and marketing of value added products from jackfruit. After the thorough hands on training, the SHG members are involved in production and marketing of jackfruit products.

The experiences of this FLD model was shared among other farmers in the locality through organising a Field day and it created awareness about enhancement of income through processing of Jack. An exhibition to display marketable products and also, a sale was organised during this field day.

KVK guided the SHG in getting market linkages such as exhibitions, fairs, local bakeries, National level conference of KVKs and International Krishimela organised by UAS held at GKVK, Bangalore, and Mahila Mahotsava organised by IIHR, Bangalore on the eve of celebration of Women in Agriculture Day at Lalbagh.

Results and Discussion

Around six products were demonstrated in the sessions along with hands on training. Table 8.1 represents the sensory scores of the demonstrated value added jackfruit products. The participants were trained with regard to the objectives of sensory evaluation. The scores ranged from 3.8 - 5.0 for the sensory attributes such as colour, flavour, taste, texture/ consistency and over all acceptability. According to the results

Table 8.1: Sensory Scores of the Value Added Jackfruit Products

Sl. No.	*Name of the product*	*Sensory parameters*				
		Colour	*Flavour*	*Taste*	*Texture / consistency*	*Over-all acceptability*
1.	Jackfruit Chips	4.0	4.1	4.1	3.8	4.2
2.	Jackfruit Papad	4.5	4.7	4.8	4.8	4.7
3.	Jackfruit RTS beverage	4.2	4.2	4.3	4.1	4.3
4.	Jackfruit Jam	4.9	4.9	4.9	4.8	5.0
5.	Jackfruit Halwa	4.8	4.9	4.8	4.9	4.8
6.	Jackfruit Mixture	4.0	4.1	4.0	4.4	4.6

[**Note:** 1. N= 20
2. Score Card: 5 – Excellent, 4 – Very Good, 3 – Good, 2 – Fair, 1 – Poor]

Table 8.2: Ranking Test for the Value added Jackfruit Products

Sl. No.	*Name of the product*	*Ranking*
1	Jackfruit Jam	I
2	Jackfruit Halwa	II
3	Jackfruit Papad	III
4	Jackfruit Chips	IV
5	Jackfruit Mixture	V
6	Jackfruit RTS beverage	VI

[**Note:** 1. N= 20]

the overall acceptability scores for the value added jackfruit products such as Jam (5), Halwa (4.8), Papad (4.7), Chips (4.2), Mixture (4.6) and RTS beverage (4.3) showed that all the products were highly acceptable. Also the products were subjected to a ranking test and the results are presented in Table 8.2. According to this table Jackfruit Jam ranked first followed by Halwa, Papad and Chips whereas Mixture and RTS beverage were ranked least.

Table 8.3: Cost Economics of the Value Added Jackfruit products

Sl. No.	Name of the product	Ingredients Cost * Rs. / Kg A	Production Cost Rs. / Kg B	Total Cost Rs. / Kg C= (A+B)	Profit (30%) Rs. / Kg D	Sale cost Rs. / Kg E=(C+D)	Market Cost Rs. / kg F
1	Jack fruit Chips	140	42	182	55	237	300
2	Jack fruit Papad	157	47	204	61	265	300
3	Jack fruit RTS beverage (Liter)	58	17	75	23	98	100
4	Jack fruit Jam	99	30	129	39	168	200
5	Jack fruit Halwa	156	47	203	61	264	300
6	Jack fruit Mixture	112	37	149	45	194	200

[**Note:** *Includes cost of packing material]

The Table 8.3 shows the cost economics of the value added jackfruit products. The cost of production of each product included the actual ingredients cost and the production cost (30 per cent of the ingredients cost which includes labour, fuel and machinery maintenance cost) and a profit of 30 per cent of cost of production was added to get the sale cost. This sale cost was then equated to the marketing cost depending upon the prices existing in the market. According to this table the jackfruit products cost ranged from Rs 100 to 300 kg. Thus, representing that the cost is very affordable for the nutri-dense jackfruit products with as much as 30–40 per cent profit that can be much relished in off season also.

Conclusion

The rural youth have high potential for entrepreneurship but lack the necessary understanding of personal traits that help in making them entrepreneurial. Their family members too need to understand the importance of entrepreneurship and provide necessary moral and financial support to encourage them to take to entrepreneurship. The entrepreneurial orientation of the youth can be enhanced through appropriate training interventions using FLD approach. Hence in this study, three small outlets were identified at Doddaballapur taluk and the production of six types of value added jackfruit products have been started. Hence, the SHG realised a considerable income through the FLD model developed by KVK in processing of jackfruit to value added products. The group had a turnover of Rs 65,000 for six months by selling the products under the brand name "SIRI PRODUCTS" in various exhibitions.

Thus, marketing of the nutritious jackfruit products as an income generating activity by the SHG for the health conscious community is promoted which in turn helped the economic empowerment of members of SHG for sustained growth.

References

1. Geeta, P. Channal, P.S. Pattar and G.K. Naidu "Pickle making – A successful microenterprise for women empowerment – A success story – International conference on Extension educational strategies for sustainable agricultural development – A global perspective held from 5-8 Dec. 2013 at Bangalore organised by UAS(B).
2. Jhamtani *et al.*, (2003) Entrepreneurial Orientation of Educated Unemployed Rural Youth. Indian Journal of Extension Education, 39 (3 and 4): pp. 123-132.
3. Shree Padre, "Prospects and Possibilities of Jackfruit – An Overview" paper published in proceedings of National Workshop on Jackfruit, 'A Multipurpose tree for changing climate', held on 21 and 22 May 2010 at Bangalore organised by UAS(B), p. 61.

9

Collective Farming—APMSS Experience

APMSS

Abstract

Agriculture is a major contributor for Indian economy. Women constitute approximately 70 per cent of the labour force in agriculture. Their role becomes pertinent at all steps of the agriculture such as land preparation, seed preservation, weeding, and transplantation and harvesting. But they do not get recognition for their work, skill and knowledge and remain invisible. Women are not considered as farmers, as they are not the owners of the agriculture land. Discrimination against women is evident in aspects like ownership, payment of wages, decision-making, marketing and control over the income. However, over the time there is a change in the status of women in agriculture with the efforts made by the Government, NGOs and civil societies. But there is still a need to make this change comprehensive to enable rural women farmers and the agricultural labourers to march towards equality and get empowered.

In this direction Andhra Pradesh Mahila Samatha Society (APMSS) has been putting efforts for over a decade. The Mahila Sanghams at grassroots level became the nodal point for facilitating this process towards the envisaged change through collective efforts in agriculture. This paper gives a detail note of this successful model of collective farming by Mahila

Sanghams from the experiences of Andhra Pradesh Mahila Samatha Society.

Introduction

Andhra Pradesh Mahila Samatha Society is launched in 1992 with an objective of empowering marginalised women through education. Women have been the primary users of natural resources, viz., land, water, fuel wood, etc. Apart from their direct involvement in agriculture, natural resources also support several of women's activities such as collection of fuel wood, fodder and water. Women are directly affected by deterioration of natural resources. On another side, many agricultural practices are unsustainable and are causing irreparable damage to natural resources. Profit being the main motivating factor; the focus is mainly on growing commercial crops rather than traditional staple crops. Women who are directly affected by this situation are unable to break out of it, as they are unable to mobilise resources such as credit, technology and information. This situation led to devise a strategy of taking the land on lease for cultivation by the Sanghams[1] with the help of Sangham fund[2] and also from the contributions of the Sanghams.

This was first experimented in Medak district. Women experienced varied levels of successes through this strategy. There was still the issue of women's access to credit and technological inputs. MS being a project for awareness generation, there was no provision for financial assistance to Sanghams on large scale. This led to develop a project, which focused on agriculture with women Sanghams as pivot with the name of "Sustainable Dry-land Agriculture with Mahila Sanghams in Andhra Pradesh", shortly called as *Samatha Dharani*[3], which was supported by UNDP through the Department of Agriculture, GoI.

1. The major objectives of Samatha Dharani are:

- Enabling women to gain access to productive resources for sustainable agriculture.
- Regenerating the natural resources base in the sub-programme area.

- Women farmers supported to achieve household food security.
- To establish an effective system to meet the information needs of women farmers.
- To integrate strategic gender interests into the process of agriculture policy formulation.

The main activities envisaged under the project are collective farming by Sanghams, giving preferences to the growing of staple crops. The project also involved Sanghams taking up activities allied to agriculture such as vermiculture, production of organic fertilisers, setting up of community grain bins and seed banks.

This was implemented in 500 villages of Medak, Mahabubnagar, Karimnagar, Nizamabad and Adilabad districts from 2000-2004.

Under this project, Sangham women used their own land, land assigned to them by SC Corporation and in few cases leased land from landlords on long-term. Almost in all cases the land was either of fallow or of low fertility. Nearly 4,000 acres of land was accessed and brought under cultivation collectively by 3,475 women across 500 villages. During this process of acquisition of land their negotiation skills enhanced to a greater extent in bargaining the land lease amount and the lease period. In spite of continuous discussions, there were apprehensions on leasing out the land on long-term basis for fear of losing ownership. However, after many discussions they realised that keeping land fallow for many years lead to more degradation and low fertility. Moreover, they also felt that if their women cultivate the land they would get some share of food grains, which is very much useful for their household consumption. Having been convinced they extended their support in leasing out the land on long-term basis.

The procedural regulations for women gaining control over land in order to begin cultivation under the programme left them with many hardships. Transfer of rights over land was not easy given the persistent patriarchal beliefs. The efforts to bring changes in these attitudes could yield positive response from men to some extent. But at the same time the cost of registration being high they have to be satisfied with signing bond papers instead of registration in their name or in Sangham's name. Same is the case with the joint pattas where the success rate of getting joint pattas was very minimal because of the administrative hurdles. This indicates fearing a change in the power equations in the society. It was a continuous process of articulation and negotiation by the Sanghams at every stage.

2. Micro Capital Assistance (MCA) and Collective Farming

Before initiating the project most of the women farmers left their lands fallow. Even when they cultivated they could not reap a good harvest. In times of drought they were completely dependent on large farmers from whom they borrowed grains on interest basis (*nagu*). In times of crop failure they would repay the value by working in the fields of the farmers without any wage. Sometimes the farmers were also indebted to money lenders at high rates of interest and unable to clear their dues.

Under this project, an amount of Rs 35000 per Sangham was given to the 500 Sanghams as Micro Capital Assistance for production of food crops. It is a revolving fund. This has assured them ready availability of investment for agriculture purpose and initiated them to go for cultivation. Due to this financial support they are able to take timely decisions and start agricultural operations. This has also saved most of their time which otherwise was spent for going around moneylenders and banks for loans.

3. Land Development

In many cases the land accessed was fallow and was not in cultivable condition it had to be first taken up for development with additional assistance. In such situation certain pre-conditions were formulated in consultation with Sanghams to take up land development activity:

- Entire land should be in contiguity.
- It should belong to family members of Sangham women.

- Land should be transferred to Sangham's name on long term lease or permanent lease (on legal advice).
- Sanghams should cultivate food crops only.

Interestingly, in 1/10th of the 51 villages the Sanghams could follow all the above conditions. The remaining Sanghams could meet either two or three of them. Therefore, these 51 villages were taken up for land up-gradation activity.

4. Agriculture Allied Activities

Even with lot of efforts to promote collective farming by Mahila Sanghams, the natural calamities have had their effect on the produce and repayment of the MCA. The women are in a desperate situation relating repayment and continuation of their collective efforts. Hence discussions were facilitated to take up integrated farming, which would reduce the cost of cultivation and provide some alternative activity during off-season. This was formulated by providing second installment of MCA to the some Sanghams. However, this was given only to those Sanghams who were not provided earlier with the funds for land development.

By using MCA some of the Sanghams, initiated agriculture allied activities like dairy, poultry, sheep raring, goat raring, setting up dal and flour mills, preparation of vermicompost, etc., for economic sustainability as well as for household consumption. By taking up these allied activities women farmers are able to create employment opportunities to one or two Sangham women continuously. This indicates women's changing role in the agricultural scenario.

5. Capacity Building and Strategies

Through Samatha Dharani capacity building has taken place at various levels and in various forms on agricultural practices, technical, organic farming and market-related issues. These include providing technical information and inputs at meetings, workshops, exposure visits, study tours and studies by research institutions. These were not off farm programmes but were part of continuous process of learning and sharing even on farms.

6. Impact of Samatha Dharani Project

The intervention yielded many results in various aspects helping women to develop a sense of solidarity. It becomes clear that working together did not only provide economic advantage but built bonds amongst these women who took decisions on everything from sowing to harvesting and marketing. These experiences brought them into the public sphere where they had to interact with markets, banks and other government institutions. In turn, this increased their awareness and self-confidence.

7. Recognition as Women Farmers

Women's knowledge and understanding about agriculture practices improved significantly. They are able to put their learning into practice. It is evident in the preparation and use of organic fertilisers and pesticides like *neem* decoction, neem cake, compost, vermicompost, etc., as also adhering to the timely activities during the cultivation.

Witnessing the enthusiasm of Sangham women, CRIDA trained some of the women farmers to improve their skills in dry land agriculture through on-farm training programmes.

Apart from agricultural activities the Sangham women, as part of their regular activities for village development, participated in village grama sabhas, panchayat meetings, Janmabhoomi, Pulse Polio progammes, back to school programme, etc. In addition they have also undertaken works like construction of drainages and laying roads. They have accessed Government schemes and acquired ration cards, houses, subsidy on seeds and farm machinery, etc.

The Department of Agriculture, GOAP, also recognised their solidarity and provided with 104 Multicrop threshers for all five districts and 34 maize shellers to Nizamabad and Karimnagar districts women farmers. These machines are much useful to them in reducing their drudgery as women play major role in threshing and shelling operations.

Samatha Dharani has helped in increased visibility to the Sangham in the villages. This enabled them to have access, control, knowledge and decision-making in agricultural practices and they gained identity as women farmers.

8. Breaking Gender Stereo Types

The project has enabled women to access improved agricultural implements like ploughs, sickles, gorru, seed cum ferti drill, dry land hand weeders, hand sprayers etc. This is not only to reduce burden of labour but also to bring within their reach the technical knowledge and better farming practices. This built confidence among the women and they acted as resource persons in spreading the organic knowledge to various groups. In addition, Multicrop threshers, Maze shellers were procured for the cluster of villages. The Sanghams are utilising them in the Samatha Dharani lands, their own lands as well as lending them to others on rental basis. This way they are able to make some economic benefit. In some instances these improved implements and their effective usage inspired the villagers, which made way for their individual procurement.

At the same time some regulations were formulated by women farmers for optimum usage of machines. Those utilising the machines should pay prescribed rent in cash or in the form of grain. Money or grain thus received would be used for maintenance expenses of these machines. The balance amount would be deposited as corpus at the cluster level emergency needs of women farmers.

9. Vermi-compost Units

Some Sanghams initially started preparation of vermicompost in small pits as part of the project intervention. Once they could witness the advantage of using vermicompost in their field, they came forward to build a permanent shed and larger pits. This is used for their crops as well and also for other farmers.

10. Seed Banks

Women farmers who have been experiencing drought conditions for the last five years concentrated on local varieties of seed, which are strong enough to withstand these conditions. Towards this they are preserving good seed from their produce.

However, this was not on a collective scale. The project component of seed banks has served this purpose. Under this a total of 1500 seed boxes were distributed to 500 Sanghams. Sangham women mainly storing seeds of green gram, black gram, red gram and other seeds for the next cropping season there by creating seed banks.

11. Towards a Change

Samtha Dharani was evolved out of Sanghams' experiences and formulated as a time bound project. Even after completion of the stipulated time the Sanghams are envisaging its continuation as regular intervention by their Sanghams. The merit of this project is reflected in the changed attitudes particularly of the family members of Sangham women who now began to look at this as an activity of the whole family.

Besides, fallow land has been brought under plough. Women succeeded in convincing the family members in selecting the crop and decision over the yield in order to keep for consumption as well as marketing.

12. Challenges

- Crop damage with lack of rainfall and pests..
- Retaining leased land is difficulty due to the land owners refusal to continue the lease once land is fertile enriched.
- Seeking the timely technical support from the department in order to get good yield.
- Sustaining the usage of seed bank and grain bins.

13. Follow up

Though the UNDP project was closed, the learnings are still being continued in many of the villages. With the gained experience through implementing this project, helped us to facilitate in other villages where Sanghams came forward to take up collective farming.

Notes

1. Sangham is a village level women's collective which will be a nodal point to take up all activities in order to empower the women.
2. APMSS provides an amount of Rs 500 per month for the strong Sangham in the form of Sangham fund for a period of three years which will be used by the Sangham women for collective activities.
3. In AP the project is known as Samatha Dharani, the name given by the Sangham women. Samatha means Equality and Dharani stands for mother Earth.

10

Meeting the Challenge of Agripreneurship with Participatory Guarantee System as an Entry for the Organic Market

Shivakumar, C.

Abstract

The concept of organic agriculture is the most vital aspect in the present day scenario and its relevance has made more and more farmers keen in knowing and adapting to their cultivation process.

The relevance of organic agriculture mainly lies in its objective to protect the soil health in general and to protect the flora and fauna in particular and thereby producing toxin free agricultural products and thus make agriculture sustainable. In the present context most of the farmers who produce are engaged in organic produce in large quantities are unable to convince the market or the direct buyers that the product is pure organic as they do not have recognised and accepted records. The main reason is that either most of them are ignorant of the certification procedures or they are unable to bear the certification costs. Since this third party certification is affordable by big farmers and restricted to only certain crops, the emergence of PGS certification gains more significance at this juncture and is more beneficial and a boon for the small and marginal farmers.

This PGS involves certification within the local farmers forming their respective local groups, where there is no dependence on a third party for certification and further the documentation can be managed in simple and local language.

The most significant aspect of PGS system is that there is a constant effort to create an environment of ecological agriculture thereby the local group member can obtain an organic mark (logo) which helps farmers to sell their produces as organic produce after completion of their conversion period.

Introduction

Structure of Local Group

Interested farmers who are in the same village or the adjoining village for easy monitoring with minimum of five members or and also sub group (PGS local group) can be made in the pre-existing group, which creates an opportunity to the other members also to enter into the PG system. There is enough scope for savings among the PGS members in the pre-existing groups for their future PGS activities

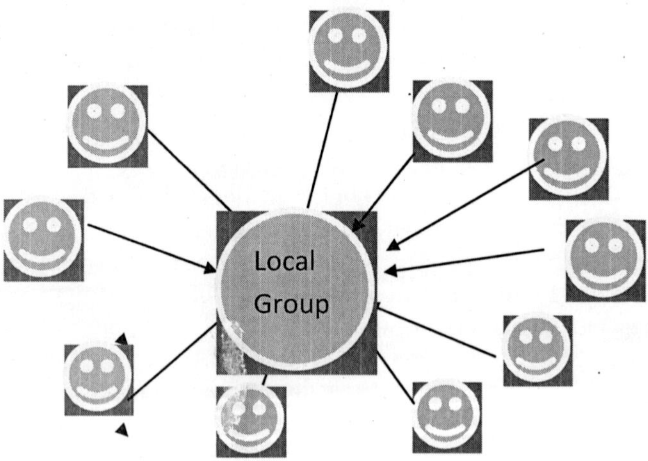

Process and Functions of Local Groups

- Interested farmers who are in the same village or the adjoining village for easy monitoring with minimum of five members or a sub group (PGS local group) can be made in the pre-existing group, which creates an opportunity to the other members also to enter into the PG system. There is enough scope for savings among the PGS members in the pre-existing groups for their future PGS activities.

- Each member should fill up the necessary information related to them in a prescribed format (Application form) and submit to the local group and also maintain a farmers pledge format and production standards by proper understanding of its contents whereby its implementation can be made easier.
- A Peer appraisal committee has to be formed with minimum of four to five members where one literate member should be identified as a convener, for the proper documentation during field inspection (appraisal). During such inspection the concerned farmer's presence is a must. The members of the appraisal committee who had visited the field, has to sign the appraisal form.
- Group has to maintain a minute book to record the proceedings of the meetings.
- Trust and honesty are the main features of the PGS system.

Challenges

- Non-availability of the local and organic seeds.
- Lack of knowledge regarding organic cultivation practices, because of the long period of conventional practices (chemical farming).
- Difficulty in grasping documentation process though the contents are in regional language.
- Conversion of all the land fragments and total land holding to organic is tedious at a stretch because it burdens the farmer to supplement the organic inputs to the whole farm at a time even though he is interested to do so.
- It may be difficult for the farmer to sell the products under PGS brand because the PGS is not so popular among the consumers.

- Lack of grass root level monitoring and regular guidance process at the level next to PGS groups among the farming community, since PGS is a new concept.
- Difficult to install processing unit at the rural level, exclusively for the PGS certified products.

The PGS farmer, in order to be self-reliant with respect to the seeds, so also in the production standards of the PGS much emphasis is laid on use of own seeds or organic or chemical free seeds thus it is very imminent to use traditional seeds.

Traditional Seeds and PGS Farmers

Seed is the most valuable input in farming. It has gained the unique status as a natural resource evolved with human civilisation. Traditional seeds, by virtue of its unique characteristics the farmers by their rich experience have recognised each of the varieties and suitable nomenclature was assigned accordingly. In certain crops like in *hulpare* ragi the word *hulu* means hay/fodder which has high silage value, and all kaddi use of local terms to accompany Latin/botanical name and the word to be underlined to indicate that it is not an English term. Varieties of Ragi like Pichakaddi, Karikaddi, Bilikaddi and Hasirukaddi where 'Kaddi' means straw and all kaddi varieties are of good fodder quality and with higher grain weight with longer shelf life and longer duration. Bennemudde ragi here benne mudde means butter which depicts softness, since this variety is very soft and with high culinary value.

In paddy niru mulugada batha means it is suited to heavy water logging conditions. And a variety called as bananthi batha, where bananthi means post pregnant i.e., the rice variety provides high nutrients at the post pregnancy stages. Certain varieties of paddy are specifically used for special occasions like marriages, *Raasi pooja* and other rituals.

Thus, each variety of different crops has its unique characteristics like drought resistance, pest and disease resistance, lodging resistance, high culinary value and medicinal properties. Thus, in order to make the farmers self-reliant, through production of seeds, conservation and multiplication of these traditional varieties is very much crucial in this context and thereby preservation of valuable local crop germplasm. The concept of seed bank is drawn from the fact that more than 60 per cent of seed requirement is met by farmer produced seeds. PGS farmers have the opportunities for the exchange of seeds to a certain extent which can be done by using the traditional seeds at the local level.

Community Seed Bank

In agriculture, the farmers are not only face problem with marketing but there are many more issues before them in their usual course of practicing agriculture. They are dependent on others for agricultural input like seeds, manure, fertilisers, pesticide and other things and also losing their local resources (seeds) and traditional knowledge which compels them to move away from the ecological agriculture system.

A community seed bank is not just a store where a seed is kept for distribution and marketing or a sophisticated storage facility which has temperature and humidity control. It is a system in the process of community culture which includes village facilities, a garden or field where traditional varieties are safe guarded. Through this system farmers have played a key role in the creation, maintenance and promotion of crop diversity with the help of the traditional skills they developed over centuries. They have been selecting crop varieties to meet specific need such as quality, resistance to pests and pathogens, adaptation to soil, water and climate. Under this system local farmers have established their own seed network to facilitate seed supply to their families and to the local markets. Community seed bank is a system composed of all of the above. Thus, it is among the major strategy for maintaining the genetic diversity in the crop.

The community seed bank in addition to seed transaction; it also facilitates the farmers by providing proper technical knowhow to adapt organic agricultural practices.

Structure of CSB

The CSB management comprises of conveners of different PGS local groups. Each convener acts as representative of each PGS group. This committee simultaneously works for management of CSB and monitoring of PGS groups at respective operational area.

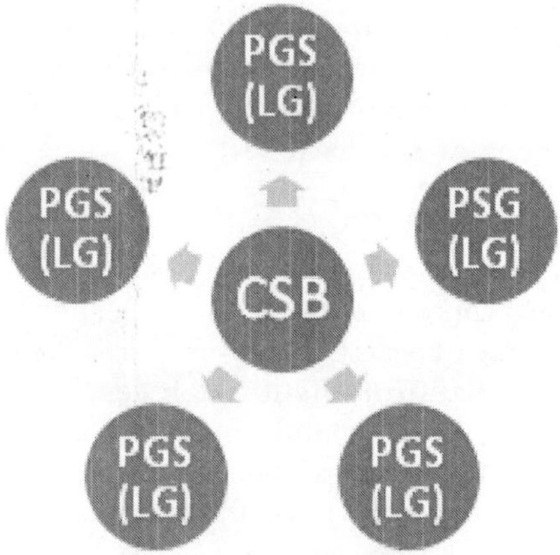

PGS Interaction with Community Seed Bank—A Model

- CSB can provide seeds in different crops and varieties to maintain crop diversity in their farming.
- Provide technical information and guidelines on crops characteristic and organic farming.
- Extend its services by providing organic input or any other required items.
- Organise training or demonstration programme for local groups of respective area.
- Take initiation in installing processing units for PGS farmers.
- Access the market facilities at local level.
- Ensure that all the formalities of PGS is complied with
- At community level CSB can popularise the concept and significance of PGS.
- Dissemination of traditional knowledge.

Crop Diversity

The CSB creates an opportunity to farmers in accessing different varieties of crops at local level and make them to enhance crop diversity in their farming system.

The crop diversity is also a vital aspect in organic farming system. It can help the farmers in multiple ways and make them self-reliant in seeds.

The CSB not only focuses on distribution of seeds but also provides valuable information on each crop and its varietal details like crop duration, straw yield, grain yield and its special characteristics. It also guides the farmers in seed selection and proper preservation techniques.

Organic Farming Related

Farmers require proper guidelines and information about conversion from chemical to organic. Further training and demonstration to farmers on organic components will be effective and helps to easily adapt to their system of practice. In addition to this regular follow up and monitoring is essential.

The CSB, based on the requirements of the farmers can initiate preparation of organic bio pesticides and bio fertilisers with the help of the other interested farmers and supply them. Such activity will help the farmers who require such components and also helps to bring an additional income to those who are directly involved in the preparation.

Local Marketing Systems

Agriculture is centralised in the rural areas and during the conversion from chemical farming to organic there is lot of requirement of organic inputs like seeds, growth promoters like *panchagavya*, vermiwash, fish oil. Biopesticide and insecticides like chilly garlic, *punchimar*and*u*, fermented plant extract (FPE), manures like vermicompost and enriched vermicompost which can be supplied by the CSB with help of interested farmers.

CSB also facilitates production and supply of seeds to PGS and other interested farming community.

Monitoring of PGS Groups

PGS is a new concept hence at the initial stages it is difficult for the individual farmers as well as the PGS group to understand and adapt it. Because of this a grass root level monitoring system is essential to monitor the PGS activities through a PGS monitoring committee at CSB level comprising of conveners of each PGS group. This committee can also involve in other PGS related activities through CSB.

Conclusion

The CSB has its unique way of dissemination of traditional knowledge and promotion of organic farming by facilitating the PGS farmers with various organic-related activities and also monitoring of PGS groups by providing proper guidelines so as to facilitate them with required marketing avenues, because the dire necessity of all the farmers is proper market for their produce both at local markets wherein more of organic inputs are involved and the processing activities so as to bring out the final organic product. From such activities along with various social processes, CSB can popularise the PGS system among the farming community. Thus, the CSB can generate its own income sources which make it financially stable and sustainable at the grass root level.

THEME-III
NGO INTERVENTIONS AND CASE STUDIES ON AGRIPRENEURSHIP

11

Production of Sugarcane Saplings:

A Successful Arti Technology for Women Agripreneurship in Western Maharashtra

Narendra J. Zende

Abstract

Appropriate Rural Technology Institute has developed 30 different technologies related to agriculture and energy, out of which seven technologies have been commercialised. Production of sugarcane saplings is one such technology which has been successfully commercialised and men and women are trained in this technology through ARTI's Rural Entrepreneurship Development Centre, located at Phaltan 415523, Dist. Satara, Maharashtra.

The technology consists of planting sugarcane single eye bud cuttings in plastic bags filled with soil after treatment and growing them in nursery for two more months. The saplings are sold to the farmers after 45 days growth. The present cost of sapling is Rs 2 per sapling. The farmer purchases 10,000 saplings per hectare to be planted at a spacing of 1 x 1 meter. By following this planting method many farmers have become successful to increase their sugarcane yield by 50 per cent.

ARTI has also standardised the loading and unloading method of saplings which has become helpful to farmers to transport more number of saplings per trip of transporting vehicle.

Women are also trained in this technology for promoting woman agripreneurship. In 2006, Mrs Dhanashri Prasad Badave of village Vidani, Tal. Phaltan, Dist Satara was trained in this technology and she has started her own nursery business in 2007. By producing 50,000 sugarcane saplings in the first year and now she is marketing 11,50,000 saplings per year. The net profit per year from this business was Rs 2,50,000 and the employment generated was 8,280 man/woman days. The details of her nursery business have been elabourated in the paper.

In 2011, under a Department of Science and Technology, New Delhi sponsored project for development of SC community people belonging to 10 villages of Phaltan block, Mr Kishore Jagtap of village Vidani, block Phaltan was trained in production of sugarcane saplings. He trained his wife in the technology and supported her to start the nursery of sugarcane saplings. Mrs Pushpa Kishore Jagtap has produced 30,000 saplings in 2011 and in 2013, she has marketed 1,60,000 saplings of sugarcane. The profit earned by her nursery business was Rs 40,000 and employment generated in her nursery was 1920 man/woman days. The progress made by this woman supported by her husband is remarkable being from poor family from SC community.

Sahyadri Tantraseva Audyogik Sahakari Sanstha Maryadit, Phaltan is also marketing sugarcane saplings on large scale since 2000. The organisation has paid 15 per cent dividend to its members for last four years. The organisation has sold 8,00,000 sugarcane saplings last year and made a profit of Rs 1,20,000 and generated employment for 3750 men/women days per year. Fifteen women entrepreneurs of village Algudevadi block Phaltan have been given the work of production of sugarcane saplings on contractual basis for the last six-seven years. This is a good example of agripreneureship for employment generation and empowerment of rural women through cooperative society's agricultural technology base.

The nursery business of production of sugarcane saplings

has a tremendous potential for employment generation and empowerment of rural women through agripreneurship because in Maharashtra sugarcane is grown on 5,00,000 hectares every year and each hectare of sugarcane field needs 10,000 saplings. There is a scope for starting about 2,500 nurseries producing sugarcane saplings each having an annual turnover of Rs 20,00,000. Even 25 per cent of these nurseries are run by women entrepreneurs; there can be employment generation of five million woman days per year.

Introduction

Appropriate Rural Technology Institute, Pune has successfully worked for the last 17 years for development of technologies related to agriculture and energy. ARTI has developed 30 different techniques out of which seven techniques have been commercialised. Production of sugarcane sapling is a such technology which has been successfully commercialised by ARTI and people are being trained in this technology through ARTI's Rural Entrepreneurship Development Center.

The technology consists of planting single node sugarcane cuttings in plastic bags filled with soil. After about 10 days, the bud spouts into single shoot of sugarcane which grows up to 30 to 40 cm in 60 days, when the saplings are sold to the farmers. Proper care is taken through need based use of fertiliser and agrochemicals.

Farmer purchases 10,000 saplings per hectare to be planted at a spacing of 1 × 1 meter. Each sapling gives out six to 15 sprouts or tillers after about 45 days thus increasing the number of tillers per hectare to 1,00,000. Because of wider spacing the crop receives sufficient sunlight and availability of nutrients, resulting in good growth and bumper harvest of 150 to 200 tonnes/ha. The farmers also purchase saplings for filling the gaps present in the conventional planting of sugarcane. ARTI has also standardised loading and unloading method of saplings, which is also important part of nursery growing sugarcane saplings.

— A farmer having 0.4 ha of land along with assured water supply can produce 15 lakh saplings per annum. The cost of each seeding is Rs 2 so the turnover of about Rs

30 lakh is possible and the net profit of Rs 3 lakh is expected in the year. From this nursery employment of about 900 men days and 3000 women days per year is possible. So it has a great potential of profit making and employment generation in the rural area where sugarcane is grown as main crop and has year round irrigation facility available.

ARTI is imparting training to men and women through its rural entrepreneurship Development Centre. In 2002 – 2005 and 2006 to 2009 many women are trained in this technology free of cost because the training courses were funded by few funding agencies like Department of Science and Technology and CAPART, New Delhi. Women also can manage well this activity of production and marketing of sugarcane saplings.

(a) Nursery of a woman entrepreneur

One woman named Mrs Dhanashri Prasad Badave from village Vidani, Block Phaltan, Maharashtra, India has received training in this technology in 2006. She has started the nursery of sugarcane saplings on a piece of her family land in 2007 by growing just 50,000 saplings in the first year. After six years of business she has successfully managed to grow about 11.5 lakh saplings per year. The details of nursery business are as follows:

Details about nursery business

Name of nursery owner - Mrs Dhanashi Prasad Badave.

Supported by her husband - Mr Prasad Vilas Badave.

Address: - Chaitanya Nursery, At Kokarewasti, Post Vidani Tal. Phaltan, Dist. Satara, Maharashtra, Pin 415523. Mobile No. 09881267472.

- Varieties grown - Sugarcane saplings.
- Varieties –CO 86032, Phule 265, VSI 03102.
- Total family land - 0.80 ha.
- Land used for nursery - 30 Are.
- Available water source—Well with 3 HP electric motor.

- Land used for growing seed cane- 40 Are
- No. of saplings sold per annum –11,50,000
- Annual turnover—Rs 35,00,000
- Approximate No. of farmers to whom saplings were sold in 2013– 400
- No. of hectares for which saplings were sold—120
- Approximate profit per year—Rs 2, 50,000

Details about employment generation

- No. of male labours employed—5
- No. of women labours employed—18
- Total No. of women days/month—540
- Total No. of man days/ month—150
- Total employment generated / year—8,280
- Do you own a transport vehicle –Yes

Nursery of a Cooperative Society

A second example is mainly for showing importance of this technology for generating employment on large scale. Sahyadri Technical Assistance and Industrial Cooperative Society Limited, Algudewadi, Block Phaltan also markets sugarcane saplings on large scale and is making profit for the last 13 years.

This organisation produces about eight lakh saplings every year and employs one woman nursery supervisor. The sugarcane saplings are produced by 14 women entrepreneurs residing nearby and the society purchases the saplings from them at the rate of Rs 0.3 per sapling. The women entrepreneurs and their family members get employment for about 20—22 days/ month or 250 days per year.

The organisation provides them land for raising saplings, water and materials required for growing saplings like sugarcane planting material, soil, polybags, agricultural instruments and implements, fungicides and insecticides required for treatment and fertilisers. The women entrepreneurs cut the sugarcane into single node pieces each one with one eye bud, then treat them with recommended fungicide and insecticidal solution and plant them into polybags already filled by them. The daily irrigation, pest control and fertilisation is done by the society employees and women entrepreneurs keep the track of saplings sold after about 45 days. Within a month of sale of the saplings, the entrepreneurs get their remuneration.

Details About nursery business

Name of the organisation - Sahyadri Tantraseva va Audyogik Sahakari Sanstha Maryadit.

Address and Phone No's - Near Ganesh nagar, Phaltan-Baramati Road, Phaltan—415523, Dist. Satara, Maharashtra. Phone – 02166 - 249874, 200246, Mobile No. 09226872459

- Land used for nursery - 4000 square meters
- Varieties grown - Sugarcane saplings, CO, 86032, Phule 265
- Available water source - Well with 3 HP electric motor.
- No. of saplings sold per year - 8,00,000
- No. of farmers to whom saplings were sold- 200
- No. of woman supervisor employed - One
- No. of women entrepreneurs employed - 14 (4 belong to SC community)
- Turnover of the organisation - Rs 28,00,000
- Profit per year - Rs 1,20,000
- Income of woman entrepreneur per year- Rs 30,000 to Rs 36,000
- Whether organisation owns any transport vehicle- No

Details about employment generation

- No. of male labours employed - One
- No. of women supervisor employed - One
- No. of woman entrepreneurs employed - 14
- No. of woman days/month - 300
- Total employment generated year - 4050 man/woman days.

(c) Nursery of a woman entrepreneur belonging to scheduled caste community

Details of nursery Business

- Name of woman entrepreneur- Mrs Padma Kishor Jagtap
- Supported by her husband - Mr Kishor Sahebrao Jagtap.
- Address - Chakradhar Nursery
- At Post–Vidani, Tal – Phaltan, Dist.- Satara, Maharashtra, PIN - 415523.
- Mobile No.0 9881267472
- Varieties grown- Sugarcane saplings.
- Varieties – Co, 86032, Phule 265, VSI 03102
- Total family Land - 1.8 ha
- Land used for nursery - 20 Are
- Available water source - Well, with 3 HP electric motor.
- No. of saplings sold in 2013 - Rs 1,60,000
- Annual turnover in 2013 - Rs 3,00,000
- Profit in 2013 - Rs 40,000

Details about employment generation

- No. of male labours employed – 02
- No. of women labours employed – 06
- Total employment generated/year - 1920

The data presented shows that there is a great potential in the production of sugarcane sapling nursery business for woman agripreneurship. The entrepreneur can make a profit of Rs 100,000 per year even if the activity is implemented on a quarter acre (10 are) of land with assured irrigation facility. This business even though run on small scale like this having a capacity of production of 300,000 sugarcane saplings per year can generate employment of about 1200 woman days per year.

This business is ideally suited for woman entrepreneurs who own about half acre land with assured water supply and if each nursery caters just to the local market, covering an area within a radius of about 10 km and supplying planting material for just 200 ha every year, it can still have an annual turnover of Rs 20 lakhs and annual profit of Rs 2 lakh. Each sugar factory has about 10,000 ha under sugarcane cultivation and Maharashtra has 42 sugar factories. In each sugar factory 50 small nurseries can flourish their business, thus in Maharashtra there is scope for starting 2000 nurseries producing sugarcane saplings. Even 25 per cent of these nurseries are run by women entrepreneurs; there can be employment generation of about five million women days per year.

THEME-IV
GOVERNMENT INITIATIVES AND POLICY FRAMEWORK FOR AGRIPRENEURSHIP AND RURAL DEVELOPMENT

12

Empowering Women Farmers Through Agripreneurship Under Mahila Kisan Saskthikaran Pariyojana

Jayaram, Killi, and D.V. Raidu IAS (Retd)

Abstract

Society for Elimination of Rural Poverty (SERP) initiated Community Managed Sustainable Agriculture (CMSA) as part of its mandate to eradicate rural poverty, since agriculture is the most important means of livelihoods for a majority of the rural poor. This initiative was taken up to address the major causes of agriculture distress - high costs of agriculture, extensive use of chemical inputs, displacement of local knowledge, unsustainable agricultural practices like mono cropping, markets unfavourable to small holders, etc.

Government of India supported CMSA under Mahila Kisan Saskthikaran Pariyojana (MKSP). One of the main objectives of MKSP is to empower women farmers through building their entreprenural capacities. Women farmers established NPM shops, custom hiring centres and market outlets to sell green inputs, pesticide free produce and machinery suitable for small holders.

There is a huge mismatch between supply and demand for green inputs, tools and implements suitable for small holder agriculture. This provides an opportunity for enthusiastic rural entrepreneurs to venture into these enterprises.

Village organisations (VOs) of SHG federations have begun to benefit from jobs and enterprises catering to inputs for sustainable agriculture and by providing services like quality control and procurement of CMSA produce. 8,556 jobs have been created in villages through the establishment of shops for supply of bio-pesticides and organic nutrients, custom hiring centres, seed banks and agricultural implements hiring centres. In addition, about 6,700 small and marginal farmers are generating additional income through the operation of vermi-composting units. 15,900 enterprises were promoted under Mahila Kisan Saskthi Karan Pariyojana (MKSP).

Introduction

Society for Elimination of Rural Poverty (SERP) initiated Community Managed Sustainable Agriculture (CMSA) as part of its mandate to eradicate rural poverty, since agriculture is the most important means of livelihoods for a majority of the rural poor. This initiative was taken up to address the major causes of agriculture distress-high costs of agriculture, extensive use of chemical inputs, displacement of local knowledge, unsustainable agricultural practices like mono cropping, markets unfavourable to small holders, etc.

Society for Elimination of Rural Poverty (SERP) is implementing the largest poverty alleviation programme in the country—Indira kranthi patham. SERP believes that poor have a strong desire and innate ability to come out of poverty, Further they have a strong sense of self help and volunteerism. They are poor on account of various obstacles - social, psychological, political and economic, and it is these obstacles which are suppressing poor people's innate abilities. SERP believes that only by building their own institutions can they unleash their innate energies and come out of poverty. The process of social mobilisation and empowerment does not happen on its own and it needs to be induced.

SERP is the state wide sensitive support institution which induces social mobilisation. SERP is an independent autonomous Society registered under Public Societies Act. The General body consists of 25 members of whom nine are ex-officio members and 16 non-official members. The Chief Minister of the State is the Chairperson and Minister, Rural Development is the Vice Chairperson of the Governing body. Non-official members are from among the participating communities and persons having experience and expertise in poverty reduction and community development sector.

Indira kranthi patham comprises of two large World Bank financed poverty eradication projects, and the SGSY programme of Government of India and State Government's interest subsidy scheme. The programme started in the year 2000 in six districts and in phases it has been expanded to all the districts. In 2008, the programme covered all villages of Andhra Pradesh and had succeeded in organising 96 lakh women in 8.1 lakh Self-Help Groups (SHGs). These self help groups have been federated into 34,500 Village Organisations (V.Os) and in turn the V.Os have been federated into 1098 Mandal mahila samakhyas (M.Ss). The Mandal mahila samakhyas have been further federated into 22 Zilla samakhyas. All poverty eradication initiatives are formulated and implemented by these institutions. The programme is present in every village of the state. The programme follows a saturation approach and 90 per cent of the rural poor are in the SHG networks. Almost 67 per cent of rural households in the state are covered.

At national level, it is estimated that 20 per cent of farm livelihoods are female headed due to widowhood, desertion, or male emigration and women in such households depend on farming for family sustenance. It is also evident that the increase in number of suicide cases of farmers in the country is another contributing factor to the enhanced rate of feminisation of agriculture. Women farmers in women-headed households are mostly not able to access extension services, farmers support institutions and production assets like seed, water, credit, subsidy etc. As most of them are not recognised as farmers, a significant many do not get included as beneficiaries to the various programmes/services of the government. Keeping this in view government of India envisaged a new scheme called "Mahila Kisan Sashkthikaran Pariyojana".

Government of India supported CMSA under Mahila Kisan Saskthikaran Pariyojana (MKSP). One of the main objectives of MKSP is to empower women farmers through building their entrepreneurial capacities. Women farmers established NPM shops, custom hiring centres and market outlets to sell green inputs, pesticide free produce and machinery suitable for small holders.

There is a huge mismatch between supply and demand for green inputs, tools and implements suitable for small holder agriculture. This provides an opportunity for enthusiastic rural entrepreneurs to venture into these enterprises.

Village organisations (VOs) of SHG federations have begun to benefit from jobs and enterprises catering to inputs for sustainable agriculture and by providing services like quality control and procurement of CMSA produce. 8,556 jobs have been created in villages through the establishment of shops for supply of bio-pesticides and organic nutrients, custom hiring centres, seed banks and agricultural implements hiring centres. In addition, about 6,700 small and marginal farmers are generating additional income through the operation of vermi-composting units. 15,900 enterprises were promoted under Mahila Kisan Saskthi Karan Pariyojana (MKSP). Graph-1, indicates the landscape of different enterprises promoted under MKSP.

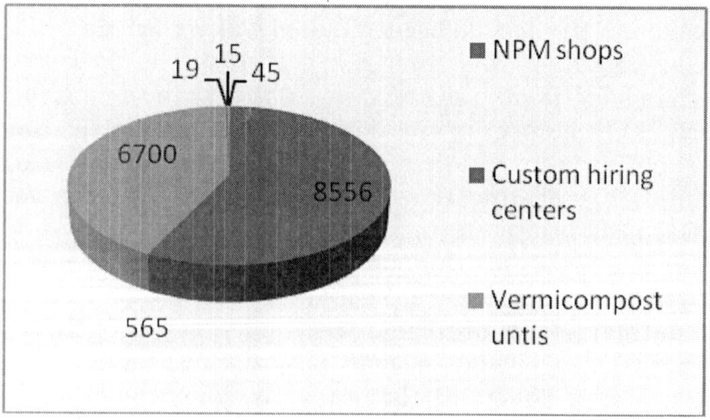

Graph-I: Landscape of different agri enterprises promoted under MKSP.

Mahila kisan who are willing to take up small enterprises were supported through micro finance. The SHGs have been able to access Rs 11,000 crores in 2012-13. In addition to the bank credit they were provided with Rs 30 Crore as revolving fund through Swarna Jayanthi Grameen Swaraj Yojana (SGSY) and Mahila Kisan Saskthi Karan Pariyojana (MKSP). The flow of this large volume of credit at a concessional interest rate of three per cent per annum has made a tremendous impact on the promotion of agripreneurship.

SERP encouraged SC/ST mahila kisan to take up these enterprises as part of inclusive livelihood strategy. Out of 15,900 entrepreneurs 47 per cent (7,535) are from SC, 23 per cent (3,673) are from ST, 22 per cent are from BC. Graph-II shows social category wise agripenures.

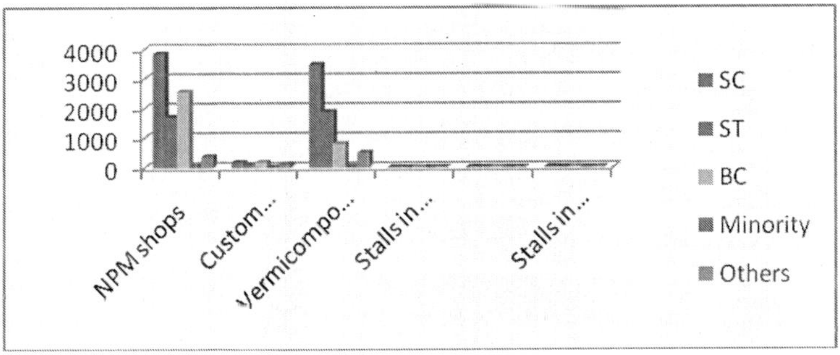

Graph-II: Social Category-wise Agripreneures.

Any woman who is keen to take up green business is provided with revolving fund and training. Women were trained on sustainable agriculture practices, usage of tools and equipment etc. Further they were handheld by the district level functionaries. They were trained for five days in three spells. Intensive training helps them in delivering quality services to the farmers in time.

Promotion of agripreneurship among women farmers is one of the main objectives of Mahila Kisan Saskthikaran Pariyojana (MKSP). Promotion of Agripreneurship is aimed at creating sustainable and decent livelihoods and reducing drudgery to women farmers. Following are the broad categories of agripreneurship promoted under MKSP.

- Farm level producers
- Green Input suppliers
- Services providers
- Food processing
- Organic outlets

Farm Level Producers

Land less agriculture labour were provided with working capital of Rs 10,000 to take up 1/2 acre irrigated land on lease. This year 40,205 women take up this enterprise. They were trained in sustainable agriculture practices. They grow Paddy through System of Rice Intensification (SRI) and vegetables. These entrepreneurs earning Rs 30,000 to 50,000 per annum in addition to food security for their household.

Green Input Suppliers

Every village organisation is provided with Rs 10,000 as revolving fund for establishment of NPM shops. Village organisations identified one of the SHG members for establishment of NPM shops. These shops supply around 20 types of botanical extracts and other green inputs required for sustainable agriculture at right time. These shops reduced drudgery in preparation of botanical extracts. So far 8,556 NPM shops were established across 22 districts creating livelihoods for 8,556 families. All NPM shop owners were trained on preparation of botanical extracts and other components of sustainable agriculture. They are also provided with manuals for preparation of botanical extracts.

Most of the NPM shop owners paid the loan amount. About 54 per cent of the NPM shops attained Rs 2000 or more per month during the peak season. NPM shop owners are actively participating in the farmer field schools (FFS) and preparing botanical extracts based on the finding in FFS. Farmers participated in FFS placing orders to the NPM shop owners.

Service Providers

Appropriate mechanisation is very critical for reducing drudgery and for meeting the shortage of labour. Custom hiring centres were established by enterpeneuring SHG women to supply farm implements to small and marginal farmers on hire. This enables the small and marginal farmers to take up farm operations on time. Small equipment like weeders, markers, sprayers, drum seeder etc., are available in custom hiring centres. There are 565 custom hiring centres across 22 districts.

Business plans were prepared for establishment of custom hiring centres. Tools and equipment required for the village were identified through consultations in the village organisation meetings. Funds required for establishing custom hiring centres were tapped from MKSP, SGSY and Integrated Watershed Management Programme (IWMP). Investments for custom hiring centres ranges from Rs 50,000 to Rs 1 Lakh based on the equipment required. Most of the entrepreneurs accessed subsidy available with department of agriculture on mechanisation.

Table 12.1 shows equipment and capital required for custom hiring centres.

Table 12.1: Equipment and Capital Required for Custom Hiring Centres

Sl. No.	*Equipment*	*No. required*	*Approximate cost in Rs.*
1.	Power sprayers	Five	85,000
2.	Tarpaulins	100	10,000
3.	Markers	3	1,800
4.	Weeders	10	6,500
	Total cost in Rs		1,03,300

These entrepreneurs were trained on business plans, usage of tools and equipment, maintenance and repairing of equipment. They fixed rents after discussing in the VO meetings. Rents vary from the equipment to equipment and based on the demand for the equipment. Average net income for the custom hiring centre owners vary from Rs 3,000 to Rs 5,000 per month. Table 12.2 shows average rent for each of the equipment in custom hiring centre.

Table 12.2: Average Rent for each of the Equipment in Custom Hiring Centre

No. of entrepreneurs opened stalls	32
No. of farmers selling their products	92
Product range	All most all vegetables
Avg Volumes	15 - 20 ton per month in each stall
Avg premiums obtained	5-10%

Small-scale Food Processing Units

150 women entrepreneurs started small scale food processing units like flour mills, neem pulverising machines. Investment, made by these women ranges from Rs 25,000 to Rs 30,000. They require single phase motors and can be established in the house itself. Through these small food processing units they are earning Rs 3000 to Rs 4000 per month.

Four women from four SHGs from Ibrahimpur village of Rangareddy district established dal processing unit with support from National Agriculture Innovation Project (NAIP). Rs 2 Lakh was provided as CIF from NAIP for procurement of Dal. Rs 4 lakh were obtained as loan from banks to establish the processing unit. They established market tie ups with "Spencers", "Safe harvest", "Hyper market" etc. They realised Rs 627/qtl. Table 12.3 provides the details of investments and profits:

Table 12.3: Details of Investments and Profits

Village	*SHG*	*Quantity procured (t)*	*Amount invested in Rs.*	*Amount realised in Rs.*	*Profit in Rs.*
Basireddipalli	Swathi	3.7	1,30,000	1,54, 471	24,471
Bompally	Mahalakshmi	1.2	44,250	53,753	9,503
Bompally	Bismilla	0.5	20,500	23,326	2,826
Ibrahimpur	Chaitanya	2.4	90,000	1,03,134	13,134
Total		**7.9**	**2,84,750**	**3,34,684**	**49,934**

Organic Outlets

Organic outlets for selling pesticide free / organic products are another enterprise promoted under MKSP. Aspiring mahila kisan are supported with Rs 10,000 to establish retail outlets. These outlets are located in Rythubazars, Zilla samakhya and Mandal samakhya offices. Outlet owners sell their own produce and or connected with 4-5 farmers and selling their produce. They sell pesticide free produce at fair price i.e., Rs 1-2/Kg premium. Table 12.4 shows the details of organic outlets.

Table 12.4: Details of Organic Outlets

No. of entrepreneurs opened stalls	32
No. of farmers selling their products	92
Product range	All most all vegetables
Avg. Volumes	15 - 20 tonne per month in each stall
Avg. premiums obtained	5-10%

Collective Marketing by SHGs

This model is developed by using the existing collection centre at Ontimamidi. This model does not require any investment except a vehicle for transport. This is one of the simplest interventions which yielded maximum benefits. This is risk free model as there is no speculation or processing involved. This model operates on its own and is self-sustaining.

15 entrepreneurs from Pochhannapet village are inspired by SHG movement and formed into livelihood groups. They started savings @Rs 100/month and raised corpus of Rs 5.4 lakh. Efforts are . . . to convert these livelihood groups into commodity interest groups. They are enrolled into PGS this year; this will enable them to access premiums for pesticide free produce.

Collection centre is the nerve centre for aggregation. Major buyers at this centre includes Reliance Fresh, More, Heritage, Big Bazaar etc. Farmers of Pochannapeta aggregate the produce of the farmers from 16 groups and sell at Ontimamidi collection centre. They hire a vehicle for transport and they attempt to mobilise funds to buy a vehicle for transport.

Average price fetched by the farmers is 30 per cent higher than the local market in Warangal and Hanumakonda. Interesting feature in this model is there is de facto "support price for tomato". Perfect weighing and zero handling charges are other attractive features of this model. Price for the commodities and required quantities are informed to farmers well in advance. Net premium achieved is Rs 24 lakhs in four months by sixty farmers.

Payment is prompt and is done through online transfers on weekly basis. Spot payment is also done for occasional suppliers.

Farmers are able to understand the market dynamics and preferences of consumers. Critical issue is surplus production in Khariff and Rabi seasons and shortages in summer months, farmers growing one or two vegetables over a large area which fetched good price in previous season. They are into production plans particularly in summer as a group so that variety of vegetables are grown required quantities as a group, supplying graded vegetables is essential feature of this initiative.

Issues and Challenges

Working Capital

Though SHGs are able to leverage various sources like banks, SGSY and others for working capital the volume of funds available is still much lower than their requirement. Hence their enterprises suffering due to low performance.

Capacity Building

Women entrepreneurs require intense capacity building and different entrepreneurs require different capacity building programmes. Developing curriculum for capacity building programmes is a challenge.

Market Linkages

Customers for these enterprises are limited and scattered, needing special focus for building market linkages. Creating awareness among the consumers and generating demand is a huge challenge.

Poor Market Intelligence and Price Discovery

Despite technological advancement, women entrepreneur are not equipped with sound market information systems on demand-supply and exact prevailing prices in different markets.

Private Players

More and more, companies are getting into retail food business. They will be happy to outsource their procurement operation to a producer cooperative, if the terms work out. This can be either the raw produce or in a processed form.

Scaling up

As the customer base is limited, increasing turnover and volumes is very difficult.

13

Agripreneurship Development and Employment Generation Under Agriclinics and Agribusiness Centres Scheme in Andhra Pradesh

M. Vinaya Kumari and P. Kanaka Durga

Abstract

In order to analyse the employment generation of agripreneures under ACABC scheme and also assess the performance of units established under the scheme, the present study was conducted in Ranga Reddy, Hyderabad and Mahbubnagar districts of Andhra Pradesh. Out of the 26 activities in which ventures are established, 11 agripreneurs covering 11 activities were included in the sample for detailed analysis. The units were categorised into five broad heads on the basis of the activities undertaken. These groups were Agri Business Units (sale of fertilisers, insecticides, pesticides, seeds, etc.), agriclinics which provide consultancy services, tractors, dairy units and nurseries. Field observations indicate that the training imparted to them was very useful especially on preparing project reports, documentation procedure and other economic aspects of running an enterprise. Significant number of villages and farmers are covered by entrepreneurs. Though other activities are taken up by the entrepreneurs supplying of agricultural inputs along with it providing consultancy services inputs is found to be major activity. It is observed that agripreneurs were able to attract farmers due to good quality inputs, expert advice to farmers regarding proper use of inputs and free consultancy services. Agripreneurs who had set up dairy units were also carrying out processing and marketing apart from milk production. Extension efforts of agripreneurs culminated in better awareness about dairy practices feed and fodder management and better production and price realisation. Agripreneurs were of the view that agribusiness centres (input suppliers) have been successful in imparting knowledge to farmers on new and scientific methods of farming, thus leading to an increase in production per hectare and farm income. Apart from providing employment to agriculture graduates, ventures set up by them have helped in providing gainful employment, both direct and indirect, to several people, depending on the nature of enterprise. On an average about three persons were employed under each enterprise. Entrepreneurs expressed view that though their business is just breaking even now they expressed a hope that they will be able to sustain in long run with reasonable profits.

Introduction

The National Agriculture Policy of 2000 has enunciated a growth rate of four per cent per annum in agriculture sector. It has grown at the rate of 3.3 per cent as per the Approach Paper to Twelfth Five Year Plan. The increase in agricultural production can be possible mainly from the growth in productivity which in turn depends on intervention of agricultural extension activities in providing farmers information, training and support for adopting improved production technologies. In order to strengthen the extension services provided to the farmers and at the same time tap the potential of these unemployed graduates, the scheme of 'Agri-clinics and Agri-business Centres' (AC&ABC) was launched on 9th April, 2002. The objective of this Scheme is to strengthen the transfer of technology and extension services by supplementing the existing extension network to accelerate the process of technology transfer to agriculture and providing supplementary sources of input supply and services and also providing self-employment opportunities to unemployed agriculture graduates. Agriclinics are envisaged to provide expert services and advice to farmers on cropping practices, technology dissemination, crop protection from pest and diseases, market trends and prices of various crops in the markets and also clinical services for animal health etc., which would enhance productivity of crops and animals. Agribusiness centres are envisaged to provide inputs such as farm equipments on hire, seeds, fertilisers and other services. Already ten years are over since the Scheme has come to vogue, it is high time now to analyse the status of agripreneurship development under the scheme and also its benefits to the farming community.

Methodology

The study will be carried out based on both primary and secondary data sources. The secondary data will be collected from the MANAGE Website on Agri Clinics and Agribusiness Centres Scheme. In order to analyse the status of employment generation of agripreneures under AC&ABC scheme and also assess the performance of units established under the scheme, the present study was conducted in Ranga Reddy, Hyderabad and Mahbubnagar districts of Andhra Pradesh. Out of the 26 activities in which ventures are established, 11agripreneurs covering 11 activities were included in the sample for detailed analysis. The units were categorised into five broad heads on the basis of the activities undertaken. These groups were Agri Business Units (sale of fertilisers, insecticides, pesticides, seeds, etc.), agriclinics which provide consultancy services, tractors, dairy units and nurseries.

Result and Discussion

The region-wise status of AC and ABC Scheme revealed that about 30709 candidates are trained during the period 2002–12 at all-India level. Of these, maximum numbers are trained in Western India followed by northern India, southern India, eastern India and Northeastern India. The same pattern can be seen even in case of number of ventures established under the scheme. At all-India level 38 per cent of the trained candidates have established ventures and 41 per cent in southern India (Table 13.1) which means the remaining 60 per cent of them who were trained have not established ventures under the scheme.

Table 13.1: Region-wise Number of Agriclinics and Agribusiness Centres Established in India from 2002-12

Region	*No.of Candi-dates Trained*	*Share in All India Total (%)*	*No. of Ventures Establ-ished*	*Share in All India Total*	*Ratio@*
Northern India	9172	29.9	3439	29.8	37.5
Southern India	6600	21.5	2727	23.6	41.3
Eastern India	4323	14.1	1295	11.2	30.0
Northeastern India	992	3.2	277	2.4	27.9
Western India	9622	31.3	3807	33.0	39.6
All India Total	30709	100.0	11545	100	37.6

Source: MANAGE, Hyder[illegible]ad.
@ Ratio of number of ve[illegible]tures established to number of candidates trained.

The state-wise analysis shows that the maximum candidates trained and established agriventures are in the state of Maharashtra followed by Uttar Pradesh (UP), Tamil Nadu, Karnataka, Rajasthan, Andhra Pradesh and Jammu Kashmir and so on. Only in four states such as in Maharashtra, UP, Tamil Nadu and Karnataka the number of ventures established is more than 40 per cent of the candidates trained. In Jammu and Kashmir and West Bengal this ratio has fallen short of 20 per cent (Table 13.2).

The ratio of number of projects sanctioned to total number of ventures established varies from state to state. However, this ratio is found to be very low in almost all states. The maximum number of ventures are financed in Assam followed by Himachal Pradesh and Karnataka (Table 13.2). It is clear from the Table 13.2 that a large number of ventures shown under the scheme are not financed by banks as these ventures probably might have established with the help of owned capital or borrowed capital either from formal or from informal sources.

Table 13.2: State-wise Number of Agriclinics and Agribusiness Centres Established in India from 2002-12

State	*No. of Candidates Trained*	*No. of Ventures Established*	*Ratio@*	*No. of Projects sanctioned by Banks*	*Ratio@@*
Maharashtra	6274	2654	42.3	237	8.9
Uttar Pradesh	5718	2585	45.2	214	8.3
Tamil Nadu	2686	1202	44.8	177	14.7
Karnataka	2454	981	40.0	221	22.5
Bihar	2378	899	37.8	98	10.9
Rajasthan	2372	834	35.2	63	7.6
Andhra Pradesh	1205	454	37.7	57	12.6
Jammu and Kashmir	1162	146	12.6	3	2.1
Gujarat	969	319	32.9	42	13.2
Madhya Pradesh	809	263	32.5	17	6.5
Orissa	504	104	20.6	7	6.7
Jharkhand	495	114	23.0	6	5.3
Haryana	417	142	34.1	19	13.4
Punjab	395	130	32.9	4	3.1
Assam	430	146	34.0	70	47.9
Himachal Pradesh	387	107	27.6	36	33.6
Manipur	354	110	31.1	6	5.5
West Bengal	326	50	15.3	6	12.0

Source: MANAGE, Hyderabad.

@ Ratio of number of ventures established to number of candidates trained.

@@ Ratio of number of projects sanctioned by banks to number of ventures established.

The units are established in 32 activities at all-India level though this figure varies from state to state. Of these 32 activities, major number of units are established under agriclinics and agribusiness centres which means supplying agricultural inputs and providing consultancy services, followed by dairy/poultry/piggery/goatary, vermicomposting, nursery, seed processing, farm machinery units and others.

Business Profile of Sample Agripreneurs

All the sample agripreneurs were possessing B.Sc. (Agriculture) degree from a recognised university. Two of the agripreneurs also possessed post graduate degree in agriculture. Majority of the sample agripreneurs belong to OC (6) and OBC (5) category. The 11 sample agripreneurs received two months training from Participatory Rural Development Initiatives (PRDIS), an NGO based in Hyderabad.

Quite a significant number of villages such as 1635 are being covered by the sample entrepreneurs. Total numbers of villages covered are 1635. On an average it comes to 168 villages per agripreneur with a range of 5 to 400 villages. Though total farmers covered per village are only 16 a significant number of farmers are covered which means their services are spread geographical. Input supply coupled with consultancy services is found out to be important activities of these ventures (Table 13.3).

Table 13.3: Business Profile of Sample Agripreneurs

	Number of Agripreneurs
Total Sample Agripreneurs	11
Total No. of Villages covered	1635
No. of Villages Covered per Agripreneur	148
Total Farmers Covered by Sample Agripreneurs	26050
Farmers Covered per Agripreneurs	2368
Farmers Covered per Village	16
Inputs Supply	7
Dairy	1
Farm Machinery Suppliers	2
Nursery Suppliers	2
Consultancy Services	8

Table 13.4: Amount of Investment Made by Sample Agripreneurs and Sources of Funds

Amount of Investment (Rs)	*Number of Agripreneurs*
More than 50 lakhs	3
Between 25-50 lakhs	2
Between 15-25 lakhs	2
Less than 15 lakhs	4
Bank	8
Middle Men	0
Owned	3

A total of eight units had been financed by Bank of Baroda, Andhra Bank, Bank of India and Canara Bank to undertake sale/supply of inputs like seeds, fertilisers, power sprayers, power dusters, knapsack sprayers, etc. These banks have provided loans ranging from Rs 5.00 lakh to Rs 72.00 lakh at the rate of interest ranging from 12 per cent to 14 per cent. Their annual turnover ranged from Rs 12 lakh to Rs 100 lakh with an average profit margin of around 10 per cent. Despite facing stiff competition from other similar units attract farmers due to good quality inputs, providing advice to the farmers regarding proper use of inputs especially fertilisers and pesticides and free consultancy services (which included repeated visits to the farmers' fields (Table 13.4).

Table 13.5: Enterprise Wise Net Income Earned and Employment Generated by Agripreneurs

S. No.	*Enterprise*	*No.of Agripreneurs*	*Investment Per Agripreneur (Rs in Lakhs)*		*Net income per Agripreneur*	*Average Emplo-yment*
			Fixed	*Operational*		
1.	Inputs Supply	6	28	17.7	3.67	12
2.	dairy	1	10	2.5	2	4
3.	farm machinery	2	10	3.5	2.5	3.5
4.	Inputs supply, Farm Machinery, paid consultancy	1	0.75	1.75	8	11
5.	Nurseries	1	32	15	5	8

The fixed investment is highest in case of nurseries followed by input supplies whereas the reverse is true in case of operational expenses. After deducting all expenses the net income per agripreneur is highest in case of undertaking all activities because of the existence of economies of scale and least in case of dairy and farm machinery. The agripreneurs who are not only employed themselves but also provided employment to four members on an average per enterprise (Table 13.5).

Summary of Findings

1. Among the 32 activities, providing input supplies and consultancy services were found to be important activities in all states.
2. Though the number of farmers covered per agripreneur is small their services are geographically distributed across different villages.
3. Despite facing stiff competition from other similar units attract farmers due to good quality inputs, providing advice to the farmers regarding proper use of inputs especially fertilisers and pesticides and free consultancy services.
4. Majority of the agripreneurs obtained bank finance for starting the ventures.
5. The net income gain to the agripreneur is though low at present, will be able to sustain in the long run with reasonable profits.
6. Due to the availability of services of agripreneurs a significant number of farmers were able to change the cropping pattern either partially or completely.

Conclusion

The region-wise status of AC and ABC Scheme revealed that about 30709 candidates are trained during the period 2002-12 at all-India level. Of these, maximum number are trained in Western India followed by northern India, southern India, eastern India and Northeastern India. Though, the objective of technology transfer has been met to some extent, yet there is a need to involve private extension staff in the entire production, processing, transporting and marketing chain. The farmers have received very little support in improving the marketing of their produce which needs to be enhanced by providing better market information to the farmers.

References

1. Chandra Shekara, P. and Kanaka Durga, P. 2007 'Agriclinics and its Impact on Agripreneurship Development' IUP Journal of Entrepreneurship Development, June.
2. Kanwath, M., Chargothra, M., Kumar, P.S. and Mishra, B.P. 2011. Attitude of the Agricultural Graduate towards Agri-clinic and Agri-business centres in Arunachal Pradesh. Indian Research Journal Extension Education. 11(1).
3. Parimaladevi, S., Husain, A.S. and Bhaskaran, S. 2006. Determinants of the effectiveness of 'agriclinics and agribusiness centres scheme' in Kerala. Journal of Tropical Agriculture. 44(1-2): 91-93.
4. Rajashekhar, K., Khan, H.S.S. and Vijaykumar, H.S. 2007. Factors Affecting Participation in Agriclinic and Agribusiness Centers programme in South India. Karnataka Journal of Agricultural Science. 20(4): (873-875).
5. Rajashekhar, K., Khan, H.S.S., Vijaykumar, H.S. and Kunnal, L. B. 2009. Problems of trained agripreneurs under the scheme of agriclinics and agribusiness centres in starting and running their agriventures. Karnataka Journal Agricultural Science. 22(1): (233-234).
6. Shekara, P.C and Durga P.K. 2007. Impact of Agriclinics and Agribusiness Centers on the Economic Status of the Farmers. The IUP Journal of Agricultural Economics. 4(3): 66-78.
7. Shekara, P.C., Malik, H.A. and Jan, N. 2011. Gender Empowerment through Agri clinics and Agri-business Centers. Research Journal of Agricultural Sciences. 2(1): 170-173.
8. Shekhara, P.C. 2003. Third wave in Indian agriculture: Introduction to agriclinics and agribusiness centres scheme. MANAGE Extension Research Rev. 10-20.

14

Studies on Women Empowerment Through Micro Finance with Special Reference to Andhra Bank

Smt Y.L. Prema Kumari

Abstract

Micro finance has evolved over the past quarter century across India into various operating forms and to a varying degree of success. One such form of micro finance has been the development of the self-help movement. Based on the concept of "self-help," small groups of women have formed into groups of ten to twenty and operate a savings-first business model whereby the member's savings are used to fund loans. The results from these Self-Help Groups (SHGs) are promising and have become a focus of intense examination as it is proving to be an effective method of poverty reduction. Against this background, a need was felt for alternative policies, systems and procedures, savings and loan products, other complementary services, and new delivery mechanisms, which would fulfill the requirements of the poorest, especially of the women members of such households.

A most notable milestone in the SHG movement was when NABARD launched the pilot phase of the SHG Bank Linkage programme in February 1992. This was the first instance of

SHGs that were directly financed by a commercial bank. The informal thrift and credit groups of poor were recognised as bankable clients. On the recommendations of the Working Group on NGOs and SHGs, the Reserve Bank advised that the banks' financing of SHGs would be reckoned as part of their lending to weaker sections and banks should review such lending. The linking of SHGs with the financial sector was good for both sides. The banks were able to tap into a large market, namely the low-income households; transactions costs were low and repayment rates were high. The SHGs were able to scale up their operations with more financing and they had access to more credit products. As a follow up of the recommendations of the NABARD Working Group, the RBI took a series of measures in April 1996 to give a thrust to micro-finance based lending.

Rise of SHGs and more formal SHG Federations coupled now with SHG Bank Linkage have made this a dominant form of micro finance in addition to micro finance institutions (MFI). Policy environment in India has been extremely supportive for growth of micro finance sector in India. Particularly during International Year of Micro Credit 2005, significant policy announcements from Government of India (GoI) and the Reserve Bank of India (RBI) have served as a shot in the arm for rapid growth.

Introduction

Micro finance has evolved over the past quarter century across India into various operating forms and at a varying degree of success. One such form of micro finance has been the development of the self-help movement. Based on the concept of "self-help," small groups of women have formed into groups of ten to twenty and operate a savings-first business model whereby the member's savings are used to fund loans. The results from these Self-Help Groups (SHGs) are promising and have become a focus of intense examination as it is proving to be an effective method of poverty reduction. Against this background, a need was felt for alternative policies, systems and procedures, savings and loan products, other complementary services, and new delivery mechanisms, which would fulfill the requirements of the poorest, especially of the women members of such households.

A most notable milestone in the SHG movement was when NABARD launched the pilot phase of the SHG Bank Linkage programme in February 1992. This was the first instance of SHGs that were directly financed by a commercial bank. The informal thrift and credit groups of poor were recognised into bankable clients. On the recommendations of the Working Group on NGOs and SHGs, the Reserve Bank advised that the banks' financing of SHGs would be reckoned with as part of their lending to weaker sections and banks should review such lending. The linking of SHGs with the financial sector was good for both sides. The banks were able to tap into a large market, namely the low-income households; transactions costs were low and repayment rates were high. The SHGs were able to scale up their operations with more financing and they had access to more credit products. As a follow up of the recommendations of the NABARD Working Group, the RBI initiated a series of measures in April 1996 to give a thrust to micro-finance based lending.

The rise of SHGs and more formal SHG Federations coupled now with SHG Bank Linkage made this a dominant form of micro finance in addition to micro finance institutions (MFI). The policy environment in India has been extremely supportive for the growth of the micro finance sector in India. Particularly during the International Year of Micro Credit 2005, significant policy announcements from the Government of India (GOI) and the Reserve Bank of India (RBI) have served as a shot in the arm for rapid growth.

2. Micro Finance in India

SHGs have spread rapidly due to their ease of replication. SHG Bank Linkage has provided the capacity for SHGs to increase their capital base to fund more members and bigger projects. Today, it is estimated that there are at least over 2 million SHGs in India. In many Indian states, SHGs are networking themselves into federations to achieve institutional and financial sustainability.

The aggregate performance as on end-March 2012 is as under.

- Saving-linked 79.60 lakh SHGs [estimated 103 million members] had savings of Rs 6,551.41 crore with Banks.
- Saving-linked exclusive women SHGs [62.99 lakh] with savings of Rs 5,104.33 crore with banks accounted for 79.1 per cent and 77.9 per cent respectively of the total.
- Share of women SHGs [36.49 lakh] and loan outstanding [Rs 30,465.28 crore] was 83.8 per cent each in the total.
- Under SGSY, SGSY-saving-linked 22.23 lakh SHGs with savings of Rs 1,395.25 crore accounted for 26.7 per cent and 21.3 per cent respectively of the total.
- Share of SGSY-SHGs [12.16 lakh] and loan outstanding [Rs 8,054.83 crore] was 27.9 per cent and 22.2 per cent respectively of the total.
- According to NABARD, SHGs have mobilised estimated savings of over Rs 22,000 crore of which nearly 70 per cent [Rs 15,400 crore] was used for internal lending. During 2011-12 alone, 11.48 lakh SHGs availed loan of Rs 16,534.77 crore from Banks and as on end-March, 2012, 43.54 lakh SHGs had outstanding credit of Rs 36,340 crore. Thus, the total pooled resources outstanding at members' level would be Rs 51,740 crore. Credit availed by SHGs along with their internal savings is revolved many times within the groups for shorter durations which makes the multiplier effect larger than the figures reported by banks.

The SBLP, which NABARD initiated as a pilot project in 1992 linking only 225 SHGs with banks, gained overwhelming momentum from 2000-01 when banks linked 81,780 SHGs and disbursed credit of Rs 114.78 crore in only one year as against linking 33,000 SHGs and disbursing credit of Rs 57 crore in seven years [1992-99]. During two decades [1992-2012], cumulative numbers of SHGs were 1,01,12,660 with cumulative loan disbursement of Rs 84,556.57 crore. Since 1999-00 till 2008-09, absolute number of SHGs progressively continued to increase with erratic growth in percentage terms, but thereafter the numbers of SHGs continued to decline, though annual loan disbursement continued to increase. This was reflected in terms of high CAGR of 39.25 per cent and 64.89 per cent for number of SHGs and loan disbursed between 1999-2000 and 2008-09 as compared with CAGR of 24.63 per cent and 45.19 per cent respectively during 1999-2000 to 2011-12.

3. Experience of Andhra Pradesh in Micro Finance

The SHG Bank linkage programme has taken firm roots in the state of Andhra Pradesh. As such there are several challenges for the banks in dealing with self-help groups but also aiming for further reductions in transaction cost. The evolving nature of Self-Help Groups would necessitate constant refining and updating of their linkage strategies.

Table 14.1: Progress Table SHG Bank Linkage in Andhra Pradesh

Name of the Bank	*Outstanding as on 31.3.13*	
	No. of a/cs	*Amount*
Allahabad Bank	3074	34.08
Andhra Bank	223917	3354.17
Bank of Baroda	8739	127.06
Bank of India	34877	245.76
Bank of Maharashtra	1230	7.57
Canara Bank	32700	402.12
Central Bank of India	12157	145.25
Corporation Bank	9079	208.12
Dena Bank	699	5.70
IDBI Bank	16	458.83
Indian Bank	66493	1188.20
Indian Overseas Bank	34410	395.29
Oriental Bank of Commerce	0	0.00
Punjab National Bank	3871	40.63
Punjab & Sind Bank	0	0.00
Syndicate Bank	78484	890.94
UCO Bank	3826	49.35
Union Bank of India	44267	532.31
United Bank of India	184	1.66
Vijaya Bank	7845	83.34
State Bank of B&J	0	0.00
State Bank of Hyderabad	78119	1333.73
State Bank of India	250372	3245.54

contd. . .

contd...

Name of the Bank		*Outstanding as on 31.3.13*	
		No. of a/cs	*Amount*
State Bank of India		250372	3245.54
State Bank of Mysore		444	5.16
State Bank of Patiala		27	0.42
State Bank of Travancore		17	0.14
Public Sector Banks	**Total**	**894847**	**12755.37**
Axis Bank		0	0.00
Catholic Syrian Bank Ltd		0	0.00
City Union Bank		543	6.87
Coastal Local Area Bank Ltd		14014	9.85
Development Credit Bank		0	0.00
Dhana Laxmi Bank		3	11.55
Federal Bank		0	0.00
HDFC Bank Ltd		0	0.00
ICICI Bank		0	0.00
Indus Ind Bank		0	0.00
ING-VYSYA Bank		6340	74.76
Jammu & Kashmir Bank		0	0.00
Karnataka Bank		0	0.00
Karur Vysya Bank		0	0.00
KBSLAB		0	0.00
Laxmi Vilas Bank		2	2.97
South Indian Bank		1	5.29
TNMB		0	0.00
Yes Bank		0	0.00
Private Sector Banks	**Total**	**20903**	**111.29**

3.1 SHG Federations/Village Organisations (VOs)/ Mutually aided co-operative societies (MACS) in Andhra Pradesh

Networking of SHGs was inspired by the felt need of the SHGs that are not able to deal with issues that are beyond their reach. SHGs having membership of 10-15 are small and informal groups. Inter group lending, ability to negotiate within higher-level structures and to gain greater bargaining power were the reasons as to why the SHG networking is required. Hence, AP Government evolved the Federations. SHGs minimum numbers of 10-15 federated at village level is called Village Organisation/SHG Federation. The group of village organisations in Mandal level will form as Mandal Samakhya also called as Mutually Aided Co-operative Societies (MACS) in Andhra Pradesh. The long-term sustainability of the SHG model may require a federal structure, without severing the linkages that the SHGs have with the local bank branches. The assumption that the federation structure should not be supplanted on the SHGs and can be addressed when the demand emerges needs reconsideration.

3.2 Micro Finance Institutions (MFI) in Andhra Pradesh

Micro Finance Institutions like SPANDANA, SHARE MOOLA, SUSMITHA etc in West Godavari, Krishna, Guntur, Prakasam and in some other districts in Andhra Pradesh have been advancing micro finance to the poor and also the members of Self Help Groups, who were already financed by commercial banks. About Rs: 1,000 crore was financed by all MFIs in the State. Private sector Banks like ICICI, HDFC, IDBI etc., have since designed innovative products and lending to these MFIs, keeping in view this sector a good business proposition.

In reality the interest rate charged by MFIs is more. Thereby many poor people are unable to repay the loan and some of them resorted to suicides. Recently in Krishna district, the District Collector ordered enquiry on the activities of the MFIs and closed down some branches of MFIs. Hon'ble Chief Minister of Andhra Pradesh advised that an official team comprising of Principal Secretary (RD), Chief Executive Officer (SERP) and Secretary (IF) to hold discussions with RBI, SIDBI and Convenor (SLBC) to study the functioning of MFIs and come up with broad recommendations to regulate their functioning for consideration of the Government.

4. Experience of Andhra Bank in Micro Finance

Andhra Bank since 1998 has been actively participating in SHG Bank Linkage Programme. Bank received the Best Performance award from NABARD consecutively for the years 2000-2001, 2001-2002, and 2003-04. The bank's SHG bank linkage outstanding as on 31.03.2013 is Rs 3354.17 crs with 223917 accounts.

4.1. Saving Products

4.1.1. AB Easy Accounts (No Frills)

To make banking facilities available to vast sections of population Andhra Bank introduced no Frills Savings A/c with name and style "AB Easy Savings Bank" account. Features of the scheme includes minimum balance of Rs 5, no charges on non-maintenance of Minimum Balance and relaxed KYC Norms.

4.1.2. Kiddy Bank Account (for children)

The scheme to the children up to the age of 18 years, minors who have completed 10 years i.e., children in the age group of 10-18 years can open these accounts in their names to be operated by themselves on production of proof of date of birth. The minimum balance is Rs 100. For minors who are below 10 years, the natural guardian should open and operate the account. At the time of opening the account, an attractive doll will be given free of cost to each account holder for depositing their savings in the doll. Accident Insurance coverage for the child and the parent with M/s. United India Insurance Co. Ltd., Rs 55 premium for a cover of Rs 1.00 lakh and Life Insurance Coverage - Life Insurance coverage to the parent in the age group of 18-55 years. The sum assured is Rs 1.00 lakh in case of natural death and Rs 2.00 lakhs for accidental death.

4.1.3. AB Abhaya Savings Scheme

Savings Bank Account with Accidental Insurance

The scheme is applicable with age limit of five to less than 70 years which covers insurance for Rs 25,000 per member with a premium of Rs 18 per member per annum. The claim document should be submitted within 180 days from the date of accident/death to the bank. Other facilities to this account includes Cheque books/International Debit card/ 24 hour ATM facility/Utility payments through ATMs/Instant Fund Transfer/ Any Branch Banking etc.

4.1.4. AB Abhaya Plus Savings Account

AB Abhaya Plus is Savings bank account with Accidental Insurance facility covering death/partial or permanent disability.

The maximum coverage is up to Rs 50000. The premium is Rs 18 per member.

Risks Covered

Nature of Disability due to accident	*Insurnce Cover Rs.*
Death	50,000
Permanent total disability	50,000
Loss of two eyes/feet/hands	50,000
Loss of any two limbs out of Eyes/hands/feet	50,000
Loss of one eye/foot/hand	25,000

4.1.5 AB Abhaya Gold Savings Account

Savings Bank Account with Accident Insurance: The account is applicable to SHG members or as joint with their spouses. The age limit is up to 70 years. Insurance cover is available up to Rs 1,00,000 per person. The premium is Rs 65 per person per annum. The claim document should be submitted within 180 days from the date of accident/death to the bank.

4.1.6 AB Jeevan Abhaya Scheme

AB Jeevan Abhaya is a Savings Bank Account launched in association with M/s LIC of India, which provides Group Life Insurance Cover with Accident Death Benefit. The scheme is eligible all those SHG members who are in the age group of 18 to 55 years. Insurance cover is available for Rs 1,00,000 in case of normal death and Rs 2,00,000 in case of accidental death.

All account holders of AB Jevan Abhaya SB account will be members of the scheme subject to their satisfying other eligibility criteria. They have to submit declaration of good health and nomination form at the time of opening of Account. Individual policy will not be issued as this is a Group Policy and there will be no Surrender value/paid up value. Administrative charges of Rs 33 per account will be charged for the scheme.

4.2. Loans Products

4.2.1 AB Housing Loans

The loan is eligible to SHG members with age group of 18 to 65 years. The loan is repayable to the maximum of 20 years. The loan is extended up to 75 per cent of cost of construction OR 80 per cent of estimated cost. The bank also extends loans to house repairs up to Rs 1.0 lac in Rural, Semi Urban Areas.

4.2.2 Dr Pattabhi Vidya jyothi Scheme: Educational Loan for Children

The loan is available for SHG member's children with age of 12-30 years for studies in India and 18 to 35 years for study in other countries. The quantum of loan to the extent of maximum of Rs 10.00 lac for studies in India and Rs 20.00 Lac for studies abroad. The margin up to Rs 4.00 Lac exempted and for the amount above Rs 4.00 lac five per cent in India 15 per cent for Studies Abroad. The security guarantee of parent taken from Rs 4.00 lacs to 7.50 lacs and for the amount above Rs 7.50 lac—Collateral Security of suitable value and guarantee of the parent. The interest concession of 0.5 per cent is given all the women under this scheme.

4.2.3 AB Vanitha Vahan

This is a facility of four wheeler/ two wheeler vehicle loan scheme exclusively for women for purchase of four wheelers on second sale. The margin will be taken at 10 per cent and the quantum of finance 90 per cent on road price for new vehicle. For the second sale vehicle 60 per cent of garage value with 40 per cent margin. The loan is repayable for four wheelers - minimum 12 months and maximum 72 months (EMI) and for two wheelers - minimum 12 months and maximum 60 months (EMI). The interest concession of 0.5 per cent will be given to all women borrowers by the bank.

4.2.4 AB Pattabhi Agricard

Facility for SHGs who are having land holdings. The card holder can draw cash and purchase agricultural inputs like seeds, fertilisers, pesticides etc., against the card. The card holder is also covered with Accident Insurance Benefit of

Rs 1,00,000 governed by the Bank's Insured Current Deposit Scheme. Insurance is optional to the borrower of the Card holders are covered under Personal Accident Insurance Scheme (PAIS). The card is provided to all SHG members who are owners of the land. The card is valid for three years. The limit is a revolving credit limit to be fixed basing on the credit requirement and the scale of finance.

4.2.5 SHG Credit Card

Andhra Bank is the first among banks in the country to introduce the credit card facility with many user friendly features for SHGs. The scheme includes SHGs who have availed finance from the bank and have repaid the same within stipulated time, and SHGs who qualify under category 'A' (70-100 marks) and 'B' category (50-70 marks) as per critical rating index norms are eligible. The Card will be issued to those groups which have reached to third/fourth level of finance with a limit of Rs 3.00 lacs with validity of three years. The facility is in the form of cash credit. During this period, the SHG can utilise/draw the limit and credit the surplus as per the SHGs convenience. The bank does not take any security up to Rs 5.00 lac. The additional benefit due to these cards is all the members of SHG will get an additional benefit of coverage of life insurance. The bank finances to SHGs for the purpose to supplement the corpus of the SHG for their internal lending purposes and to take up micro enterprises/economic activities by the SHG or its members.

The advantages to SHGs: The advantages to SHGs include that the card will be useful for immediate identification at counter of the branch, as it contains Loan No., S.B A/c No., and names of all SHG members. The card will serve as identification of SHG, to all concerned Government departments and in the public functions.

4.2.6 Financing to Village Organisations/Federations

VOs/Federations are SHGs minimum numbers of 10-15 federated at village level is called Village Organisation. The group of village organisations at Mandal level will form as Mandal Samakhya also called as Mutually Aided Co-operative societies (MACs) in Andhra Pradesh. The scheme features include availing this facility the group should be registered under AP MACS Act, 1995. SHGs should have got its accounts audited by a Chartard Accountant during last two years and placed the audited financial statements before its General body within a period of six months from the close of relevant accounting year. The Federation should have filed annual returns before the statutory authorities in accordance with provisions of relevant laws.

The bank sanctions to VO one or two credit limits i.e., for trading activity and also for onward lending to SHGs as per the proposal submitted by the VO/Federation. The VOs who are having bank account for the period of six months are eligible for the finance. The Federation should have mobilised the share capital (thrift) in full from member SHGs and there should be no arrears in its collection. The quantum of finance will be 10 (Ten) times of the net worth of the VO (or) 80 per cent of estimated/projected Micro credit plan, whichever is less the loan is given with 20 per cent margin. The Corpus and the Book debts available with the Federations will be both Primary and Collateral security for the limit to be financed by the Bank as the Federations will not have any fixed assets.

4.2.7 Scheme for Financing Matured SHGs for Farm Production and Investment Activities

The scheme is formulated with an objective of the scheme is to facilitate the members of matured SHGs to meet their credit requirement for farm production and investment activities and to enable them to diversify their income generating activities. Bank extends finance to target Group of all matured SHGs, which are three years old or have availed a minimum of two cycles of bank loan and repaid completely are eligible. The scheme includes the insurance coverage of Individual Self Help Group members with Janashree Bima Policies, which covers their life and also with Swasthya Bima Policies which covers their health.

4.2.8 AB Mahila Soubhagya-Debt Swapping to Rural and Urban SHGs

To provide institutional credit to Self Help Groups (SHGs) to repay loans of their members taken from non-institutional lenders (private money lenders). The scheme is launched with an objective of the scheme is to facilitate the members of SHGs to meet their debts (from non-institutional lenders) through bank linkage. Advantages of the scheme includes to make the SHG members to come out of the clutches of money lenders and replacement of high cost loans with bank finance. The eligibility for the loan is as per the corpus and (or) Micro Credit Plan (Note: Micro Credit Plan includes the components like Investment credit needs for economic activities and Social needs like Health, Education, marriage, house, house repair etc., which is subject to maximum of 10 per cent of investment credit needs as calculated above). 50 per cent of the eligible loan amount as calculated above, (or) to the extent of debt whichever is lower, as additional term loan. For new SHGs, which have completed at least for six months of their existence with regular savings and internal lending. The eligibility of loan is four times of savings/corpus (or) Rs 50,000 whichever is higher. 50 per cent of the eligible loan amount as calculated above (or) to the extent of debt whichever is lower, as additional term loan. The loan is repayable in three to five years in monthly installments with gestation period of six months. The bank does not take collateral security up to Rs 5.00 lakh per group. Individual Self Help Group members are covered with Janashree Bima Policies, which covers their life and also covered with Swasthya Bima Policies with their health.

4.3 Insurance Products

4.3.1 SHGs-Life Cover: Janashree Bima Yojana Scheme-life Coverage for SHGs

All those SHG members who are aged between 18 to 59 years are covered in this policy. The age proof can be obtained from Voters list/Ration card/Multipurpose card or certificate issued by the Government agency connected with the activity of Self Help Groups. The member of the Self Help Group (SHG) has to submit a data cum application to the SHG. All the data forms cum applications pooled from SHGs' are to be submitted to the concerned Bank. The annual premium payable is Rs 100 per each member. An equal amount of premium Rs 100 will be adjusted from the Social Security Fund set up by the Corporation making the total premium Rs 200. The claim will be settled by the bank on receipt of the information from the member. The benefits includes that an assurance shall be affected on the life of each insured member under one year Renewable Term Assurance plan. Death due to any reasons (both Natural and Accidental Death) and disability is covered for the Sum Assured as detailed below.

S. No.	*Particulars*	*Amount of Claim in Rupees*
1.	On death	20,000
2.	Death due to Accident	50,000
3.	Total and permanent disability due to accident	50,000
4.	Total and Irrecoverable loss of two limbs or loss of sight of both eyes or one eye or one limb.	50,000
5.	Loss of one limb	25,000

4.3.2 SHGs Health Cover

Swasthya Bima Policy-health Cover for SHGs (For members of Self Help Groups and other credit linked groups)

The scheme will be operated jointly with M/s United India Insurance Company Ltd. Members of Self Help Groups and other credit linked groups who are below poverty line and availed credit from Andhra Bank are eligible under this policy. The members should be in the age group of 15–65 years. Premium payable per each member is Rs 140. The benefits include:

1. Hospitalisation expenses are payable under the policy up to an amount of Rs 10,000 subject to Policy terms and conditions.

2. Transportation cost of Rs 200 is payable per Policy period subject to admissibility of claim.
3. Reimbursement of Rs 30 per day of hospitalisation towards cost of meals subject to be maximum of Rs 150 per policy period and subject to admissibility of claim.
4. Pre-existing of diseases is not payable under the Policy. However Policy is subject to 30 days waiting period for diseases and subject to exclusions of diseases not covered under policy during 1st year.

4.4 Case Studies Financed by Andhra Bank

Case Study 1: Laxmi Priya Self Help Group in Pandurangapuram Village, Khammam Dist., Andhra Pradesh: Manufacturing and export of Rumy caps.

Started by 11 women of all communities including SCs/STs. Initially they saved Rs 1 per day per head. Prepared papads and other eatables. When corpus was Rs 10,000 they raised a loan of Rs 10,000 from Andhra Bank. They started stitching garments for women. They got training for making Soft Toys from the Dept of Women and Child Welfare, Government of AP. They secured a bank loan of Rs 1,00,000 when corpus was Rs 30,000. They started making soft toys and hosiery items and RUMY caps.

Further loan of Rs 1,24,000 was taken when the corpus was Rs 38.000. Group received export order for Rumy caps from Thailand. From a stage where they were dependent on their husbands who used to earn Rs 20 to Rs 30 per day as daily wages, these women now earn Rs 1000 to Rs 3000 per member per month. They display their products in various exhibitions and are thankful to the bank, government departments for the help extended to them in making them self-reliant and economically independent.

Case Study 2: Fashion Designing and Garment Making Project, East Godavari District.

The Government of India under Swarnjayanthi Gram Swarozgar Yojana (SGSY), a centrally sponsored poverty alleviation programme, sanctioned a special project titled Fashion Designing and Garment Making Project with a total outlay of Rs 23.97 crores for the benefit of 13,680 rural Self Help Group (SHG) women in East Godavari District. The Project is under implementation in East Godavari District through District Rural Development Agency (DRDA) for the last two years.

The details of the Project are:

Total project outlay	:	Rs 23.97 crores
SGSY subsidy	:	Rs 12.00 crores
Loan from Banks	:	Rs 11.97 crores
Women assisted	:	13,680 members
Training components	:	Fashion Designing and Garment manufacturing

Manufacturing

Batik, Tie and Dye, Kalamkari Printing, Embroidery

No. of women trained	:	About 6,000
Period of training	:	75 days

Infrastructure available

The District Rural Development Agency, East Godavari is having Training and Technology Development Centres (TTDC) at Amalapuram, Samalkota and Rajahmundry to an extent of five acres each. The DRDA constructed buildings with an amount of Rs 150 lakhs each to cater the training needs of the Project.

Common Facility Centres are established at the above three TTDCs and necessary machinery and equipment including specialised machines are placed at the centres for training as well as executing the orders. 18 satellite Common Production Centres are also established at major towns in the District with an amount of Rs 10 lakhs each at which the women trained under the project are taking up garment stitching work. Each centre is equipped with 60 to 100 single needle machines.

Details of various types of Garment stitching completed:

1. Women tear-away pants exported to Zordan – about 18,500 pieces

2. Neck and Head bands exported to Korea and Japan – about 1,50,000 pieces
3. T-Shirts, Women Jackets, Swimmer dresses, aprons and Bermudas – About 43,500 pieces
4. Laced pillow covers exported to UAE – about 30,000 pieces
5. GT Skirts and silky top night wear exported to USA – about 3,000 pieces
6. Lace sofa and diwan pillow covers exported to USA – about 4,000
7. 1,500 Bed sheets and pillow covers
8. 2,000 pieces of Air Force staff uniforms
9. 2,00,400 seeds bags to AP Seeds Development Corporation
10. 15,000 shoulder bags supplied to AP Forest Department
11. 67,395 uniforms to AP Social Welfare Residential School Society through APCO
12. 40,120 uniforms to the boarders of BC Welfare hostels
13. 25,698 uniforms to the boarders of SC Welfare hostels
14. 3,000 uniforms to the boarders of ST Welfare hostels
15. Closing ceremony dresses to participants of Afro Asian Games held at Hyderabad.

Local buyers have entered in a Memorandum of Understanding (MOU) with the District MACS Federation for production of various types of garments. The Common Facility Centres and Common Production Centres are allotted to the buyers for taking up stitching of orders duly providing machinery, equipment and operations who were trained under the Project.

Case Study 3: Lace Park of Narsapuram

The unique handicraft is making millions of Dollars of Foreign Exchange to the Lace Exporters of the area. Since these two lakh women are in decentralised sector the DRDA West Godavari at the request of the District Administration mobilised these women and in the first phase it could mobilise 10,000 Women in the 1000 SHGs and then, these SHG are federated at Village level as Village level Mutually Aided Cooperative Societies and at District level they have been federate as Lace Park at Narasapuram. 51 village level societies and District federation have been registered. State Government sanctioned an amount of Rs 100 lakhs under IIDC. Women participated in national level and state level exhibitions and won the appreciation.

- Total Sales : Rs 46,65,45
- Total Production Value : Rs 56,33,660
- No. of exhibitions participated : 19
- Total sales conducted in exhibitions: Rs 10,54,385
- Export Order : One export order executed through Parameswari Textiles, Karur.
- MOU : Undertaken MOU with Parameswari Textiles, Karur.
- Steps taken for : Applied for ISO certification.

Case Study 4: Sri Sai Jyothi Mahila Group, Chundur

The group was formed in the year 1998 with 15 members. Most of the members are agricultural labourers. After forming the group, they mobilised Rs 1,10,578 as savings since inception. They availed finance from Andhra Bank, Chundur and took up the activity of (Soft Toys) Doll making. Chundur branch financed twice. Currently, the members stopped going to fields and began to make the dolls at their houses resulting in them generating considerable income and their economic status is improved a lot.

Case Study 5: Manasa Dwacra Group, Emani

The group was formed in the year 1994 with 15 members. They could save nearly Rs 1,12,000 since inception. Initially, the group took the bank loan from Andhra Bank Emani branch for Rs 90,120 for Dairy farming. They promptly pay the dues. Besides dairy farming, they also indulge in Agarbathi manufacturing. Their economic status improved. The group received appreciation from the State Government.

Rural Kiosk by Mother Theresa Group, Kovvali: (Case Study 6)

Name the SHG	*Mother Theresa SHG*
Name of the village and District	Denduluru, West Godavari Dt.
Date of opening SB account at the branch	08.01.2004
Purpose of the loan	To establish unit of Rural KIOSK under SGSY loan
Building site donated by	Sri V. Someswara Rao
Construction of building done by	Government of AP with the help of AP State Housing Corporation
Group contribution	Rs. 25,000
Contribution by DRDA	Rs. 25,000
Bank Loan	Rs. 2,50,000
Back end subsidy under SGSY	Rs. 1,25,000
Total Cost	Rs. 3,00,000
Details of machinery, other furniture and stocks	Xerox machine. Computer, Furniture and stocks of the dept. stores
Repayment period	Five years
Present status or repayment	Regular
Officials visited	The then Governor of AP Sri Susheel Kumar Shinde
Gross income per month	Rs. 15,000
Net income/month	Rs. 4,000
Training support by	National Informatics Center, Eluru
Future Plans under kiosks	Collection of Telephone bills

Services available at Kiosk

1. Issue of caste, income nativity and residence certificates by charging Rs 10 per certificate.
2. Collection of electricity bills in and surrounding villages. Group gets Rs 1.50 per bill from the Department.
3. Collection of Gram panchayat house tax and water tax dues.
4. Xerox copying works @ Rs 1.00 per copy.
5. Departmental store for selling mostly DWACRA products such as pickles, jute bags, masala powders, etc.
6. Internet services and computer classes for school children.
7. Collection of postal RDs on commission basis.

8. Acting as agents to ANL courier services.

The centre has become:

1. A Model rural KIOSK in the District.
2. Proved that dedicated and collective teamwork of rural women folk can create miracle in the village.
3. Marketing of SHG products.

Case Study 7: Sai Sakthi Podupu Sangham: Waddepalli mandal, Mahaboobnagar dist, AP Bima Banyans

Sai Sakthi Podupu is a group of 15 members of SHG specially formed by the DRDA Mahaboobnagar District of Andhra Pradesh. This group is formed to have homogeneous group with an aptitude to work together and like-minded members for specialised activity i.e., banyans manufacturing. The group members are basically from agricultural families having agricultural land and carrying agriculture as main occupation. Date of incorporation of the group: 12.10.2002. The group has started as Small scale Industry Group has got the marketing facilities from DRDA and DWACRA Bazaars and exhibitions. The group is a progressive and model functional group, which has taken innovative activity.

Case Study 8: Padmavathi Self Help Group-Weavers, Peddatamarapalli

The group members belong to the weavers community. In 1995, the group was formed with 13 members. They availed bank finance from Andhra Bank Peddatamarapalli branch under SGSY with the loan amount of Rs 80000. With this, their economic status was improved and the group is getting good income and regularly repaying the loan installments.

4.5 Micro Finance in Development of Rural Economy and its Impact on Women

A recent World bank-NCAER Survey on rural access to finance indicates that 70 per cent of the rural poor do not have a bank account and 87 per cent have no access to credit from formal source. India has an extensive banking infrastructure comprising over 30,000 rural and semi urban branches of commercial banks over 14,000 branches of RRBs, around 12,000 branches of DCCBs and nearly 1,00,000 cooperatives credit societies at the village level. There is at least one retail credit outlet on an average for about 5,000 rural people, which translates into one outlet for every 1,000-households. Access in terms of rural branches increased from 1,833 in 1969 to around 30,572 at present. The population per rural branch declined from 2,01,854 in 1969 to 16,000 at present. The proportion of borrowings of rural households from institutional sources increased from seven per cent in 1951 to more than 60 per cent at present.

During the current year banks are targeted to achieve nearly 3,00,000 groups. In the years to come NABARD will have to use its resources including the Micro Finance Development and Equity Fund (MFDF), to support innovation in products, services, and channels, to introduce incentives for banks to build qualitative and profitable micro finance portfolios and promote product innovation for multiple requirements of the poor. The future of rural poverty alleviation is the investment in all aspects of rural development. Small working capital loans for petty trade, artisans and micro business activities in rural areas are a growing part of MFI portfolios.

The 2005 year of Micro Credit is an opportunity to highlight the perspective of finance for the poor. The international year was proclaimed by the United Nations to bring focus on the poor their entrepreneurship and highlight a useful tool help them move out of poverty. As many know, the poor are not poor because they cannot manage their money; they are not poor because they cannot manage their business activities and are not profitable; they are poor because their resource base is too small.

5.1 Impact of Micro Finance on Women

5.1.1 Political

One of the key benefits of SHGs is women's empowerment and this can be seen with the number of women involved in public affairs. While the number of women actually involved in politics is still very low. Their presence today is affecting the perception of women and their role in the political arena. They are being recognised as an important group with serious concerns. The role of SHGs is both as an inspiration and as a financer. Impoverished women develop greater language and financial skills through the SHG, which provides the building blocks for higher levels of confidence to engage the world. SHGs not only empower its members but also wield a powerful political role as a group as well.

5.1.2 Social Harmony

Broadly defined, social harmony encompasses the equality and integrity of relationships between different social groups. To frame the following analysis, SHGs typically consists of the social groups like Schedule Caste (SC), Scheduled Tribe (ST), Minorities (MN), Backward Caste (BC) and Other Caste (OC). The composition of SHGs are sometimes exclusively one particular social group or a mix. The impact of SHGs on social harmony has also been mixed.

5.1.3 Social Justice

While there has long been a dispute resolution mechanism in villages, in the past it was controlled by men. Now, there are instances of women, SHG members, being involved in resolving disputes. Whether or not the women are working for their own interests or in the case for justice varies, regardless SHGs' impact on the political arena is certainly being seen also in social justice, albeit in a slow and evolutionary process.

5.1.4 Community

Recent analysis has shown that the impact that SHGs have on the community at large have been minor. There have been few instances of significant contributions from SHGs to education, family planning, eradication of child labour and hygiene. This demonstrates that given the opportunity, SHGs, assuming they have the capacity, can act as a director of community development. The perception of taking of a women's based organisation taking a leading role for the betterment of the greater good has monumental impacts on the local community.

5.1.5 Livelihoods

Livelihood, meaning a person's economic activity, is an area that is vitally important to SHGs. The loans that SHG members receive are intended to improve their livelihoods so that they can receive greater and steadier cash flows. In rural areas, livelihoods range from agriculture farming, animal husbandry, dairy and various other goods and services activities. Experience has shown that SHGs have improved livelihoods to the extent of providing the leveraging needed to start an enterprise. However, the interventions to introduce new livelihoods or refine existing ones that could yield better economic results were done by external agencies.

5.1.6 Poverty

The impact of micro finance on poverty reduction, which is an integral part of the development process of rural economy, has been significant. Some of the following empirical findings include:

- Micro finance has empowered women by enhancing their contribution to household income increasing the value of their assets and generally given them better control over decisions that affect their lives.
- Micro finance has reduced the incidence of poverty through increase in income, enabled the poor to build assets and thereby reduce their vulnerability.
- There are reports that households that have access to micro finance spend more on education than non-client households.
- It has contributed a reduced dependency on informal moneylenders and other non-institutional sources.
- In certain cases micro finance has reduced child mortality, improved health especially among women.
- The way micro finance impacts overall poverty reduction in a given country is then shaped by the nature of poverty in that country. India has over a quarter of its population below the poverty line. The World Bank reports that India is still home to some 260 to 290 million poor, numbers that rise to 390 million if poverty is measured by the international standard of those living on less than US$1 dollar a day. Almost half of India's poor,

approximately 133 million, are concentrated in three states: Uttar Pradesh, Bihar, and Madhya Pradesh. Rural areas in India are home to three quarters of India's poor, which is strengthened by the increasing urban/rural disparities. There are substantial disparities within the country as the gulf between the rich and poor widens. The Indian government's poverty reduction strategy focuses on infrastructure, social development (especially education and health), and rural livelihoods.

6. Road Ahead

6.1 By Banks

- Encourage outsourcing of some of the banking services aimed at rural poor with required policy framework. SHG federations/Village Organisations shall be permitted to act as business correspondents, (intermediaries) for delivery of financial services to the rural poor, as these groups are already linked with the banks. Each village to identify the teachers, post offices, NGOs, VVV (Village Volunteer Vahini) Clubs, etc., to use them as Business Facilitators and Correspondents. The outsourcing one of the step in financial inclusion strategy and the banks to adopt outsource some of the banking services in certain areas to reduce transaction cost both in lending and recovery through Business Correspondents / Facilitators. Entire written off loans in rural areas should be outsourced for recovery so that they will be included in further lending.
- Develop insurance products suitable to the members of SHGs/Village organisations.
- Providing micro pension schemes to the SHG/village organisation members may be thought of in tie up with insurance companies. Insurance companies may come forward to cover the rural poor with less premium amount.
- All women who are not included into banking fold through SHGs to be linked.
- To outreach the IT enabled services in rural areas, the

concept of Common Service Centers (CSCs) basically "Rural Computer Kiosks" may be adopted. Under this scheme, first preference will be given to SHGs and unemployed youth to start "Rural Kiosks'. The rural kiosks will offer basket of Government-to-citizen and business-to-customer services, which includes accepting electricity bills, house taxes, updated market information, birth certificates, land records, internet services, etc. Already, some of the banks in India have started financing to Rural kiosks. Government is planning to digital expansion of 1,00,000 Rural Kiosks by 2008 through public, private partnership (PPP) mechanism. This will provide employment to 1,00,000 people directly and 2-3 lakh additional indirect jobs in rural areas with total outlay of Rs 5,742 crs. These will cater 6,00,000 villages, i.e., one kiosk to six villages.

- Banks to give Smart Cards to SHGs.
- Buyers and sellers meets can be arranged by the banks to sell the products prepared by rural people/SHGs/ farmers.
- Banks to open exclusive micro finance branches not only in rural areas but also in urban areas to serve credit needs of urban poor.
- Banks to establish Rural Development Institutes in the Districts through out the country to give capacity building trainings of various on going schemes to SHGs, rural unemployed youth, SHGs, farmers, etc.,

6.1.2 By State Governments

State has to provide right kind of policy framework for encouraging SHGs /Federations /VOs, apart from investing on education and health needs of these groups.

6.3 By NABARD

State has to take initiatives on conducting entrepreneurial development programmes (EDPs) to SHGs/VOs/Federations on a continual basis. NABARD has to continue to formulate policies and new schemes for SHGs/Federations/VOs on a continual basis.

6.4 Others

- Thrust on promotion of quality SHGs on a large scale, with special focus on comparatively backward regions with the active support from NGOs.
- Designing suitable training and exposure programmes for all the staff members of banks and for capacity building of SHGs in association with the NGOs.
- Providing promotional assistance to partners for promotion and nurturing of SHGs.
- Widening the range of SHG promoting agencies by integrating SHG approach in social sector development programmes of the development agencies and the Panchayat Raj Institutions (PRIs).
- Large scale dissemination of the concept of Self Help Groups among the rural masses.

7. Conclusion

Micro finance SHGs in India helps banks to increase the number of accounts and inculcate banking habits in rural places especially women. The performance of the SHG model exceptional in providing savings-based mechanism for internal group credit to meet household needs. On terms of micro finance initiatives and number of players in the field, India has become a major country in the world. The success of micro finance interventions should be taken advantage of bringing about greater integration with rural development endeavours.

Banks have to strengthen the micro finance intermediaries such as SHG Federations/Village Organisations, fund these organisations to create rural delivery channels, provide continual training in puts, and utilise their services for delivery of financial services to the financially excluded rural populations to achieve the ultimate goal of eradication of poverty by inclusive growth of rural economy. If the banks utilise the services of these SHG Bank linkage model as business correspondents/Facilitators the above mentioned effects will continue on the society thereby financial inclusion strategy will be materialised for the development of the rural poor and society.

Bibliography

1. Micro Finance and Rural Development: Engineering Economic Growth by K.V Kamath MD, ICICI Bank.
2. Speech dated July 31, 2006 Dr Y.S.P. Thorat, Chairman, (NABARD) on financial inclusion-NABARD chief moots three pillar plan.
3. Speech by V. Leeladhar, Dy. Governor, RBI on 02.12.2005 Taking banking services to common man-financial inclusion.
4. Agro Business: Micro finance and Rural Development by M.S. Kapur, CMD Vijaya Bank.
5. Linkages between formal and informal financial institutions to extend financial service to poor people by Marie Kirsten.
6. Two Decades of SHG-Bank Linkage Program by Dr Amrit Patel, August 6, 2013.

15

Impact of Self Help Approach on Women Empowerment–A Comparative Analysis on SC and Non-SC Women from Selected States

R. Chinnadurai

Abstract

Kudumbashree (Kerala); Kudumbashree is today one of the largest women-empowering projects in the country. Launched by the Government of Kerala in 1998 for wiping out absolute poverty from the State through concerted community action under the leadership of Local Self Governments. The programme has 37 lakh members and covers more than 50 per cent of the households in Kerala. Built around three critical components, micro credit, entrepreneurship and empowerment, the Kudumbashree initiative has today succeeded in addressing the basic needs of the less privileged women, thus providing them a more dignified life and a better future.

Stree Shakthi (Karnataka): It was launched throughout the State during 2000, by the Directorate of Women and Child Development in Karnataka. The programme is designed to provide special impetus to the empowerment of rural women in the State through formation of self-help groups (SHGs). The aim of the project is to empower women economically and socially by organising them into self-help groups. At present 1,40,000 self-help groups have been formed in the state with 20.731 lakh women members being organised in these groups till January 2010, and the members have saved an amount of Rs 835.25 crores. A total of 1,24,008 groups have availed bank loans to the extent of Rs 1,125.59 crores and internal loan of Rs 1906.00 crores has been disbursed to take up various income generating activities. Rs 73.00 lakhs was released as incentive for 1460 groups to take up income generating activities. Rs 56.00 lakhs has been paid as incentive to Anganawadi workers for monitoring Stree Shakthi groups.

Mahalir Thittam-Tamil Nadu : This Project, more popularly known as Mahalir Thittam, is implemented by Tamil Nadu Corporation for Development of Women with the support of Non-Governmental Organisations (NGOs) and Banks. It is functioning through a network of Women Self Help Groups (SHGs), established and monitored with the assistance of NGOs, initiated in the year 1997-98. There are 4,89,008 SHGs formed till December 2010 covering 75,66,497 women members. Total savings of the SHGs is Rs 2,973 crores having a credit of Rs 10,658.16 crores. The project also plans for the growth of SHG movement with a view to promote sustainability.

All the three models discussed have a more or less similar goal, objective, approach and strategy for women's empowerment through self-help with group formation, skill building and income generating activities. Implementation of the programme in partnership with NGOs and CBOs, internal saving and bank credit linkage are the common characteristics of the different models aimed to study.

The present paper is based on a study with the objectives to study the development interventions of three different models of women empowerment. Impact of development intervention on social and economic status of women and establish a comparative analysis of development in different models on SC and non-SC women.

Study Indicators: The issues focused in the study are to understand the after effect of SHGs i.e., Change in Women's

Participation in Public Events, Change in Employment Pattern, Participation in Political Decision-making, Participation in Electoral Roles, Changing role in Household Responsibilities, Household Decision making, Preference of Expenditure, Change in Education, Change in Income Status, Change in Poverty status, Change in Household Assets, Change in internal and external Mobility, Community recognition on women, Change in household utility, Change in knowledge, attitude and skills, etc.

Study Area: Study was conducted in Kerala, Karnataka and Tamil Nadu.

Sampling Procedures: To study the special efforts and significant features of different models, the three states mentioned above were purposely selected. Two districts from each state were selected namely, Kottayam and Idukki districts in Kerela, Dindigul and Ramanathapuram districts in Tamil Nadu, Kolar and Mandiya districts in Karnataka. The districts were selected on the basis of few indicators of development (one backward and one moderately developed district), Concentration of SC population (More SC populated Districts) and SHG performance (availability of group-based economic activities). Two blocks from each district were selected with similar parameters used for selection of the districts. In the third stage two GPs were grouped in to three categories namely, having only non-SC villages, only SC villages and combined populated villages. One SHG each from non-SC and SC alone Gram Panchayats, and two SHGs (one SC group and one non-SC group) from combined GPs were selected. From each group two office bearers with purposive sampling and eight women members with random sampling were selected. In total, 10 members from each group arriving 40 women from each block were identified. From each state 16 groups covering 160 women were covered. Suitable semi-structured interview schedule was prepared and pre-tested in Tamil Nadu. The interview schedule covered all aspects related social, economic and political empowerment with the adequate coverage of various indicators pertaining to the study objectives. It covered 480 SC and non-SC SGSY beneficiaries from three states.

Introduction

Introduction and effective implementation of social reforms and enactment of women protection legislations made commendable progress on the development of women over a period of time. Those efforts enabled Indian women to secure legal and political equality, enter professions and occupy positions of power and this has led to a myth that, 'unlike some of the Asian societies, women possess a very high status in India. In reality, six decades after independence and planned development, the position of women has worsened considerably in every sphere, with declining sex ratios, declining economic participation rate and growing gaps in life expectancy and mortality rates between men and women. Though the Constitution proclaimed equality and radical social reforms, prevention of child marriage, encouraging widow remarriage and equal sharing of parental property under the Inheritance Act, made important departures yet ancient fabric of Indian men dominated the social structure. But mere enactment of laws does not change in attitudes, and ironically, these advances in social legislation have acted as a disservice to women. Recent efforts of various national, international and grassroots feminist organisations compelled the governing institutions on gender sensitisation to focus on implementation of women development strategies and programmes to fetch due share of fruits of development in India.

The secondary position of women in the men dominant society is a hurdle for the entry of women into economic roles this created a complexity of problems in rural women. Firstly, in the unorganised sectors 'sexual division of labour' resulted in women occupying less paid occupations. Mass turn out of women in MGNREGS manual labour work is a live example that men do not engage in low paid jobs even though they are unemployed. Indian social custom bind women to the household responsibilities, child care and other unpaid agriculture works. By defining woman's responsibility to family care, their inclusion into the labour market is made inevitable and the inadequate incomes of males or absence of male earners, at certain levels encourages deviant behaviour and results in the pervasive notion of the woman worker as a supplementary earner irrespective of the contribution of the resources to the household and the time and energy spent. Thus, a woman who earns as much as 50 per cent or sometimes 100 per cent of the household income is still regarded as a supplementary earner. And almost in all cases and in all levels they do not get equal wages for equal work, nor do the conditions of work offered to them take into account their dual roles. The need to combine productive work with her reproductive role and family responsibilities means that a woman's choice of work is often dictated by what is feasible and easily available, and this need for flexibility is frequently exploited by the labour market and is easily used as another excuse to pay low wages to women. Amongst the poorer sections of the rural community, women are frequently expected to shoulder the burden of the survival of their families. Women tend to work for longer hours and contribute more than men in terms of total labour and energy spent by the household. Women are principally engaged in agriculture or in the unorganised informal sector as construction workers, petty hawkers and vendors and in traditional home-based occupations such as basket and mat weaving, bidi making, lace making, *agarbathis*, etc.

As noted, development efforts have not made much significant improvement on the life style of 30 per cent of rural population. This deprived community has become the victim of all socio-economic, political and natural problems arising in the country. Material and financial deprivation of the poor trap them into vicious circle of poverty and hinders their development. In the recent years, self-help approach has been introduced in order to boost the rural economy, and financial institutions are encouraged to take part in the process of poverty alleviation. Various studies evidently establish that majority of the rural poor still do not have access to credit from formal sources. Credit access to asset less rural poor in India is a near impossibility due to various procedural obstacles in the formal institutional credit sources. In order to meet the rural poor's credit requirements and empower women in the country, Government of India started a major flagship programme called SGSY and provided micro credit to all such poor women in need of credit. Many state governments also followed similar approach on their own or sometimes amalgamated with SGSY. In this backdrop, this study was conducted to analyse the inputs, process and results of three different models on women socio-economic development in the respective states with special focus on SC women beneficiaries, comparing to non-SC women. For a brief understanding, the models from three states are given.

Field Data Presentation on Important Parameters of the Study

Table 15.1: Pertaining to Education, Occupation and Landholding of the Respondents

Study Parameters	*Particulars*	*Category*		*Total*
		SC	*Non-SC*	
Education	Illiterates	122 (25.4)	66 (13.7)	188 (39.2)
	Primary	59 (12.3)	38 (7.9)	97 (20.2)
	Middle Class	28 (5.8)	55 (11.5)	83 (17.3)
	High School	20 (4.2)	38 (7.9)	58 (12.1)
	Hr. Sec.	11 (2.3)	22 (4.6)	33 (6.9)
	Graduation	-	18 (3.76)	18 (3.7)
	PG and above	-	3 (0.6)	3 (0.6)
	Total	**240 (50)**	**240 (50)**	**480 (100)**
Occupation	Agriculture	25 (5.2)	82 (17.1)	107 (22.3)
	Animal Husbandry	80 (16.7)	105 (21.9)	185 (38.5)
	Labour	135 (28.1)	53 (11.0)	188 (39.2)
	Total	**240 (50)**	**240 (50)**	**480 (100)**
Status of Landholding and Size	1-2.5 Acre	17 (3.5)	55 (11.5)	72 (15.0)
	2.5 - 5 Acre	8 (1.7)	27 (5.6)	35 (7.3)
	Landless	215 (44.8)	158 (32.9)	373 (77.7)
	Total	**240 (50)**	**240 (50)**	**480 (100)**

Table 15.2: Pertaining to Annual Income of Respondents Before and After Joining in SHGs

Study Parameters	*Particulars*	*Category*		*Total*
		SC	*Non-SC*	
Annual income before joining in SHGs	No income	-	40 (8.3)	40 (8.3)
	3,000 -5,000	27 (5.6)	-	27 (5.6)
	5,001 -8,000	48 (10.0)	28 (5.8)	76 (15.8)
	8,001 - 11,000	83 (17.3)	62 (12.9)	145 (30.2)
	11,001 -13,000	61 (12.7)	71 (14.8)	132 (27.5)
	13,000 -15,000	11 (2.3)	39 (8.1)	50 (10.4)
	Total	**240 (50)**	**240 (50)**	**480 (100)**
Annual income after joining SHGs	5,000 -10,000	51 (10.6)	-	51 (10.6)
	10,001 -15,000	65 (13.5)	66 (13.7)	131 (27.3)
	15,001- 20,000	71 (14.8)	77 (16.0)	148 (30.8)
	21,001 -30,000	39 (8.1)	67 (13.9)	106 (22.1)
	30,000 and above	14 (2.9)	30 (6.2)	44 (9.2)
	Total	**240 (50)**	**240 (50)**	**480 (100)**

Table 15.3: On Group Performance of Respondents Before and After Joining in SHGs

Study Parameters	*Particulars*	*Category*		*Total*
		SC	*Non-SC*	
Stability of the Group	Stable	70 (14.6)	115 (24.0)	185 (38.5)
	Increased	-	-	-
	Decreased	170 (35.4)	125 (26.0)	295 (61.4)
	Total	**240 (50)**	**240 (50)**	**480 (100)**
Years of experience	1-2	20 (4.2)	20 (4.2)	40 (8.3)
	3-4	110 (22.9)	110 (22.9)	220 (45.8)
	5-6	105 (21.9)	105 (21.9)	210 (43.7)
	Total	**240 (50)**	**240 (50)**	**480 (100)**
Frequency of meeting	Weekly	62 (12.9)	158 (32.9)	220 (45.8)
	Fortnightly	36 (7.5)	20 (4.2)	56 (11.7)
	Monthly	142 (29.6)	62 (12.9)	204 (42.5)
	Total	**240 (50)**	**240 (50)**	**480 (100)**
Attendance of the group meeting	All	60 (12.5)	185 (38.5)	245 (51.0)
	Majority	105 (21.9)	55 (11.5)	160 (33.3)
	Some members	75 (15.6)	-	75 (15.6)
	Total	**240 (50)**	**240 (50)**	**480 (100)**

Table 15.4: Data About Decision Making Process of SHGs

Study Parameters	*Particulars*	*Category*		*Total*
		SC	*Non-SC*	
Decision in the meeting	All members	75 (15.6)	138 (28.7)	213 (44.3)
	President	57 (11.9)	6 (1.2)	63 (13.1)
	Link Worker	56 (11.7)	21 (4.4)	77 (16.0)
	NGO Facilitator	36 (7.5)	16 (3.3)	52 (10.8)
	Mixed	16 (3.3)	59 (12.3)	75 (15.6)
Process of Decision Making	By consensus	59 (12.3)	192 (40.0)	251 (52.3)
	By voting	-	-	-
	Group Ref	108 (22.5)	-	108 (22.5)
	Link worker/ facilitator in consultation with members	63 (13.1)	19 (4.0)	82 (17.0)
	Link Worker/ Facilitator/ Representatives (Mixed)	10 (2.1)	29 (6.0)	39 (8.1)

Table 15.5: Data on Awareness of the Respondents Before and After Joining in SHGs

Study Parameters	*Particulars*	*Category*		*Total*
		SC	*Non-SC*	
Knowledge and Awareness of SHG's Activities	Meeting Calendar	116 (24.2)	175 (36.5)	291 (60.6)
	Rules and Regulations	122 (25.4)	179 (37.3)	301 (62.7)
	Group Records	122 (25.4)	161 (33.5)	283 (59.0)
	Cash in hand	124 (25.8)	164 (34.2)	288 (60.0)
	Balance in Bank	118 (24.6)	144 (30.0)	262 (54.6)
	Outstanding Loan	122 (25.4)	170 (35.4)	292 (60.8)
	Total Capital of the Group	137 (28.5)	164 (33.2)	301 (62.7)
	Savings of Group	143 (29.8)	146 (30.4)	289 (60.2)
	Total loaning of Group	125 (26.0)	156 (32.5)	281 (58.5)
	No. of Members taken loan	151 (31.5)	207 (43.1)	358 (74.6)
	Members repaid loans	127 (26.5)	186 (38.7)	313 (65.2)
	Name of Bank	203 (42.3)	240 (50.0)	443 (92.3)
	Income of Group	140 (29.2)	159 (33.1)	299 (62.3)
	Objectives of Group	164 (32.1)	217 (45.2)	381 (79.4)
	Achievements of Group	129 (26.9)	208 (43.3)	337 (70.2)
	Constraints of Group	137 (28.5)	202 (42.1)	339 (70.6)

Table 15.6: Data Related to Purpose of Savings and Ownership of Economic Activities Engaged by the Beneficiaries

Study Parameters	*Particulars*	*Category*		*Total*
		SC	*Non-SC*	
Main Purpose of savings	Social Security	8 (1.7)	71 (14.8)	79 (16.4)
	Food Security	135 (28.1)	32 (6.7)	167 (34.8)
	Education	35 (7.3)	68 (14.1)	103 (21.4)
	Medical	14 (2.9)	-	14 (3.0)
	Marriage	18 (3.7)	-	18 (3.7)
	Emergencies	-	16 (3.3)	16 (3.3)
	Agriculture	-	43 (9.0)	43 (9.0)
	Asset Building	30 (6.2)	12 (2.5)	42 (8.7)
Ownership of Economic Activities	Individual	204 (42.5)	183 (38.1)	387 (80.6)
	Group	36 (7.5)	57 (11.9)	93 (19.4)
	Total	**240 (50)**	**240 (50)**	**480 (100)**

Table 15.7: Data pertaining to Type of Economic Activities Engaged by the Respondents and Changes on Socio-Economic Status after Joining SHG

Study Parameters	*Particulars*	*Category*		*Total*
		SC	*Non-SC*	
Economic Activities	Agriculture and Allied Activities	73 (15.2)	73 (15.2)	146 (30.4)
	Animal Husbandry	40 (8.3)	40 (8.3)	80 (16.7)
	Hotel Business	22 (4.6)	22 (4.6)	44 (9.2)
	Handicrafts	10 (2.1)	10 (2.1)	20 (4.2)
	Speices Powder Production	45 (9.4)	45 (9.4)	90 (18.7)
	Brick Making	15 (3.1)	15 (3.1)	30 (6.2)
	Confectionery	15 (3.1)	15 (3.1)	30 (6.2)
	Grocery Shop	20 (4.2)	20 (4.2)	40 (8.3)
	Services	-	-	-
	Total	**240 (50)**	**240 (50)**	**480 (100)**
Changes on Socio-Economic Status after joining SHG	Mobility	115 (24.0)	170 (35.4)	285 (59.4)
	Recognition in Family	167 (34.8)	160 (33.3)	327 (68.1)
	Recognition in Community	62 (12.9)	127 (26.5)	188 (39.4)
	Interaction with Outsiders	126 (26.2)	213 (44.4)	339 (70.6)
	Literacy/ education	110 (22.9)	196 (40.8)	306 (63.7)
	Access to Health Services	105 (21.9)	185 (38.5)	290 (60.4)

contd...

contd...

Study Parameters	*Particulars*	*Category*		*Total*
		SC	*Non-SC*	
Changes on Socio-economic Status after joining SHG	Access to Immunization	53 (11.0)	92 (19.2)	145 (30.2)
	Access to Sanitation Facility	95 (19.8)	227 (47.3)	322 (67.1)
	Access to Credit Sources	198 (41.2)	240 (50.0)	438 (91.2)
	Asset Building	174 (36.2)	240 (50.0)	414 (86.2)
	Family Income Increase	164 (34.2)	240 (50.0)	404 (84.2)
	Skills	75 (15.6)	181 (37.7)	256 (53.3)
	Voicing your Concern	122 (25.4)	167 (34.8)	289 (60.2)
	Nutrition Awareness	66 (13.7)	189 (39.4)	255 (53.1)
	Family Planning Awareness	75 (15.6)	205 (42.7)	280 (58.3)
	Girl Child Development Awareness	152 (31.7)	225 (46.9)	377 (78.6)
	Health Awareness	115 (24.0)	220 (45.8)	335 (69.8)
	Decision Making Related to Child Centered	127 (26.5)	203 (42.3)	330 (68.8)
	Family Economic Decision Making	93 (19.4)	173 (36.0)	266 (55.4)
	Participation in Development Programmes	201 (41.9)	218 (45.4)	419 (87.3)
	Participation in Political Decision Making	66 (13.7)	113 (23.5)	173 (37.2)
	Contest in Elections (PRIs)	8 (1.7)	19 (4.0)	27 (5.7)
	Education of Children	86 (17.9)	131 (27.3)	217 (45.2)
	Individual Income Increase	179 (37.3)	240 (50.0)	419 (87.3)
	Choice of Expenditure	55 (11.5)	147 (30.6)	202 (42.1)
	Role of Household Activities	44 (9.2)	79 (16.5)	123 (25.7)
	Others	121 (25.2)	213 (44.4)	334 (69.6)
Main problems related to functioning of SHGs	Lack of Skill	37 (7.7)	24 (5.0)	61 (12.7)
	Inadequate Finance	192 (40.0)	217 (45.2)	409 (85.2)
	Lack of Co-operation	165 (34.4)	123 (25.6)	288 (60.0)
	Lack of Market	85 (17.7)	88 (18.3)	173 (36.0)
	Repayment	55 (11.5)	10 (2.0)	65 (13.5)
	Leader Dominance	114 (23.7)	52 (10.8)	166 (34.6)

Source : Data collected from the field; Figures in the parenthesis are percentages.

Major Findings and Suggestions

(a) Personal Particulars of Sample Population

- Majority of respondents i.e., 41.4 per cent were in the age group of 36-45 years, followed by 27.5 per cent were in the age group of 26-35. Middle age group people volunteer in more numbers to join the SHG movement and function actively. Regarding the marital status of the respondents 82 per cent are married. Only married women are encouraged to join in the SHGs.

(b) Family Particulars of the Respondents

- The study found 63.7 per cent of families are headed by male, only 25.0 per cent of families are headed by woman, it is also due to various compelled circumstances like absence or non-existence of husband.
- Overall educational attainment shows better achievement among all the three states as reported by 62.4 per cent as literates. But analysis on the state-wise and category-wise education attainment is very poor except for the state of Kerala. Especially, among SC communities in Karnataka around 71 per cent are illiterates, in the case of Tamil Nadu 61 per cent are illiterates. Education level is far better among non-SC women SHG members. Among literates around 20 per cent studied only primary schooling, followed by 17 per cent middle school, 12 per cent upto high school. Among 37.6 per cent illiterates, SC women constitutes 24.4 per cent which shows very big gap among SC and non-SC women.

(c) Particulars of Employment and Income of the Respondents

- Among the sample population 79.4 per cent are engaged in self-employment and remaining 20.6 per cent are working as labourer in their groups. Previous status of employment reveals 22.3 per cent respondents engaged in agriculture activities (SC 5.2 per cent non-SC 17.1 per cent) as farmers, followed 38.5 per cent (SC 16.7 per cent, non-SC 21.9 per cent) in animal husbandry and 39.2 per cent respondents worked as agriculture labourers. Majority women's income before joining SHG was in the range of Rs 8,000–13,000 only. Status of income after joining SHG rose to the range of Rs 10,000–30,000.

- Interestingly after joining in the SHGs around 31 per cent of women equal representation from both SC and non-SC earn Rs 15,001-20,000, another significant 22.1 per cent of people earn an appreciable income of Rs 21,000–30,000. It is to be concluded that economic avenues created under different models of all the three states made positive change in terms of access to employment opportunities and assurance to regular flow of income.

(d) Particulars of the Household Decision Making

- Among the study population more than 57 per cent said that husband is the sole decision-maker in the family. Self-decision-making among SC women shows better position in Karnataka, worse in other two states. non-SC women have opportunity to share with men for joint decision-making.

(e) Respondents Attitudes towards Social Issues

- Responses on the attitudes towards certain social issues reveal, 31.5 per cent (SC 14.2 per cent, non-SC 16.0 per cent) accepted for give and take of dowry for marriage. Inter-caste marriage was encouraged by 48.7 per cent, for inter-religion marriage also accepted by majority in Kerala, 51 per cent (SC 21.5 per cent, non-SC 29.6 per cent) agreed to encourage love marriage and 42.7 per cent (SC 16.9 per cent non-SC 25.8 per cent) would like to encourage for widow re-marriage, 38.3 per cent (SC 11.0 per cent, non-SC 27.3 per cent) reported acceptability to appreciate divorces on unavoidable circumstances. There are around 83 per cent respondents reported positively for family planning, followed 94.4 per cent towards job reservation for women and 61.9 per cent supported to punish the wicked husband.

(f) SHG Functioning and Impact

- Drop out noticed very high in SC groups reported by 81.5 per cent in Karnataka and 75 per cent in Tamil Nadu and more drop outs even among non-SC groups in Kerala. Around 46 per cent women, representing equal number from SC and non-SC category joined in SHG before three-four years, around 44 per cent joined before five-six years, only around eight per cent are being member of SHG for one-two years.
- Forty three per cent said that local NGOs motivated them to join SHGs and facilitated to avail financial assistance from government and loan from bank.
- About the schedule of periodical group meetings, 45.8 per cent reported they conduct weekly meetings, followed by 42.5 per cent reported they conduct meetings once in a month. Fifty one per cent of respondents replied all the members attend the meetings. Around 33 per cent said majority members take part in the meetings. In the case of SC groups, pressure or facilitation is needed from outside by like NGOs 75.0 per cent in Tamil Nadu and by the project implementation units in Kerala 87.5 per cent, in Karnataka 81.5 per cent by both institutions.
- Decisions with consent of all the members prevails more among non-SC groups in Karnataka 51.25 per cent and in Kerala 85.0 but less in Tamil Nadu 36.25 per cent. Link worker or NGO facilitator take leading role in taking important decisions particularly in SC groups, it was agreed by 39 per cent in Karnataka, 45.0 per cent in Tamil Nadu.
- Among the SC and non-SC groups, more than 50 per cent are having knowledge and awareness about the various process related to group functioning. Majority members having awareness about group meeting calendar (58.2 per cent), group rules and regulations (60.2 per cent), information about group records (56.6 per cent). Group's financial transactions are known to more than 50 per cent of the members like cash available in the hand 57.6 per cent, cash balance at bank 52.4 per cent, outstanding loan 58.4 per cent, total capital of the group

60.2 per cent, savings and disbursed loans 57.8 per cent and 56.2 per cent respectively.

- Main purpose of savings for 34.8 per cent majority from SC group (28.1 per cent) save money for their future food security, followed by 21.4 per cent, majority from non-SC groups save money to meet the educational expenditures of their children, 16.4 per cent, again majority 14.8 per cent from non-SC category expressed for the purpose of social security.

9.7 Types and Impact of Training

- Only around 55.6 per cent reported that they have attended training. The training gave confidence building for 47.2 per cent (SC 16.2 per cent, non-SC 31.0 per cent), skill development for 43.4 per cent (SC 17.0 per cent, non-SC 26.4). Regarding banking relationship 51 per cent (SC 20.0 per cent, non-SC 31.0 per cent) said that the training motivated to open personal savings accounts. Interaction with government officials during training helped to build good rapport; it is reported by around 50.0 per cent (SC 21.4 per cent, non-SC 28.4 per cent). Training curriculum also includes awareness building on various RD programmes and their benefits. For 43.6 per cent (SC 17.6 per cent, non-SC 26.0 per cent), training helped to gain knowledge on the beneficiaries rights and their entitlements. Other outcomes like managerial skills 44.0 per cent (SC 18.0 per cent, non-SC 26.0 per cent), enhanced income and opportunities for 52.4 per cent (SC 21.4 per cent, non-SC 31.0 per cent).
- Evidence shows that, the trainee's decision-making skills have increased enormously as it was reported positively by 54.4 per cent (SC 21.0 per cent, non-SC 29.4 per cent) in participation in family decisions, improved participation in planning and implementation of development programmes said by 33 per cent (SC 13.4 per cent, non-SC 19.6 per cent). After joining into SHG movement majority respondents have got benefits under various RD prgorammes like IAY, TSC, NREGS and other state

government programmes. It was reported by 47.0 per cent (SC 24.2 per cent, non-SC 22.8 per cent).

- Majority group members i.e., 77.4 per cent (SC 40.8 per cent, non-SC 36.6 per cent) engaged in individual economic activities.

9.8 Impact of SHG on the Socio-economic Aspects of Beneficiaries

- It was reported by majority of the respondents (59.4 per cent) that they have very good mobility within the district on various purposes after joining in SHGs. As per the version of 68.1 per cent women are well respected in the family as well as in the community 39.4 per cent. Recognition in the family is better for SC members too but society recognition is very poor. Around 70.6 per cent responded that they have freedom to interact with outsiders on business related activities.
- Participation in SHGs improved attention to education of 63.7 per cent families in the study region. Importantly, awareness level has increased to significant-level on various issues especially health care and prevention of deceases. It was agreed by 60.4 per cent on access to health services, 30.2 per cent towards access to immunisation, 67.1 per cent access to sanitation and 91.2 per cent on access to institutional credit.
- Economic improvement of respondents' family through SHGs were examined and noticed a positive change on various aspects. It can be also understood through consent by 86.2 per cent on asset building, increase in family income 84.2 per cent and improvement in nutritious food intake. Skill development was one among the major tangible impact of the SHG movement which created livelihoods for the respondents was agreed by 53.3 per cent.
- SHG helped members to control over family savings (48.7 per cent), development of self confidence (58.3 per cent), increase in awareness level (64.0 per cent). The level of feeling among SC members about society's perception is very low in all the models of SHGs.

- Majority member in Karnataka and Kerala involved in Shramadhan (62.3 per cent) and public awareness generation (76.9 per cent) programmes. Majority groups are also participating in RD programmes. Around 45 per cent are also involved in the campaigns against social issues at their village level.
- Major problems in functioning of SHGs as revealed by the respondents are listed, among them inadequate finance and lack of internal co-ordination becoming prominent in all the states as reported by 85.2 per cent and 60.0 per cent respectively. Lack of market network both within and outside the service regions hurdles the progress of micro enterprises as reported by 36 per cent respondents. Dominant behaviour of the group leaders is a major problem for majority groups in Karnataka and Tamil Nadu. Existences of all the above problems are severe among SC groups comparing to non-SC groups.

1. Suggestions

- Repetitive memberships have to be verified among different groups and schemes. It is identified one member of SHG is being member in many groups. Such people dilute the group's interest of unity and growth. Efforts must be made at the time of group formation to organise women who have real zeal to work together for economic prosperity. Adequate ground work has to put to organise women having equal economic and social status. It helps to avoid few people's domination or suppression in the group.
- Duplication of schemes with similar objectives and cliental allow women to disintegrate the groups of existing to other schemes. Integration of similar programmers and convergence will enable the mission to strengthened and concentrated delivery towards achievement of targeted objectives.
- Seriousness on appraisal of business proposals to suggest merits and demerits of such activities by analysing future prospect is the need of the hour in all the regions of the study area. Priority has to be given to agro-based like

agri-input on agro-processing activities may have more success in the rural areas being majority beneficiaries are farmers or agriculture labourers. Success and sustainability possibility is very high only for group-based activity, therefore strengthening of group activities and discourage of individual activities are essential.

- Training need assessment is vital before conducting suitable training to the beneficiaries more number of training programmes in different aspects of group functioning and management of business activities to be ascertained. Continued and periodical business trade and marketing related training will boost the group member for further growth.
- Majority of the groups in all three states engaged in individual oriented economic activities by dividing the total fund or bank loan by all the members which becomes meager amount insufficient to invest on new economic activities. It hurdle the sustainability of activities and ultimately become defunct or disintegration of groups. Insistence is required to adhere to the guidelines of the scheme especially to organise group-based economic activity.
- Majority of the group members spend the money meant for economic activity on unproductive activities like meeting expenses on festivals, family ceremonies and other rituals. Hence, proper monitoring and follow up by the facilitating agency is needed to insist the members to spend the money on earmarked purpose.
- Many production oriented economic activities of the SHGs face a number of problems of recurring of raw materials, stocking, quality control and marketing. Inability or lack of field experience and knowledge compelled to become sick unit lead to dormant. Proper and timely guidance, required capacity building will improve the functioning of the units.
- Survey of defunct groups and dormant economic activities has to be done for finding ways and means to revive and restore. Proper facilitation is required on periodical

conduct of weekly meetings not only just to disburse and collect of loans or subscriptions but enable them to discuss personal and social issues to enlarge the awareness level and achieve empowerment. Rotation of leadership of the groups has to be ensured.

1.1 Suggestions Specific to the SC Groups

- Poor SC women in rural areas live with acute poverty facing many problems like illiteracy, ignorance, lack of awareness, lack of capital, lack of skills etc., suitable package of counseling and motivation are required to convince them to organise as groups and to do further activities.
- Imparting of functional literacy is essential for SC women to handle the group in problem situation. Adequate dosages of financial inputs are required to run the business without fail. Longer duration of training from development of entrepreneurial abilities and trade-related skills to be conducted. Refresher training also required for SC to update the knowledge and skills according to the need of the society. Orientation on futuristic plan and thinking to be imparted for planned efforts of economic development.
- Continuous hand holding support is required to facilitate SC groups to transact with outside agencies till empowerment is achieved. Adequate care and follow up is required to avoid deviations of utilisation of scheme fund and encourage them to organise group-based activities and arrangements have to be made for regular source of income.
- Creation of tangible assets under the schemes like rearing of milch and meat animals, establishment of provisions shop will prolong the survival period of economic activity which motivate them to have better care and improvement of the activities. The bankers also should put eye watch on the functioning of SHGs, if necessary, facilitate needed help in the areas of guidance, technical inputs, finance and accounts etc.

2. Conclusion

All the above three models are having more or less similar goal, objectives, approach and strategy for women's empowerment through self-help with group formation, skill building and initiating income generating activities. Implementation with partnership of NGOs and CBOs, internal saving and bank credit linkage are the common characteristics of the different models aimed to study. The micro-finance facility extended through groups has significantly contributed in improving their financial conditions and taking up of viable income generating activities. The SHGs are not only providing credit, but also empower women socially and economically. They encourage women to participate in decision-making in the household, community and local democratic sector and prepare women to take up leadership positions.

References

1. Bisoyi Tanuj Kumar, Rural Credit Regional Rural Banks and Mirco-Finance, 2010.
2. RBI 2007, Report on Trend and Progress in Banking in India 2006-07.
3. FWWB. India 2008, Annual Report 2007-08.
4. Sa-Dhan-2008, "Quick Review" 2007-08 in India.
5. NADARD-Annual Report 2007-08 SHG Bank Linkage Progress.
6. Government of India, Ministry of Finance 2008, Economic Survey, New Delhi, India.
7. Micro Finance-Self Employment and Poverty Alleviation by Sangita Kamdar, Himalaya Publication.
8. Fisher Thomas and M.S. Sriram, 2002, Beyond Micro Credit Putting Development Bank into Micro-finance.
9. Deshmukh-Randive Joy 2004, Womens Self-Help Group in Andhra Pradesh- Participating Poverty Alleviation in Action.
10. Gariyali, C.K. and Yettivel S.K. 2003, Women own- The Self Help Movement of Tamil Nadu.

16

Entrepreneurship in Women for Pro-Poor Growth and Gender Equality

Sathyavani Gandham

Abstract

"Empowering women is a prerequisite for creating a good nation, when women are empowered, society with stability is assured".

—**APJ Abdul Kalam**

In this vibrant world, women entrepreneurs are a considerable part of the global expedition for sustained economic development and pro-poor growth. In India, planning commission, central and state government recognised the importance of women to be in the mainstream of economic development. In particular, the development of entrepreneurship in women is seen as the appropriate way to address the poverty at grassroots level and to achieve gender equality. Industrial policy of government of India has highlighted the need for entrepreneurship programmes for women to enable them to start small scale industries. Women in India are struggling for entrepreneurial freedom even after 65 years of independence. Due to the vast gender disparities and poverty in India, women have not been widely recognised as entrepreneurial resource. This paper focuses on the gaps in the mechanisms developed for the empowerment of the women to eradicate poverty and also the gender issues which became strong hurdles for promoting entrepreneurship in women, for pro-poor growth and for boosting gender equality in current scenario.

Key words: Women Entrepreneurship, Pro-poor Growth, Gender Equality.

Introduction

In this vibrant world, women entrepreneurs are a considerable part of the global expedition for sustained economic development and pro-poor growth. The industrialisation, urbanisation and social legislation processes have undergone many changes but the social perspectives on women remained as it is, especially in rural milieu. In many rural societies, women are responsible for household provisioning like food crop production, gathering fuel, hauling water, caring for children and the aged. In return, men are expected to meet certain cash requirements of the household. This division of labour affects women's ability in all directions. Ultimately it led to the poverty and imbalances in human development also became a major barrier to the growth of the nation.

Women are a significant entrepreneurial force whose contributions to local, national and global economies are far reaching. Women produce and consume, manage businesses and households, earn income, hire labour, borrow and save, and provide a range of services for businesses and workers. Women represent an increasing proportion of the world's waged labour force and their activity rates are rising (OECD, 2006). Women are an important human resource of the nation and every state should try to utilise them as mediators of economic growth and development. Encouragement for women entrepreneurship is one of the ways for that. In India, the number of micro, small and medium enterprises (MSMEs) has been continuously rising, up to almost 30 million in 2010. The percentage of women-owned MSMEs is around 13 per cent (OECD, 2012). But unfortunately it is seen that the traditional mind set of the society and negligence of the state and respective authorities are important obstacles in the women entrepreneurship development in India.

Women are a major untapped entrepreneurship resource. The evidence in many studies shows that women entrepreneurs lag behind men not only in numbers, but also in other terms too (Kanazawa, 2005). A fraction of this gap is likely to be due to poverty and gender inequality. Poverty is a crucial problem facing all developing and underdeveloped countries in the modern world. It is felt that the problem of poverty can be solved through a concerted effort towards pro-poor growth strategies by the State. Feasible opportunities can be provided to the deprived and the destitute by means of lending asset creating facilities. Women households are the cruelest victims of deprivation and destitution. So any poverty eradication programmes must aim at improving the standard of living environment of the women communities and gender equality is not just about economic empowerment. It is a moral imperative, it is about fairness and equity, and includes many political, social and cultural dimensions. Gender equality, however, is also a key factor in self-reported well-being and happiness across the world (Nidheesh, 2009).

Need for the Study

Self Help Group (SHG) formation is a women centred programme to enable and enlighten the poor women in India to realise their potential and strengthen them to contribute to the development of their family, community and in turn society as a whole. The SHG movement started in 1980's in India, but still there are women who didn't participated in any income generating activity though she is a member in the SHG. The bank loan amount was distributed among the women in the group instead of initiating a collective task for income generation. The bank linkage helped them to fulfill their familial needs but not to their development as entrepreneurs on large. If we observe the below picture, it is seen that still there are areas and women who have not covered under SHG programme.

The main familial needs fulfilled by the SHG women are:

- **Employment to husband:** If he is unemployed, the loan amount was utilised for purchasing an Auto or for any other livelihood.
- **Education of the children:** As most of the women in SHGs were illiterates they recognised the need of education and started providing education to their children.
- **Marriage of the daughter:** Though dowry is prohibited through an enactment it is an undercurrent in the present society.
- **Construction of house:** It is an important need to the common man.
- **Investment for agriculture:** In most of the cases the families who depended on agriculture will go for land lease and the loan amount is utilised for that.

If the women had crossed all the above, then only they started thinking on investing for additional income generation. Most of the investments of the rural women are on agriculture-based activities like milching animals, sheep rearing, selling vegetables, kirana shops (where men can sit and sell but not the women) etc. It is mainly due to the social visualisation and illiteracy.

According to NABARD, 2012-13 report:

Sr. No.	Particulars	Achievements	
		Physical (No. in lakh)	Financial (₹ in crore)
1	**Total number of SHGs saving linked with banks**	**73.18**	**8217.25**
(i)	Out of total (of which) exclusive Women SHGs	59.38	6514.87
(ii)	Out of total (of which) SGSY SHGs	20.47	1821.65
2	**Total number of SHGs credit linked during 2012-13**	**12.20**	**20585.36**
(i)	Out of total (of which) exclusive Women SHGs	10.37	17854.31
(ii)	Out of total (of which) SGSY SHGs	1.81	2207.47
3	**Total number of SHGs having loans outstanding as on 31 March 2013**	**44.51**	**39375.30**
(i)	Out of total (of which) exclusive Women SHGs	37.57	32840.04
(ii)	Out of total (of which) SGSY SHGs	11.93	8597.09

From the above table it is observed that 59.38 lakhs SHGs are exclusive women SHGs linked with savings, 10.37 lakhs

SHGs were linked with credit during 2012-13 and 37.57 lakhs SHGs were having outstanding loans. The remaining 11.44 lakhs were with good savings and credit record means 19 per cent of the SHGs were involved in the entrepreneurial activities so far but what about the rest of the SHGs?

Till now very few efforts have been made in exploring the women Entrepreneurship in India. Earlier the Government of India (GoI) has initiated Swarnajayanthi Gram SwarozgarYojana (SGSY) for the upliftment of women and as well as to develop entrepreneurship among women. SGSY was primarily designed to promote self-employment oriented income generating activities for the Below Poverty Line (BPL) households in the rural areas. If this programme is for poor people, why there is a need to form separate SHGs under SGSY? The benefit can be provided to the interested people in the existing SHGs. From the above data it is also observed that no specific women groups were identified under SGSY. Due to such all things the programme could not achieve 100 per cent results. Later it is further developed and converted into a mission called 'National Rural Livelihood Mission'. Most of the business ran by women in rural surroundings were purely gendered and the capacity building too was done in the areas intended for women socially. Therefore, there is need of continuous attempt to inspire, encourage, motivate and co-operate women for becoming entrepreneurs, also creating awareness among women about the various areas to conduct business.

Objective

- To identify the gaps in the mechanisms developed for the empowerment of the women to eradicate poverty.
- To study the impact of assistance by the government on entrepreneurship in women.
- To appraise the factors responsible for encouraging women to become entrepreneurs.

Methodology

The study focuses on extensive study of secondary data collected from various books, National and international Journals, publications from various websites which focused on various aspects of Women Entrepreneurship and also the personal observations of the author while working at the grassroot level.

Literature Review

Human capital is a constraint on Pro Poor Growth. Lowering high levels of inequality is important for poverty reduction as well as for improving other aspects of social well-being (DFID, 2004). Sex-segregated labour markets are associated with higher gender wage inequality (Cartmill, 1999; Tzannatos, 1999), which distorts investment in human capital, prioritising male income earners and undercapitalising women earners. Promoting pro-poor growth means enabling a pace and pattern of growth that enhances the ability of poor women and men to participate in contribute to and benefit from growth. India is not exception to inequality, the social traditions and superstitions play enormous role which differ from society to society.

In India, according to Mehta and Mehta, 2011, women live protected lives. A woman is taught to depend on the male members of her family from birth. She is not allowed to take any type of risk even if she is willing to take it and has ability to bear it as well. They are even less educated, economically not stable nor self-dependent which reduce their ability to bear risks and uncertainties involved in a business unit. The old and outdated social outlook to stop women from entering in the field of entrepreneurship is one of the reasons for their failure. They are under a social pressure which restrains them to prosper and achieve success in the field of entrepreneurship. The development of women entrepreneurship is very low in India, especially in the rural areas.

Women are working to earn livelihood along with men since times immemorial, their contribution in monetary term remain unaccounted or if at all accounted it is given very low value. It doesn't mean that women do not possess the capacity. In fact, women even the illiterate rural ones practice and use all the tools and techniques of efficient management. A woman has diversified functions to perform in the family as user, conserver, protector and creator/promoter of resources. But now-a-days the women are playing multidisciplinary roles:

Multiple Roles of Women

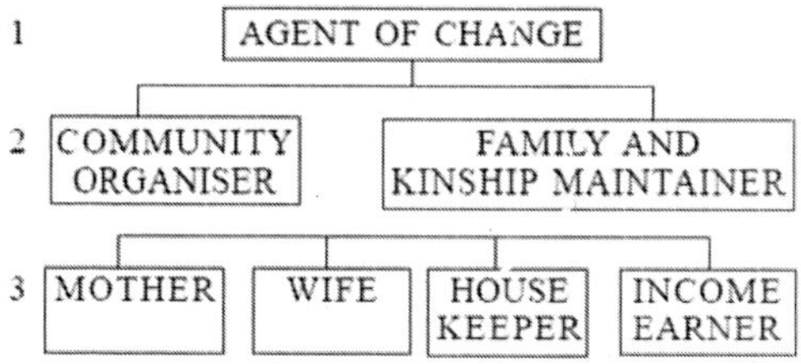

1. Less known, completely ignored
2. Known, less explored
3. Well known, well explored

Despite women's increased participation in the labour market over the past half-century, they remain substantially underrepresented as entrepreneurs. When asked, fewer women than men say they would prefer to be self-employed. When they do chose to become entrepreneurs, more often than men, they cite a better work-life balance and/or economic necessity as the main motivation for starting a business. At times of high unemployment, women-owned businesses make a key contribution to household incomes and economic growth. Entrepreneurship is equally important in developing countries for job creation, innovation and growth. Fostering entrepreneurship is a key policy goal for governments in all countries; there are shared expectations that high rates of entrepreneurial activity will bring sustained employment creation. Moreover, thriving new enterprises can boost the development of new products, production processes and organisational innovations (OECD, 2012).

Entrepreneurship amongst women has been a recent development. The entrepreneur is a person who has enterprising quality, takes initiative and establishes an economic activity or enterprise. Starting and operating an enterprise involves considerable risk and effort on the part of the entrepreneurs, particularly in the light of high failure rate. The enterprises started by women are so greatly influenced by the decisions and desires of the members of the family (Rajani and Sarada, 2008).

The emergence of women entrepreneurs and their contribution to the national economy in urban locale is quite visible in India. The number of women entrepreneurs has grown over a period of time, especially in the 1990s. Micro-finance programmes have significant potential for contributing to women's economic, social and political empowerment. Access to savings and credit can initiate or strengthen a series of interlinked and mutually reinforcing 'virtuous spirals' of empowerment. Microfinance development has emerged as major strategy to combat the twin issues of poverty and unemployment that continue to pose a major threat to the polity and economy of both the developed and developing countries. A number of agencies-Government as well as Non-Government Organisations- are, today involved in micro-finance development initiatives (Jyotish, 2006).

Women in India have developed over time more recognition of their capacities as entrepreneurs, but social conditioning still weighs heavy on their initiative and self-confidence. Lack of time and capital limit the potentials of women to start risky ventures. Today's world is not static it is dynamic; more women i.e., educated, urban women are deciding to launch their own business for a variety of reasons:

1. To achieve for independence and flexibility.
2. To better balance work and family.
3. To make optimum use of technical education and qualifications.

Women are segregated into different categories basing on their nature of work.

- Women in organised and unorganised sectors.
- Women in Traditional and Modern Industries.
- Women in Urban and Rural areas
- Women in large scale and small scale Industries.

The third category of women entrepreneurs are Illiterate Women, Financially week and have no knowledge about entrepreneurship and business. This category is the rural women, who initially enter into business arena to fulfil their familial needs and for better economic position (Shanta).

Major Bottlenecks for Rural Women Entrepreneurship

Rao (2007) observed in his study that poverty and illiteracy are the basic reasons of the low rate of women entrepreneurship in our country. The educational level and professional skills also influence women participation in the field of enterprise.

Gender inequality is still prevalent in many parts of the country yet. Women are looked upon as *abala*, i.e., weak in all respects. In a male-dominated society, women are not treated equal to men that act as a barrier to woman's entry into business. A kind of patriarchal male-dominant social order is the building block to them in their way towards business success. Male members think it a big risk financing the ventures run by women. The greatest deterrent to women entrepreneurs is that they are women.

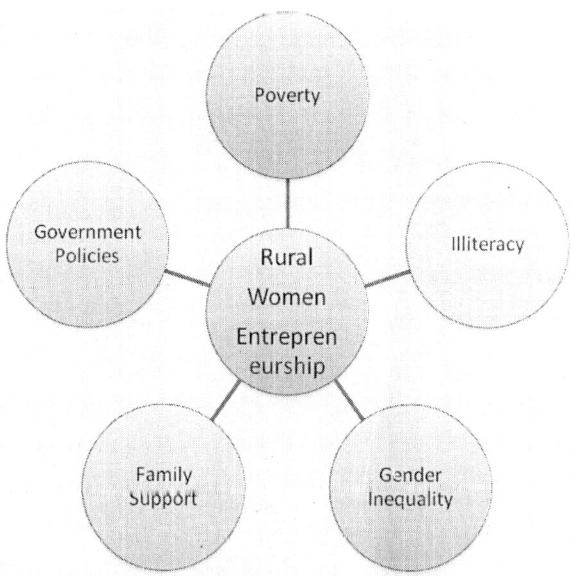

Women's family obligations also bar them from becoming successful entrepreneurs in both developed and developing nations. The financial institutions discourage women entrepreneurs on the belief that they can at any time leave their business and become housewives again as Indian women give more emphasis to family ties and relationships. Married women have to make a fine balance between business and family. The business success also depends on the support the family members extended to women in the business process and management.

Government of India has introduced the policy measures to promote the status and the level of female entrepreneurs in the country. There has been increasing turned in number of women owned enterprises in India, but despite government efforts, substantial growth could not be achieved. They should be provided easy financial help without putting unrealistic conditions by banks and financial institutions (Kothawale, 2013).

Government Policies and Initiatives

India is the country with the largest number of policy initiatives specifically targeting women entrepreneurs. A particular focus has been put on the initiative of SHG to raise the financial status of BPL families, to eradicate poverty and for human development by including women. But this programme has not focused much on education of women in the early stage of the initiative and not started parallel. So women achieved financial status but they are far from the mainstream.

Later SGSY has been introduced to increase self-employment among the BPL households. But due to inefficient capacity building this programme could not attain 100 per cent results.

Another programme called 'Sakshara Bharat' was implemented to enhance the functional literacy rate among the age group of 15-80 years, in which no specific space for SHG women. If it is made compulsory for them at least some of the women in SHGs would have been conquered the fear of illiteracy.

The other and recent programme is NRLM. The objectives of the NRLM are Universal social mobilisation, Formation of people's institutions, Universal financial inclusion, Training and capacity building, Enhanced package of economic assistance for setting-up of micro enterprises and larger role for Self Help Groups (SHGs). Training and capacity building under this programme ensures that the poor are provided with the requisite skills for managing their institutions, managing their livelihoods, for enhancing their credit absorption capacity and credit worthiness. Even this programme is not focusing on the identification of entrepreneurial skills and innovative nature among women and providing assistance accordingly. The skill building component under this programme is concentrated only on the requisite skills for managing their institutions, managing their livelihoods but not for grabbing the new opportunities or to open doors for women to accelerate in many other fields where women were prevented by gender disparity. Hence, there is a need to refurbish the policies of the government for pro-poor growth and gender equality.

Implications for Women Entrepreneurship

- Promote positive societal attitudes toward entrepreneurship, and in particular, women's engagement in entrepreneurship.
- Support women's business growth with technical assistance and education.
- Provide specific training to staff in charge of programme design and delivery. Respond to the financial and technical support needs of women entrepreneurs wishing to increase the scale of their businesses.
- National Entrepreneurship Strategy for building the enabling environment for entrepreneurship development and includes creating and strengthening institutional mechanisms for policy implementation and monitoring.
- A conducive regulatory framework which enables entrepreneurs to successfully create, manage, expand and operate a business.
- Policies should be based on a systematic analysis of the factors that prevent or discourage entry of women entrepreneurs into the market, and limit growth of female-owned enterprises.

Conclusion

Resurgence of entrepreneurship in women is the need of the hour emphasising on rural women strata of population, spreading awareness and consciousness amongst women to outshine in the enterprise field, making them realise their strengths, and important position in the society and the great contribution they can make for their nation as well as the entire economy. Women entrepreneurship must be molded properly with entrepreneurial traits and skills to meet the changes in trends, challenges, global markets and also be competent enough to sustain and strive for excellence in the entrepreneurial arena. If every citisen works with such an attitude towards respecting the important position occupied by women in society and understanding their vital role in the modern business field too, then very soon we can pre-estimate our chances of out beating our own conservative and rigid thought process which is the biggest barrier for pro-poor growth and gender equality.

References

1. Arakeri Shanta V., Women Entrepreneurship in India, Vol. 1, Issue No. 3, ISSN 2277-1182.
2. Cartmill, R.S. (1999), "Occupational Sex Segregation in Global Perspective: Comparative Analyses of Developed and Developing Nations", CDE Working Paper 99-12, Center for Demography and Ecology, University of Wisconsin-Madison.
3. C.P.Kothawale, 2013, Women Entrepreneurship Development: Problems and Prospects, Vol. 2, Issue-I, May, ISSN 2321–0397 (Online).
4. Department for International Development (DFID), Pro-poor growth Briefing Note 1, February, 2004.
5. Jyotish Prakash Basu, 2006, Microfinance and Women Empowerment: An Empirical Study with special reference to West Bengal, www.igidr.ac.in/.../mfc.../Jyotish% 20 Prakash% 20Basu_submission_55.p...ý
6. Kanazawa, S. (2005), "Is discrimination necessary to explain the sex gap in earnings?" *Journal of Economic Psychology*, Vol. 26, No. 2, pp. 269-87.
7. Mehta, Anita and Mukund Chandra Mehta, 2011, "Rural Women Entrepreneurship in India: - Opportunities and challenges." Paper presented at the International

Conference on Humanities, Geography and Economics (ICHGE 2011), Pattaya, December 2011.

8. NABARD, 2013, Status of Microfinance in India report 2012-13.
9. N. Rajani and D. Sarada 2008. Women Entrepreneurship and Support Systems, Stud Home Comm Sci, 2(2): 107-112.
10. OECD, 2006, Promoting Pro-poor Growth Private Sector Development, Enhancing Women's Market Access and Promoting Pro-poor Growth.
11. OECD 2012, Gender Equality in Education, Employment and Entrepreneurship: Final Report to the MCM, C/MIN(2012)5
12. Shanmukha, Rao Padala. 2007. "Entrepreneurship Development among Women: A case study of self help Groups in Srikakulam District, Andhra Pradesh." *The ICFAI Journal of Entrepreneurship Development* 1(1).
13. Tzannatos, Z. (1999), "Women and Labour Market Changes in the Global Economy: Growth Helps, Inequalities Hurt and Public Policy Matters", World Development, No. 27, No. 3, pp. 551-659.
14. Vijay Kumbhar, 2013, Some Critical Issues of Women Entrepreneurship in Rural India, European Academic Research, Vol. I, Issue 2/ May, ISSN 2286-4822.

ABSTRACTS

Theme-I: Agripreneurship for Women Employment and Empowerment

1

Women Agri-Producer Companies for Sustainable Rural Development in Northern and Eastern India

P. Naidu, U. Ghate, H.N. Behera and R. Ingle

Women-led agri-enterprises can enable development of the poorest section of the society, as we notice from agriculture landscapes in northern and eastern India, whom the agriculture and cooperatives development of the western and southern India bypassed so far. Women's role in agriculture is high but remains ignored and they suffer from (a) lack of decision-making powers,(b) virtually non-existent property rights and (c) inequitable benefit sharing. Northern and eastern Indian women can adopt the producer company model to emulate the cooperative's success as in western and southern India. These worked on agri-production or agri-marketing that is more complex while we suggest the agri-inputs production is a growing and low-skill, women friendly niche in the northern and eastern India, with focus on vegetables. We found this during two agri development projects in backward regions in India- Amravati district (Maharashtra) and Bolangir district, Odisha. There is huge scope for dairy and vegetables as lucrative sectors due to the malnourishment and growing economy and as women find these comfortable. Organic manure, vermicompost, biopesticide, biofungicide, bioherbicide and growth boosters (root bacteria) and value addition as appropriate. Mahila Kisan Sashaktikaran Pariyojana (MSKP-women farmer development scheme) of Government of India Rural Development Ministry is promoting such initiatives.

Economic sustainability hinges on incentivising the farmer groups to buy from these microenterprises, by way of facilitating myriad of (a) government schemes e.g. shade net, bore-well etc., (b) providing small zero interest loans for income diversification e.g. apiculture, (c) providing capacity building trainings such as PGS organic certification, (d) providing secure market linkages and (e) in some cases contract farming.

Environmental sustainability is ensured by way of focus on organic production systems, and auxiliary benefits of IED intervention includes: (a) diversified food basket as a direct result of crop diversification, (b) improved lifestyle as a result of additional disposal income and (c) better medical and education as a result of increased income. Since the money stays within the village, every participating household benefits and overall rural development is progressive.

This model of community clusters where men and women pursue their traditional roles more optimised and efficiently, could lead to equitable and sustainable development, than mere promotion of Women Self Help Groups (WSHG) or farmer (men) clubs, as prevalent.

Biography

Utkarsh Ghate

He is director of CCD NGO in its northern India work in the poor state of Chhattisgarh, Madhya Pradesh, Orissa and eastern Maharashtra. He has a doctorate in botany and two decades of experience in rural development in agriculture, forestry and livelihoods. He has about 25 scientific publications, with 50 per cent in international journals. Micro-enterprise development is his expertise, besides biodiversity, climate change, organic farming and sustainability.

Pulikesh Nydu

He is agriculture programme coordinator of CCD NGO in the state of Orissa and Maharashtra in Balangir and Amaravati districts respectively. He has a doctorate from Germany and studied in Africa before beginning his career in India recently where he has his ancestral roots. Women empowerment. enterprise development and organic farming are his interests. He has travelled globally, with about a dozen publications.

Hemabati Nandan Behera

He is field coordinator of CCD NGO in the Agriculture and non timber forest products development with a decade of experience.

Rajkumar Ingle

He is field coordinator of CCD NGO with two decades of experience. He manages the project of Agriculture department of Maharashtra Government in Amaravati district. Panchayati Raj governance is his experience, besides agriculture development.

THEME-II
TECHNOLOGIES FOR WOMEN EMPOWERMENT AND EMPLOYMENT

2

Agripreneurship in Food Processing

Mahila Samakhya

Increase in population is the greatest threat to the survival of humanity leading to an ever-increasing gap between population growth and food supply. According to FAO, in its annual report "The State of Food Insecurity in the World 2002", estimates that there were around 840 million undernourished people in 1998-2000, 799 million in the developing countries, 30 million in the countries in transition and 11 million in the industrialised countries. In order to arrest the situation, much attention has been given on the exploitation and utilisation of unusual food plants. In such a situation it is important to develop suitable processing technologies for edible, non-timber forest products (NTFPs), which can be a potential source of nutrition.

NTFPs are the backbone to the Indian forest economy contributing over 50 per cent to the forest revenues. According to a report, the export earnings from NTFPs are about US$1,331 million. Some of the major edible NTFPs of India are sal seeds, mahua flowers and roots, myrobalans, Bamboo shoots, mushroom, etc. Among these, mahua flowers are one of the most important NTFP, playing a major role in the tribal economy. Large numbers of mahua trees are found in the states of Uttar Pradesh, Madhya Pradesh, Orissa, Jharkhand, Chhattisgarh, Gujarat, Andhra Pradesh, Maharashtra, Bihar,

West Bengal and Karnataka. The estimated production of mahua flowers is more than one million tonne in the country. In many states government organisations like Tribal Development Co-operative Corporations (TDCC) and Girijana Cooperative Corporation (GCC) in Andhra Pradesh purchase the flowers at a minimum support price to set aside the collectors from the exploitations of the middleman. However, due to lack of suitable post-harvest processing technologies, most of the flowers get decomposed in the godowns. At present the only industrial utilisation of these flowers is in production of liquor, which is illegal in most of the states.

To find out the potential of mahua flowers in food industry, Asha proposes value addition to fresh mahua flowers for developing a number of food products like juice concentrate, jam, jelly, sauce and mango-mahua leather. http://youtu.be/NKITk3IM8Yw http://youtu.be/jQkuggoASdY http://youtu.be/EVIsNII0fI4

Mahua grows in abundance in Bhadrachalam agency areas of Khammam district, Andhra Pradesh. A single tree produces 20 to 200 kgs of seeds every year which can be used to extract oil. The oil which is considered very well for care of skin can be used for making washing soaps. The seed cakes obtained after extraction constitute very good fertiliser. The mahua seeds can be collected by women and children of the every family. The oil extraction process can be carried out by a Village Organisation of Srama Sakthi Sanghas (V.O.). The oil expeller is a mini unit of about 1.5 lakhs investment which will be owned and managed by the V.O. Since Handmade Washing Soaps will be used by the tribal women in their respective village it will not take long to promote some village based units in the area.

Objective

Increase the employment and income generation potential for the Mahua collector's women and children apart from providing an affordable source of nutrition. Provide tribal women with simple tools and equipments for improved processing of NTFP at their household level for their own consumption and marketing. To promote income generation activities for sustainable livelihoods linking with conservation of forest resources and environmental protection. Women will get good price for their collected and processed products besides supplying nutrient food to their children. Women will be capacitated to make their own washing shops using Mohua Oil for their domestic use and for marketing.

3

Challenges and Opportunities Facing Women Agripreneurs in India

S.A. Arul

Development of location specific cost effective technology and agriculture practices are vital for optimal agricultural production. The world of agriculture is changing fast technologically, commercially, economically and ecologically. Agriculture challenges in India are four fold: need for enhanced production and productivity; need to address the issues of equity and uneven development; need to understand and address issues of sustainability and the last challenge is to enhance profitability in agriculture. A farmer needs to be linked with the agri-business systems, Research Institutions, Public Administration, working with the other farmers, open market and other limited partners.

The challenge of agricultural transformation has been felt as the need of the hour by the Government of India and the concept of Agriclinic and Agribusiness has been emerged as a major initiative towards agricultural development. The following are the core professional values and skills that shape the whole form of Agriclinics and Agribusiness.

(i) Strengthening the Agricultural Extension System in the rural and urban areas.

(ii) Mainstream the farming community with current farming. trends, farming techniques, market price upgradation.

(iii) Creation of employment opportunities for the Villagers.

(iv) Supply chain management for the farmers.

(v) Agricultural insurance for the farmers.

Role of Manage in Promoting Women Agripreneurs

MANAGE has been playing a key role in promoting Agripreners since 2002. The scheme has been implemented across the country and ventures have been established in more than 53 categories related to agriculture and allied sector. The scheme has created dual impact in terms of generating employment in the country. Direct impact has been created by the scheme by providing self-employment to the Agri graduates through the set up. These ventures in turn have generated employment for others. MANAGE, through ACABC programme has enabled huge amount of Agri graduates to become potential leaders in the field of agriculture. Majority of the unemployed graduates have found themselves with increase in income and a social upliftment in their professional and personal lives. Most specifically the ACABC scheme has really enriched the farming community with better guidance on recent agriculture technologies, farming methods etc. Agripreneurs have also generated lot of employment opportunities for the farmers.

About VAPS

This Nodal Training Institute (NTI) – Voluntary Association for People Service (VAPS), Tamil Nadu is one of the Organisation approved by Central Ministry of Agriculture and Co-operation through MANAGE, Hyderabad to conduct the Agri-Clinics and Agri-Business Centres Scheme (ACABCS), Training Programme for the candidates with stipulated qualifications from the State of Tamil Nadu and UTs of Puducherry and Andaman/Nicobar Islands. This NTI has so far trained 1842 candidates and among them are women candidates. In Tamil Nadu totally 464 women candidates has been trained and 171 of them have established their own Agri/Horti/Fisheries/Forestry/AH/Value Addition related projects with or without Bank finances.

Agriculture and Women Agripreneurs

The concept of Agriclinic and Agribusiness centre scheme has played a significant role in the lives of men and women professionals in the field of agriculture. The past one decade in India, there is a transformation in the agricultural arena in terms of agricultural productivity, technology, input supply to the farmers, knowledge upgradation to the farmers and Agricultural extension. The contribution of agri professional especially the women has eminent contribution towards these agricultural development.

The involvement of Voluntary Organisations/Non-Governmental Organisation /KVK/SAU dealing with Agri Extension Training with qualified trainers has really gone a long way with appropriate support to resources, capacity building and facilitates to participate actively in the process of the empowerment of women in agricultural related activities.

Despite several success of women professional in agriculture, they face threats and challenges in many occasions. Women agripreneurs struggle hard to promote their business as fast as men agripreneurs. The societal restrictions such as free mobiles for women have further been identified as hinderence to their business development. This paper discusses both the opportunities and challenges of women agripreneurs in the arena of agriclinics and agribusiness.

Challenges

- Family needs secured jobs with prescribed work time schedules.
- Family hesitant to take up risky business especially by women which needs all time work and movement; and needs to meet different people at different times and places.
- Banks hesitant to finance for women insists for 40 lakhs security even for 5 lakhs loan.
- Banks insists that the husbands/parents be a co-applicant and sign the documents.
- In one case of the value added products supply, the purchasers are not easily believing the women for the supply the required quantity at the required time.
- After a very hard work only the supplier has to become a manufacturer.

- Farmers are not believing at the first instance the recommendations provided by the women Agripreneur.
- In case of women Agripreneurs, so far the family properties are not shared among the girl children, hence, they are finding great difficulty in providing securities.
- Most of the Bank Staff are not aware of the ACABC Scheme.

Opportunities

Agribusiness gives a viable opportunity for women in Agripreneurs in terms of economic empowerment. The personal income which women get through Agribusiness gives them a personal strength and confidence. As far as VAPS ACABC Experience is concerned, Majority of Women Agripreneurs Expressed that they feel empowered of becoming a leader in the field of agriculture. In many occasions they have also expressed that seeing the farming community give them satisfaction to a minimum level.

- When the woman also becomes an Entrepreneur/MD for a manufacturing company her social status increases.
- Once the farmers are satisfied, they always come to the women agripreneurs for services both for inputs and advice.
- Couple Agripreneurs find the job very easy and progress is achieved within a short time.

Instead of job seekers, women Agripreneurs became job-providers and enhanced their face-value amongst family members and also in the society which increased their self-confidence.

Conclusion

Role of women Agripreneurs in agriculture has got significant impact in the lives of farming community. They have gained transformation in socio-economic arena. Though lot of opportunities have been created for women Agripreneurs women face lot of challenges in practicing Agribusiness at a large scale level such as gender disparities and gender discrimination in Agribusiness. Hence strategies for gender mainstreaming in the field of agriculture is the need.

4

Solar Food Processing Technology for Sustainable Livelihood for Rural Women

Suresh I., Srinivasa Reddy M. and Shyamala R.

Women make essential contributions to agriculture and rural economic activities in all developing country regions. In rural areas, about 83 per cent women workers were engaged in agriculture in 2004-05, either as cultivators or labourers, as compared to 67 per cent male workers. Employment is critical for poverty reduction and for enhancing women's status.

Ongoing focus on use of renewable energy and attention to rural women's leadership and their contribution to sustainable development is very encouraging. One such opportunity is use of solar energy to process fruits, vegetables and agricultural commodities at farm level. India is the second largest producer of fruits and vegetables with only four per cent processing. It is estimated that about 20 to 25 per cent of fruits and about 30 per cent vegetables are spoiled due to lack of processing.

Farm level processing of fruits and vegetables and making available to market will make significant impact on economic status of the rural women. However, lack of village-based technologies and power crisis will create a great hurdle to this strategy.

Recently developed innovative solar cabinet dryer by Society for Energy Environment and Development has developed the processes for 70 products for value addition and long shelf life which can offer a sustainable solution to this problem. Solar cabinet dryers can be an excellent means to process fruits, vegetables and other agricultural commodities in the production areas. Solar dehydration processes of fruits and vegetables are presented in this paper and they can be effectively processed at the farm level by the rural women as an income generation activity. This cabinet dryer uses zero energy cost and can offer clean and hygienic process. Adoption of these solar cabinet dryers can offer clean environment processing and thus promoting Green Energy applications. These technologies are relatively simple and can be easily followed by illiterate personnel with adequate in-house training and in our training programmes. These trained women in the rural areas can use this technology as a solution for livelihood where uninterrupted power is always an issue to do any commercial drying process. Successful adaptation of solar cabinet dryers can stimulate sustainable economic growth to rural women. This paper discusses also the cost economics of starting a microenterprise by self-help groups of rural women in processing the horticultural produce grown in the villages.

THEME–III
NGO INTERVENTIONS AND CASE STUDIES ON AGRIPRENEURSHIP

5

Women Entrepreneurship in Production and Marketing of Herbal Medicine

G. Gopal Reddy and B. Lavakumar

Sri Aurobindo Institute of Rural Development (SAIRD), at Gaddipally village in Nalgonda district of Andhra Pradesh with financial assistance from the Andhra Pradesh Netherlands Biotechnology project, Hyderabad initiated the introduction of Herbal medicine for curing some of the common ailments by encouraging individual herbal gardens, community gardens and helping them by training and providing necessary technical knowhow to market the products. It has gained some popularity by our participation in various exhibitions like annual Horticulture show, district level exhibitions, all-India industrial exhibitions at Exhibition grounds Bio melas and other religious gatherings at district level. We have exhibited them and provided some free samples in the beginning for popularising the herbal medicines, particularly for curing constipation, pain oil for curing knee joint pains, herbal tooth powder, Triphala as an energy booster, Madhunashini for diabetic patients etc. These are gaining popularity and there is a good market now. We have also conducted school health programme for the benefit of children in two dozen villages and popularised these medicine. We have taken license from the department of Ayush, Government of Andhra Pradesh for producing and marketing 12 shastric herbal medicines. With this experience we have also established one demonstration unit with 100 different herbal plants at Rural Technology Park at NIRD campus, Rajendranagar, Hyderabad in collaboration with APNL Biotechnology Programme, IPE, OU, Hyderabad.

Necessary training, supply of the planting material and support for obtaining license for marketing herbal products can be provided, provided the government also takes interest and responsibility specially for the Self-Help Group (SHG) members through providing financial assistance for training, production and marketing. This can be popularised on a wider scale to provide better healthcare at a much cheaper cost than allopathic medicine. This has an additional advantage because being herbal there is no side effect and specially in remote areas where healthcare is not available by allopathic doctors which is expensive and out of boundary for majority of rural population. Herbal medicines go long way to improve health condition of rural population at affordable price. This needs all encouragement from all concerned sections of society including government, semi government and voluntary agencies.

THEME–IV
GOVERNMENT INITIATIVES AND POLICY FRAMEWORK FOR AGRIPRENEURSHIP AND RURAL DEVELOPMENT

6

Extension Strategies for Increasing Agripreneurship Amongst Women Farmers

Ravinder Naik Vankudothu, Rabindra Nath Padaria and Shridhar Patil

Women comprises major agriculture work force. The contribution of women in agriculture is significant. Since time immemorial, their contribution towards agriculture remains to be at higher level. Various studies have indicated that, majority of the women (85 per cent) are dependent on agriculture (NCW, 2006). Their role in various activities of the farming (Bala, 2003) varies from land preparation (32 per cent), seed cleaning and sowing (80 per cent), inter-cultivation activities (86 per cent) and post harvest activities (84 per cent). Although their contribution to world food production is maximum (80 per cent), they receive only 2-10 per cent of the extension services (FAO, 2005), the point which deserves special introspection to be made. Apart from this, poor access to resources, poor access to information, poor access to market and risk factors are the major constraints faced by women in agriculture (Devi, L. 2007). Majority of the extension strategies and programmes are oriented towards men farmers and their capacity building leaving a narrow space for the women farmers. If proper initiatives are taken, women can be the best examples of successful entrepreneurs as they have in-built qualities of entrepreneurship such as common sense, ambitions, team work, hard work etc., (Madhuri, T., 2011). There are many activities of agriculture that could be taken up as an enterprise such as Vermicompost, Floriculture, sericulture, food processing etc., which are fairly suitable to women folk. There is a need to shift our focus from concentrating men farmers to that of women farmers as their contribution is maximum in food production. Extension machinery working at grassroot level should concentrate to provide capacity building and motivate them to take up various enterprises as per their interest, suitability and availability of resources. There is a need to design extension strategies towards this end. The institutions such as Krishi Vigyan Kendra, Rural Development Agencies and NGO partners should come out with new strategies focussing women farmers. Various location specific, and need-based capacity building, vocational and self employment programmes could motivate the women farmers to make their mind towards agripreneurship. It should be remembered that agriculture is no longer going to be profitable unless it is taken from a business point of view, for this, women could play catalytic role by helping themselves.

7

Invisible Face and Food Security: The West Bengal Experience

Suparna Ganguly

Agriculture is an important tool for reducing poverty and increasing growth. And women are playing a vital role at every aspect of agriculture like planting, sowing, weeding, and harvesting etc. Not only that they are also responsible for the primary seed keeping, conserving and managing an incredible variety of India's vital food crops. According to the Food and Agriculture Organisation "women produce between 60 and 80 per cent of the food in most developing countries and are responsible for half of the world's food production." This paper tells about the contribution of women in agriculture as well as food security in West Bengal. Though most of the agricultural women are not getting the recognition as 'Farmers' rather than the 'labour', but they are performing the role of primary food providers for their families and alleviating hunger and malnutrition by this way. Not only that, they are also key players behind the expansion of commercial agriculture as well as nations' economic growth. Major part of this study has been done in ethnographic mode.

Conclusions

The post liberalisation period saw an active participation of women in agriculture giving way to feminisation of agriculture. During this time, the work participation rate of women rose to 30.2 per cent in 1992 but gradually experienced an alarming plunge at 19.2 per cent in 2012. Analysis reveals that women have started withdrawing from agriculture activities and have started moving into more decent jobs which are more agripreneurship oriented. Consequently there was a movement of women into the world of business, trade and commerce which has produced successful entrepreneurs in various business activities. However, women's participation in the business world is much lower than as was expected. A comparison of the women participation rate in India with that of the developed countries reveals that, women participate actively in business and trade activities without any restrictions. But the Indian society burdened by many social and cultural restrictions on women maintaining a low degree of women's participation in entrepreneurial activities. With this view in the offing the two-day National Seminar on Agripreneurship for Employment and Empowerment of Rural Poor Women was held on the 30th and 31st of January, 2014 (*copy of the time table enclosed*).

It is quite encouraging to find that women with a definite agenda have acquired good positions in the business world like Indra Nooyi (CEO of Pepsi Co); Dr Kiran Mazumdar-Shaw (Chairman and Managing Director of Bioon Ltd.); Anu Aga (Chairperson of Thermax Engineering); Sulajja Firodia Motwani (Joint Managing Director of Kinetic Engineering Ltd); Ekta Kapoor (Head of Balajji Telefilms); Priya Paul (Chairperson of Appeejay–The Park Hotels chain of boutique hotels).Yet, most of the women, in rural India are either illiterate or semi-literate and are unable to gain proper support in this field. Women involved in entrepreneurship in agriculture face lot of problems in India which are related to socio-economic aspects, skill development, and problems related to family support, leadership etc., as were flagged by the researchers. Discussion emerging from the seminar reveal that the paradox of entrepreneurial skill, lack of awareness on existing technologies, absence of direct ownership of property, low ability to bear risk, negligence by financial institutions, lack of self-confidence, lack of professional education, mobility constraints and financial freedom constitute the major problems of women entrepreneurship development in India.

In the backdrop of the discussions from the papers presented following perceptions and conceptions reflect on the theme Agripreneurship for Women Employment and Empowerment:

1. Women are an important human resource of the nation and are the mediators of economic growth and development. Therefore, there is need for continuous attempts to inspire, encourage, and motivate women entrepreneurs.
2. Most of the SHGs have reached the second level of their maturity wherein they are seen taking up entrepreneurial activity in the farm sector in rural areas like sericulture, floriculture, seri poly clinics, running the Mini Dal Mills etc., which are a source of employment and economic empowerment.
3. KVKs are working capacity building on skill oriented vocational training programmes with the SHGs and are able to bring in successful interventions for economic gains through agripreneurship in women.
4. Agrienterprises are able to fetch 3-4 lakhs income per year.
5. Even though the loans are released, lack of appropriate working capital is a hindrance in running the enterprise on a sustainable basis.
6. Adoption of appropriate technologies can help in economic empowerment of the women in agripreneurship.

7. Technology based interventions have successfully notified an annual turnover of Rs 35 lakhs per year.
8. Role of institutions like cooperatives go a long way in creating employment for women. For example five million women days were created in Maharashtra during the lean season.
9. Agrienterprises are started because of a necessity and not as an opportunity. The people in the rural areas are forces which is a pull factor leading to motivation in the society. But women agripreneurs face a lot of road blocks which are in the form of gender stereotypes.
10. Policy removes biases against women but is difficult to overcome in reality.
11. Government interventions facilitating certain concessions have helped the agrienterprises to take off, for example, the cooperative by name Sankalp could establish outlets for sale of organic products with the help of BAIF which took care of the rentals for the units. Today the turnover of Sankalp is Rs 45 lakh per year and Rs 18,000 per month is the income.
12. Constraints and challenges for women in enterprise development are because of lack of knowledge management. Forward ever backward never should be the prime principle.
13. Following the principle of three M's- Money, Management and Marketing will help fructify in gaining women employment and empowerment as is exemplified in the launch of agrienterprises based on renewable energy sources in agro-food processing.
14. Reclamation and Regeneration of natural resources through collective farming employed through women groups is an intervention for women employment and empowerment as it also gives scope for allied activities.
15. Region specific agriculture products are a potential source of agripreneurship for women as in the case of Arunachal Pradesh which is famous for bamboo-based enterprises

16. Agriculture enterprise facilitation centre-promoting organic pesticide through community participation has turned out to be an innovative agri-enterprise in Chhattisgarh.
17. A shrink in the extension workers is the order of the day but the way forward is by the involvement of NGOs.

Major challenges emerging from the presentations are:

1. As women devote most of their time to take care of their family there is an absence of balance between family and career obligations.
2. Despite having excellent entrepreneurial abilities women are unable to create additional income on a sustainable basis.
3. Support extended by the family members to women is an important issue.
4. Financial freedom given to women is also very poor, especially in less educated rural families. Which hooks on social ethics and traditions and has become a vicious circle of dependency.
5. Lack of Direct Ownership of the Property for women. Very few women have a right to property.
6. Initiatives of the governments should be more in the form of gender equality and advancement of women.
7. Paradox of Entrepreneurial Skill and Finance of "have and haven't" is evident.
8. Low Risk Bearing ability in rural women is also another hindrance. Women in India are dependent on the male members. She has no stake in any discussions and not allowed to take any risk.
9. Financial Institutions, Banks are important financers of entrepreneurs. Negligence by these institutions and non-accordance of the credit to women entrepreneurs has been another barrier, in the light of a supposed non-performing asset in future.
10. All these hindrances add to Lack of Self Confidence and create a strong mental block.

11. Mobility is another factor effecting women entrepreneurial development. They are not ready to leave their place for business activities.

Suggestions

1. Awareness programmes should be conducted on a mass scale with the intention of creating awareness among women.
2. Awareness should also create knowledge to assess individual skills and capacities.
3. Most women shy away from entrepreneurial activity as they lack capacities. As a sequel to it women lack entrepreneurial bent of mind. Therefore, there is a need to make them realise of their capacities including risk bearing capacities.
4. Educational levels and professional skills influence women participation in entrepreneurship.
5. Banks need to change their attitude while disbursing the loans to the poor women agripreneurs; disbursement of the information on the bank schemes, credit, loan, and capacity building interventions by the bank should be the focus of the bank.
6. Agriculture technologies like Green House Farming, Drip Agriculture should be promoted as was in the state of Gujarat which today is the highest producer of Banana in the world.
7. Technology transfer must be emphasised because it is not happening in tot.
8. There is a need to protect our agriculture first. Till now no national level budget has been proposed for agriculture, however, AP stands out in introducing this budget
9. SHGs should be trained to preserve the seeds through seed bank.
10. Farmers attaining more than 60 years of age should be given pension @ Rs 3,000 per month to encourage them.

11. Every farmer should be given the right to open an account at zero balance.
12. Every farmer should get Kissan credit card along with Kissan health card.
13. Since tenant farmers are not able to access loan from banks, joint liability groups of the farmers should be formed from which banks can give loans to the tenants.
14. The numbers of women farmers are growing today. Therefore, measure should be taken to build capacities of women for marketing interventions.
15. Small and marginal farmers should form groups from which agripreneurship should be developed which will strengthen food security.
16. Solar motor pump sets with subsidy should be promoted to offset electricity problems in the rural areas.
17. Women experiences on agripreneurship should be updated.
18. Conduct TOT for women farmers and stakeholders like officials, unions, and farmers for information dissemination on agriculture programmes.

Index

G

J

K